YARNED *and* DANGEROUS

YARNED *and* DANGEROUS

SADIE HARTWELL

KENSINGTON BOOKS
www.kensingtonbooks.com

This book is a work of fiction. Names, characters, places, and incidents either are products of the author's imagination or are used fictitiously. Any resemblance to actual persons, living or dead, events, or locales is entirely coincidental.

KENSINGTON BOOKS are published by

Kensington Publishing Corp.
119 West 40th Street
New York, NY 10018

All Kensington titles, imprints, and distributed lines are available at special quantity discounts for bulk purchases for sales promotion, premiums, fund-raising, educational, or institutional use.

Special book excerpts or customized printings can also be created to fit specific needs. For details, write or phone the office of the Kensington Sales Manager: Kensington Publishing Corp., 119 West 40th Street, New York, NY 10018. Attn. Sales Department. Phone: 1-800-221-2647.

eISBN-13: 978-1-61773-719-0
eISBN-10: 1-61773-719-4
First Kensington Electronic Edition: December 2015

ISBN-13: 978-1-61773-717-6
ISBN-10: 1-61773-717-8
First Kensington Trade Paperback Printing: December 2015

10 9 8 7 6 5 4 3 2 1

Printed in the United States of America

To all of the yarn goddesses and gods out there:
May your yarn never tangle, and may you
always have more than enough to finish.

Acknowledgments

To Mike and Will, for making my life as close to perfect as it ever needs to be.

To my mom, sisters, and aunts, for being my most enthusiastic cheerleaders, and for listening to me prattle on about books. Love you, ladies!

To my agent, John Talbot, my editor, John Scognamiglio, and the dedicated folks at Kensington, thanks for your help and guidance as this book came to life.

And as always, to the members of the Connecticut Chapter of Romance Writers of America, the finest writers' group of this or any other time.

Sometimes I follow directions exactly as written.
And sometimes I knit what the yarn tells me to.
Either way, a pattern forms.

—From *The History of Needlework* by Cora Lloyd

Chapter 1

"Don't ask me to do this. Please." Josie Blair set her coffee mug down on the table. Hot brown liquid sloshed over onto the mess of papers spread across the surface, which served as a desk as well as a place to eat. "Darn it." She crossed the floor of her tiny Brooklyn kitchen, opened a drawer, and pulled out a paper towel.

"There's no need to swear at me," her mother said.

"Sorry. And 'darn it' isn't exactly a cuss, Mom. It wasn't directed at you." Josie began to blot at the mess. She took a deep breath. "I can't go back to that hick town to take care of Uncle Eben. I barely remember him." Her cat, Coco, twined around her feet. She reached down and stroked the soft black fur. Coco allowed the petting for a moment, then trotted off on her little white paws.

"The man is recovering from a broken leg. And he's grieving. He and Cora weren't married long, but they cared about each other. There isn't anyone else, Josie."

"Only because he's scared off every visiting nurse in the county."

Her mother grinned. "As soon as I get back, I'll relieve you. It'll only be a couple of weeks."

Right. A couple of weeks of drop-dead boredom. "Mom, all you have to do is cancel your cruise. Simple." Josie felt awful even as she said it and wished she could take it back.

Her mother, bless her, didn't seem to mind. "It's nonrefundable, as you well know. You said you've got vacation time coming. Why not take it in the country? Connecticut will be beautiful this time of year, with all the snow."

Josie poured herself a fresh cup of coffee and filled her mother's mug. She set a plate of cookies from her favorite bakery in Greenwich Village in front of her mother, selecting a macaroon for herself.

"You can bring some work with you," her mother continued. "Uncle Eb lives in the boondocks, but he has electricity and a telephone. Your computer will work. Cora's yarn shop has to be closed up, and Eb can't do that alone."

Josie's eyes fell on the pegs she'd installed near the front door. On one peg hung a classic camel Burberry coat she'd found in a consignment store. Around the collar of that coat hung a lacy scarf, hand-knit of yarn in the colors of the ocean—azure, aqua, and green. Cora, her great-uncle's wife, had sent Josie the scarf just before she died in the car accident that injured Eb. Guilt pricked Josie's gut. She had never met Cora, and she never would now.

Josie looked at her mother and felt her resolve crumbling. The last place on earth she wanted to go was back to Dorset Falls, where she'd lived for a couple of years as a teenager. But her mother had sacrificed so much to raise Josie alone on a teacher's salary. If anyone deserved a Mediterranean cruise, it was Katherine Blair.

"I'll drop you at LaGuardia tomorrow so you can catch your flight to Italy. Then I'll head up to Connecticut on Sunday," Josie said, dropping a kiss into her mother's highlighted hair.

Katherine smiled, gratitude evident in her eyes. "That's my girl."

Her girl hoped she wasn't making a big mistake. And wondered whether her car would make it all the way to the Litchfield hills.

Josie switched off the radio. She'd been out of range of any listenable station for miles, and the combination of the static, the drone of the tires of her ancient Saab, and the bright glare of the sun made her head ache. Unfortunately, her aspirin were packed away in her tote bag in the backseat. She'd finished her coffee around New Rochelle and her diet Mountain Dew somewhere around New Haven, so there was nothing to swallow the pills with anyway.

She was also rather urgently in need of a rest stop, which were few and far between on this interminable stretch of highway. Not only could she not recall how far back the last rest stop had been, she could not recall the last time she'd actually seen a commercial building along this road.

According to Antonio, the deep, Italian-accented voice of her portable GPS unit, she'd arrive at Uncle Eben's place around eleven a.m. if she didn't stop for lunch. Why couldn't all men be like Antonio? He was always calm, and kind, and he never got mad at you if your plans changed. He understood if you had to go a different way for a while. He just recalculated the route and gave you your next direction, all with that same smooth, nonjudgmental voice.

Unlike some people I know. Last night's argument with Otto still had her fuming.

"You have got to be kidding me," Otto had said, pointing a yak kabob at her over dinner. "The magazine goes to press in ten days, and you're leaving now? Unacceptable."

Josie took a bite of her asparagus risotto, letting the cheesy richness melt on her tongue before she answered. His stare was making her uncomfortable. She should have loved her job. Otto Heinrich was a well-known, some said brilliant, fashion designer, and as his assistant she had nearly unlimited access to him. If she wanted to sell her own designs someday, she couldn't ask for better experience. Still, Otto had his moods and he often took his frustrations out on Josie.

"Jennifer can handle anything that comes up. She knows the magazine as well as I do."

"She's not you. When are you going to take this job seriously?" He stabbed his fork into the pile of whole grain pasta on his plate and began a vicious twirl. He shoved the pasta into his mouth and let his eyes rest on her chest as he chewed.

God, she hated him when he was like this, all snotty and self-righteous. And lewd. "My collection is coming along just fine." Okay, that was kind of a fib. She'd been working on designs for next fall, but her drawings stunk and she knew it. She had a great eye for fashion and a talent for writing about it, but it was becoming apparent, after a Master of Fine Arts degree she was still paying for and would be for years to come, that she might, possibly, not be a designer.

"I find it hard to believe that you'd rather go take care of some old geezer you hardly know than work with me." Otto whipped his head around, and his shiny blond ponytail swung out in a wide arc, barely missing a passing busboy. Otto had better hair than she did. "Waiter! Another glass of this wine, please."

"He's family, Otto," she said, crossing her arms defensively. "He's old, and he needs me." So what if she hadn't seen Uncle Eben in years? She would get to know him now, that was for sure. Maybe her memories of his crotchetiness weren't accurate. Maybe he'd turned into a big sweetie in his old age, with a faithful, friendly dog by his side. *It would be nice to have a dog,* she thought. *I could take it for walks along Uncle Eb's quiet country road, and not worry about picking up after it.*

"What about me? Don't I count for something?" Otto almost, but not quite, managed a convincing pout. "We could be very good together, you know." He ran a finger up her arm.

Josie recoiled. Otto was an equal-opportunity lech, gawking unabashedly at every woman in the Haus of Heinrich offices. She knew for a fact that he'd been sleeping for months with the receptionist, a dark-haired sylph with modeling aspirations. Up until now, other than a few lascivious glances that Josie had ignored, he'd behaved himself around her. But since he broke up with Anastasia, something had changed, and he'd been dropping hints to Josie, which she'd also ignored. If she had to guess, she'd say that Otto probably didn't like the idea that Josie had a life and obligations that didn't revolve around him and his company. And he was arrogant enough to think his Germanic charms would be enough to keep her in New York and working for him forever.

But no job was worth doing . . . that. She'd studied hard and worked hard to get where she was, and she was not going to become Otto's Flavor of the Month no matter how much she needed the income. Anger bubbled up, and she swallowed it down. "No, we couldn't be anything together." Purse slung over her shoulder, she stormed off toward the front of the restaurant, then stopped and returned to the table.

Otto sat back in his chair, smiling. There was a sound of leather-on-leather as his hand-tailored jacket scraped against the upholstery. "If you leave again, don't come back."

Josie picked up her plate of risotto. She hefted the plate. It was made of good, solid white china. There was still a lot of food left on it, and, if she threw it at him, it would make a very satisfying mess. It might even hurt. Certainly, the leather suit jacket would be ruined.

Otto's face went serious again. "Don't do anything we'll

both regret, Josie," he warned. She looked at the plate again, and the delicious cheesy aroma drifted up into her nostrils.

"Miss?" She addressed the server passing by with a tray of drinks. "Could I get a to-go box?" Turning to Otto, she said, "I quit."

"You can't quit." He threw back the rest of his wine. "You've already been fired."

Chapter 2

WELCOME TO DORSET FALLS. Josie passed the sign and drove into town. Her spirits sank. The place was far, far worse than she remembered. Almost every brick and glass storefront downtown was empty, their windows covered in brown paper. She glanced up to see a sign over a corner shop. MISS MARPLE KNITS. *That must be Cora's place,* she thought. There couldn't be two yarn stores in a village this size. No Starbucks. No nail salon. No department store.

Josie sighed. It was only for a few weeks. When she got back to New York, she would convince Otto to give her her job back—he would have fixated on someone else by then—and she would apply herself in earnest to those designs. She was sure she could do it. Pretty sure, anyway.

"We can do this, too, Coco. I think." Josie's tuxedo cat yawled from her carrier in the backseat as Josie turned down a side street and drove back out of town.

"Arriving at destination, on left," Antonio said a few minutes later.

Josie slammed on the pedal, and the Saab fishtailed on the

gravel road. She reversed as far as the mailbox, which consisted of a lidded bucket made of some kind of dull gray metal welded onto a pole. LLOYD was hand lettered in black paint across the front of the receptacle.

The driveway was narrow and opened out onto snow-covered lawn on either side. "What are those things?" Josie said out loud. Coco didn't answer. Numerous weirdly sculptural rusty bits of metal stuck up from under the snow, while strange lumps dotted the front lawn. She rolled to a stop in a graveled area at the side of the house as a huge, shaggy beast barreled off the front porch and barked loudly at the driver's side door. Josie jumped back involuntarily. Coco hissed and began to scratch at the sides of her plastic prison. Only glass stood between them and Cujo, who looked ready to maul them to a bloody pulp.

Great, she thought. *Trapped. Now what?* Josie looked around the front seat for something she could use as a weapon, but realized she couldn't do much damage with the wadded-up potato chip bags and candy wrappers that littered the passenger seat. Could she poke the thing in the eye with the straw from her gutbuster Mountain Dew?

"Jethro!" a voice commanded from the front porch. Josie's eyes followed the huge yellow dog as it ran toward the source. An elderly man dressed in a faded plaid flannel shirt unbuttoned over a gray thermal Henley stood propped up on crutches. He wore a pair of dusty green utilitarian pants, the left leg shortened and frayed over a white fiberglass cast. "Down," the man ordered, and the dog obeyed, dropping to the deck and panting, tail wagging.

Josie drew a breath and willed her heart rate to return to normal. The engine was still running. She could back out of the driveway and head right back to New York, without even getting out of the car. Even from this distance she could see her great-uncle's furrowed forehead and the fact that he was glaring at her from underneath a formidable set of gray, hairy eyebrows.

"Well, ain't you coming in?" the man yelled. "The dog don't bite. Unless I tell him to."

She lifted her chin and opened the car door. Josie Blair was no sissy. She'd lived in New York City for more than a decade. She could handle this old man and his slavering canine too.

Smile plastered on her face, Josie exited the car. "Uncle Eben? It's been a long time."

"Not long enough, missy," he said, pointing a crutch at her. "I don't need you here, and I don't want you here."

"You haven't changed a bit, Unc. Just as charming as you were when I was a kid." Josie set the cat carrier on the semi-frozen ground, opened her trunk, and pulled out a suitcase and her laptop bag. She could come out for the rest, including a small litter box and Coco's special organic food, once she settled in.

"Hmmph," Uncle Eb snorted. "And you've still got a smart mouth. You'll have to carry in your own gear. I got a busted flipper."

She made her way past some cylindrical wire cages stacked up around desiccated brown plants loaded with some rotten orbs that might once have been tomatoes. The porch of the old house sagged, but seemed solid enough beneath her fur-lined clogs. She kept her distance from the dog, whose tail was now wagging furiously.

"You might as well come in." The man pivoted and opened the screen door, then the heavy wooden inner door, and clumped inside. The screen door slammed shut behind him, leaving Josie outside.

"Old coot," she muttered.

"Nothing wrong with my hearing, sweet pea."

The front door opened into a good-sized room with no discernible purpose. There was a large wooden table in the center, surrounded by wooden dining room chairs. Both the table and the chairs were piled high with newspapers, junk mail, and other detritus. If this was a dining room, no dining had taken place here recently. Eb sat down in a burnt-orange velour recliner positioned by the front window, and dropped his crutches on the floor beside him. Jethro lay down at his feet and let out a doggie sigh.

"Can you cook?" Eb said.

Josie dropped her suitcase to the floor with a thunk. "If by cooking you mean opening packages of frozen food and putting them in the microwave, or running a Keurig machine, then yes. I'm a great cook." She shrugged out of her fleece jacket, unwound the scarf from around her neck, and deposited both on top of a Vermont Country Store catalog on the closest chair. Coco took off like a shot when the door to her carrier was opened, and Josie wondered when, if ever, she'd see her again. But the cat had been a stray when Josie took her in, so it was a good bet she could take care of herself.

Eb's eyes lit up. "What's that?"

"What's what?"

"That Kyoorick machine. What does it do? Is it a farm tool?" Eb shifted around and repositioned his broken leg. "I ain't as spry as I used to be, and I need my tools."

Josie smiled. "That's a kind of coffeemaker."

"Oh. Well, I need my coffee too. But the only kind of coffeemaker you'll find here sets on the burner and perks till it's done. I wouldn't mind some coffee, come to think of it." He pulled a newspaper and a pencil out of the side pocket of the recliner. A little cloud of dust rose up and dispersed into the winter sunlight streaming in through the window. "And maybe some lunch."

She sighed. This was why she was here. To take care of Eb. She was determined to make the best of it. "Which way's the kitchen?"

Eb didn't look up from the paper, but penciled something onto what appeared to be the crossword puzzle. He gestured vaguely toward the opposite wall.

Josie followed his gaze. There were three raised-panel doors set in the wall. What was behind Door Number One?

"Not that one, missy. That's my room. The middle one."

She turned the knob and pushed open the door. A blast of hot air hit her, presumably coming from the enormous woodstove blazing away in the center of the room. A drip of sweat ran down her nose, and she wiped it away with her sleeve.

"Leave that door open, wouldja?" Eb called from the other room.

Gladly, if it would dissipate some of the heat. She pulled the wool sweater over her head, adjusted her T-shirt, and dropped the sweater on the counter. A search of the painted wooden cupboards yielded a can of tomato soup. She checked the expiration date. It was still good, and it had a pull top, which was also good because there was no sign of a can opener. All the kitchen drawers were full, and the last one she'd pulled open had been full of mousetraps and a package of poison. Perhaps Coco could make herself useful around here, if she weren't torn to shreds by Jethro first.

Still, this was a nice room. It appeared to have been painted recently, a soft buttery yellow. The light in this part of the house came in through wavy glass panes and accumulated on the wide golden pine boards of the floor. The bottom half of the window was covered in a snowy openwork crocheted curtain. Josie bent to examine the lovely piece, fascinated by the tiny stitches and complicated pineapple pattern. *This must be Cora's,* she thought, and felt a twinge of sadness. Poor Cora had started to make this old house a home, but never had the chance to finish the job.

Josie squirted some dish soap into a saucepan she found in the sink, grabbed a paper towel, and began to wash it. A few minutes later, she had the soup bubbling on the stove and had located bread and a package of cheddar cheese wrapped in brown paper and tied in string in the refrigerator. Grilled cheese, she decided, and set to work. Gourmet cook she was not, but this she could handle.

She returned to the dining room and cleared off two chairs and a corner of the table by depositing the stacks on the floor. "Lunch is ready, Uncle Eb."

He huffed. "I like to eat here in my chair."

"Well, today you eat at the table. Come on, I'll help you up." She offered him a hand, which he didn't take.

His eyes cut to the lunch on the table. "Where's my coffee?" he growled.

"You'll have to give me a lesson on that thingie. I made tea instead. After lunch I'll go into town and shop." *And buy a real coffeemaker,* she thought.

Eb sat down with a mild grunt and began to spoon up the soup. "You ain't shoppin' today," he said, dipping a corner of the grilled cheese into the bowl.

"Why not? The stores are open, right?" Not that she'd actually seen any stores.

The old man tore off a crust of the sandwich and tossed it at Jethro, who caught it in midair and came over to the table, sniffing. "You ain't got time."

As far as Josie could tell, she had nothing but time for the next two weeks. For all his blustering, maybe her great-uncle just didn't want to be alone. A feeling she could sympathize with. New York was a city with millions of people, but when she went back to her apartment at night, it was just her and Coco.

"I'll be back soon, and I'll bring us back a nice hot dinner." She wondered what takeout was available in town, then decided it didn't matter. As long as it was hot, maybe containing gravy, Eb would probably be satisfied.

"We've got chores to do, missy. Then you can drive me into town, and I'll show you what you need to do at the shop."

Chores? She hadn't even unpacked yet. This didn't sound good.

A half hour later Josie found herself sitting behind Eb on a four-wheeled, camouflage-painted contraption that looked like a golf cart on steroids. She held onto the handles down by her hips for dear life, feeling as though at every bump and rut she would be propelled off the ridiculous machine and into the field that surrounded them. Dirty water sprayed up as they hit a deep puddle. "Nuts!" she said. "These are brand new jeans. And my fur clogs!"

Did Eb even have a washing machine? She hadn't gotten a chance to see the rest of the house, let alone find out where she would be sleeping. Probably in some upstairs room, uninhabited for years—uninhabited by humans, anyway. There was no telling what kind of nasty things resided in that old farmhouse. She shuddered, glad once again for Coco's mousing prowess.

A few hundred yards from the old farmhouse, Eb pulled to a stop at a small barn covered in weathered gray-brown boards. He swung his good leg over the seat. "Well, ain'tcha gonna help me?" he snapped. "I can't use crutches on this bumpy ground."

She got off the machine and let Eb lean on her. "Fine. Don't get your union suit in a bunch, Eb."

Eb snorted. "For your information, I wear Fruit of the Looms, just like every other self-respecting farmer in these parts. And now that you mention it, you can pick me up a package when we go into town. Now get a move on."

TMI. Josie grimaced, counted to ten, then backwards to one, as they made their way to the doorway of a shed that appeared to be tacked on to the main structure of the barn. A dull clucking sounded from behind the door as she opened it. A flutter of feathers assaulted her, causing her to jump back. No mistaking a chicken coop, even for a city girl.

"Now grab a basket and go collect the eggs."

Josie stared at Eb, then looked down at her feet. The hens exploded upward, settled down to the coop floor, and marched out the door into the sun. Josie gulped. "You want me to touch eggs that haven't been washed yet? Ones that have just come out of a chicken's . . . you know what?"

Eb's prodigious eyebrows pulled together into a large, hairy caterpillar.

"Can't you find somebody else to come in and help you? Someone who knows what she's doing?"

"Ain't nobody else. Everybody's got day jobs. The neighbor's grandson's been coming over to take care of the chickens for me, but now I've got you, and he can go back to those crazy critters he's got. Hay, melons, and pumpkins in the summer and fall, maple syrup in the winter, eggs all year round. I gotta make enough money to pay the taxes, otherwise I lose the farm. Simple."

She wondered what constituted a crazy critter. This farm had been in the family for more than two hundred years. She couldn't let Eb lose it. But Eb had no children, and it would probably have to be sold once he died anyway. She felt a little stab of . . . something at that thought. Curious.

Eb's eyes narrowed. "Where do *you* think eggs come from?"

"I know where eggs come from," Josie said. "The supermarket, in nice clean containers." She took a deep breath, wondering if she'd regret it. But the air smelled like sweet straw instead of bird excrement, which she'd expected. She poked a finger into one of the long boxes lined with hay. A warm, smooth object found its way into her hand, and she pulled it out, placing it into the padded basket. Eb prodded her with a crutch from the sidelines as she fished around again and again until she'd found all the eggs. *My queendom for some hand sanitizer*, she thought.

"You sure you got 'em all? Now put some fresh straw down

on top of the old and let's get these wiped down and into the cartons. We've gotta deliver them to the store."

Josie resisted the urge to wipe her hands on her jeans. "What store?"

"Downtown. Wash up over there, and let's get going. We're late."

Chapter 3

Dougie's General Store was located on Main Street in a building that had housed a hardware shop when Josie had lived in Dorset Falls as a teenager. After her dad died—a long, slow, painful death from cancer—she and her mom had moved here so Katherine could teach at the local high school. They rented a cute little Victorian a few blocks from the center of the village. When Josie graduated, she went to New York and never looked back at Dorset Falls. Katherine Blair moved on to a permanent position in a private school in Westchester County.

Josie had made friends in high school, but gradually lost touch with everyone over the years. So she was surprised—pleasantly so—to find someone familiar behind the counter. Lorna Fowler greeted them as they walked in. Lorna had aged well, not that she was any older than Josie. Her hair was back to its natural dark color, pulled back into a glossy braid. Josie remembered one night when Lorna had slept over. The girls had dyed stripes into their hair with powdered drink mix—Lorna, blue; Josie, hot pink; mothers, livid. She smiled and gingerly set her box of eggs on the counter.

"Josie?" Lorna said. "Is that you?" Her face broke into a broad smile, and she came around the counter, enveloping Josie in a hug. Josie stiffened, then relaxed and hugged Lorna in return.

Eb hobbled toward the back and parked himself at one of the café tables. "Can't a man get a cup of coffee around here?" he called, leveling an accusing glare in Josie's direction. She resisted the urge to roll her eyes.

"Coming right up, Eb," Lorna said. "This morning's donuts are sold out, but I've got some fresh gingersnaps." A low grunt of acquiescence sounded. Turning to Josie, Lorna said, "Don't go anywhere—I'll be right back. I want to hear all about New York."

Josie looked around. The store was certainly countrified. The area to the left of the sales counter was lined with aisles flanked by shelves containing basic groceries—canned soups, boxed macaroni and cheese, and a small selection of dish detergents were visible from where she stood. A small table sat at the end of one of the aisles. Brightly colored mittens were arranged neatly on the fire-engine-red tablecloth.

Josie walked over to examine them. The child-sized mittens, each pair held together by a matching cord, were beautifully done with perfectly uniform stitches. Josie was no knitter, but she knew quality work when she saw it. She wished she knew a kid she could buy them for, but none of her friends back in the city had children, or were likely to anytime soon. Kids certainly weren't on her personal radar, although at thirty she was aware that her biological clock might possibly be ticking.

A sign on the table read: HANDMADE BY THE DORSET FALLS CHARITY KNITTERS ASSOCIATION—ALL PROCEEDS BENEFIT THOSE IN NEED. The price was half what Josie would have expected to pay in a New York boutique. She reached up and fingered the scarf around her neck, the one Cora had sent her.

Cora had almost certainly been one of the Charity Knitters, or at the very least she had provided them with supplies.

"Beautiful, aren't they? And the money goes to all kinds of good causes," a crisp voice said behind her. Josie straightened and turned. The woman was in her sixties, tall and angular with silvery gray hair cut in a severe pageboy, a pale, heavily powdered face, and bright red lipstick. "I'm Diantha Humphries, the president of the club that makes these items."

Josie felt as if she'd been punched in the gut. Of all the people in this town whom she could run into, it had to be Diantha Humphries. The mother of her high school boyfriend, Trey. A mother who thought her darling son could do no wrong—and could do a lot better than dating the pink-haired daughter of a schoolteacher.

Diantha's eyes disappeared into a squint. "I know you, don't I?" she said. Recognition dawned, and her eyes flew open. "Josephine Blair. What a . . . surprise."

Apparently bygones were not going to be bygones.

Josie squared her shoulders. "Mrs. Humphries. How nice to see you again." *Not.* She forced a smile to her face. "I hope you are well," she said sweetly.

"What brings you back to town?" Diantha's lips pursed so tightly it appeared her face might crack from the pressure. "Trey's married, you know."

Oh, for the love of Ralph Lauren. Trey had been a jerk in high school, and Josie would bet dollars to the donuts the store had sold out of this morning he still was. "I'm here temporarily. To help my uncle close up Cora Lloyd's yarn shop."

Diantha visibly relaxed. "Oh. When is your going-out-of-business sale?" Her eyes took on a glint that was almost greedy. "You could simply donate the stock to the Charity Knitters Association, you know."

She could, but it wasn't hers to give. And she wasn't at all enthused about doing any favors for Diantha.

"Well, that's up to Eb. The store and its contents belong to him now."

Diantha's face took on a calculating expression. "It's too bad about Cora. Such a horrible accident." She tapped a long, blood-red nail on her chin. Josie felt her hopes tick up a notch. So there *was* a nail salon somewhere around here. "You know, I've thought about opening up my own yarn shop. Perhaps you—or Eben—would consider letting me take over the lease and buy the stock?"

Josie bristled. She glanced at Eb, who was glaring in their direction. Whether his annoyance was directed at her, Diantha, or someone else was impossible to tell. "Uh, I'll talk about it with my uncle, and one of us will get back to you."

Diantha's face relaxed. "You do that." She pulled a creamy business card from her purse and pressed it into Josie's hand. "My number's on there, along with my e-mail address. I expect to hear from you soon." She turned and left the store.

Josie moved to the back of the store and sat herself down across from Eb. He pulled a set of keys out of the pocket of his canvas Carhartt jacket and scooted them toward her. "Here are the keys for the shop. Go on over and get started. I'll be over when I'm done with my coffee."

Get started with what? She had no idea. She called out to Lorna. "I'll be back, and then we can catch up." Lorna waved at her, smiling broadly, and poured Eb another cup.

Josie stood in front of Miss Marple Knits, a block from the general store, past several empty storefronts. The door was painted a bright, cheerful blue, which contrasted with the sad sign posted on it: CLOSED UNTIL FURTHER NOTICE. She tried several keys until she found the one that turned the lock. Bells tinkled as she stepped over the threshold into a dark room. It was late afternoon, and the natural light was fading. She felt around on the wall near the door for a switch and was rewarded with illumination.

The shop was moderately sized. Perpendicular to the big front window sat a sofa upholstered in a floral pattern. Two wingback chairs and a coffee table covered in knitting magazines completed the sitting area. Josie's eyes moved around the room. One wall was hung with what appeared to be tools and supplies. Josie recognized knitting needles and what must be crochet hooks in various sizes. Cubbies lined two walls, and each cubby was filled with yarn in a riot of colors. She reached out and ran her hand across a skein of dark green yarn—wool, she could see from the paper label—and resisted the urge to rub it across her face.

She'd always loved fabrics and the fashions that could be made from them, but this was different. There was something elemental about the yarn she held in her hand. Something close to the earth that nurtured the grass that fed the sheep that produced the wool that made the yarn that would someday make a garment. Suddenly sorry she'd never learned to knit, she wondered what it would feel like to create a beautiful thing, stitch by stitch. The shop felt warm, inviting, almost like the hug she'd received from her old friend Lorna.

Josie shook it off. She was here to nurse her great-uncle back to health, close up this store, and get back to New York, where she belonged.

The bells over the door rang again. A group of ladies, none under retirement age, blew in with a cold wind that ruffled the pages of the knitting magazines on the coffee table.

They began to disperse around the shop, heading straight for the cubbies and baskets full of yarn. One came toward her and thrust out a gloved hand. Josie stood there, her mouth hanging open. What the heck was going on?

"Hello, dear," the woman standing in front of her said. She pulled back her hand when Josie didn't take it. "You wouldn't know me, but I was a friend of Cora's. Lillian Woodruff."

Josie shook her head to clear it. "Nice to meet you, Lillian. Uh, you all know the shop is closed, right?"

Lillian laughed, her tightly permed gray hair bouncing around her head. "Closed? No such thing as closed. I was downtown and saw the lights on in the shop, so I called all my friends. Look at these knitters, ready to buy." She swept her hand grandly around the room. "You *are* having a going-out-of-business sale, aren't you?" Lillian was matter-of-fact now, even a little bossy, the façade of the sweet old lady gone. "Isn't that why you're here?"

What was it with the women in this town? Cora had only been gone six weeks, and they'd descended like vultures on the shop. Each skein of yarn was a siren calling to them, Josie supposed. Maybe they couldn't help themselves. But it didn't make her feel any less defensive. It was certainly disrespectful to Cora, and Josie wasn't about to let them get away with it. A dozen years in New York City had taught her everything she needed to know.

"I'm not selling the inventory."

Lillian frowned. "Perhaps I didn't understand you." Her face cleared. "Ah, you're going to donate it to the Charity Knitters Association. A noble sentiment. But unnecessary."

"Unnecessary, how?" Josie's radar was pinging like crazy. Something was going on here.

"Because I'm going to make you and Eben an offer—a very generous offer—to buy the business and everything in it." Her moon-shaped face got even rounder when she smiled.

"I've already had an offer." Josie smiled back.

Lillian's eyes darkened. "Who?" She began to twist the scarf around her neck. "Cora always planned to sell me a share of Miss Marple Knits, you know."

Josie didn't know. Couldn't know. But somehow, despite the fact that she'd never met Cora, Lillian's statement didn't ring true. Josie made a decision.

"Ladies," she said, using her New York voice. "There seems to be some misunderstanding. The shop is being closed, but the inventory is being sold online. Through an auction site. So you can all leave now." She looked pointedly at Lillian. "There's no sale."

Lillian glared. "Diantha got to you first, didn't she? Or maybe you've got some rich New Yorker on deck who thinks she can swoop in here and change everything?" The woman's breath was coming faster and harder now. "You'll be sorry," she hissed. "Who do you think you are, waltzing back into town and taking charge? You're probably trying to fleece poor Eben for everything he's got, now that Cora's gone." She smoothed the scarf around her neck. "Well, you won't get away with it. I'll see to that." Lillian stormed toward the door. "Come on, ladies. Nothing to buy here."

The women looked confused, but set their shopping baskets on the floor. They left in a haze of disappointment that was almost palpable.

Josie blew out a breath. "Sorry, Cora," she said aloud. "They just rubbed me the wrong way."

She went behind the polished wooden counter, so antique-looking it was probably original to the shop a hundred years ago, to look for a red marker. Maybe if she added some bold lines around the CLOSED sign, people would get the hint.

The door bells jingled yet again. "Give me a break. Don't these ladies understand the word *no*?" Josie straightened. "We're—"

"Is the coast clear?" Eb entered the store, a bit clumsily with his crutches.

"Oh, it's you." Josie hurried over and sat Eb down in one of the armchairs. "I thought it was those ladies coming back."

"Kicked 'em out, didja? Good job." He seemed impressed. "That pack of she-coyotes has been plaguing me since right after poor Cora died." Eb's face clouded over. He and Cora hadn't been married long, but who knew how long they'd known each other before that? Her death had clearly affected him more than he would probably ever admit. But Eb wouldn't appreciate overt sympathy. Josie knew that much about him already.

"Thanks for the warning."

"You're welcome. Now let's head on home. There's a storm coming in, and we gotta get Jethro inside."

Josie glanced toward the windows. The light coming in was now gray, and the air felt heavier, she realized. She hoped Coco had found a comfortable spot to curl up in, maybe near the woodstove.

"Eb, I'll start boxing up the yarn and things tomorrow, then start listing everything on the Internet. Maybe I can sell it all at once to another yarn store, and we'll have this done quickly." She thought about Diantha's offer, then Lillian's. It would certainly make things simple to sell to one of them. But a feeling had taken root in the pit of her stomach—the feeling that Cora wouldn't want that. It was crazy. Josie had never even met Cora and couldn't possibly know what she would have wanted.

Eb was watching her intently from underneath his formidable brows. "You'll do what's right, missy. I'm sure of it."

At nine thirty the next morning, Josie arrived at Miss Marple Knits. Since she hadn't chosen a bedroom yet, or even unpacked, she'd spent the night on the living room couch under a warm hand-knit afghan. The animals were fed, Eb was breakfasted and settled in with his morning crossword, of which he seemed to have an endless supply, the kitchen was cleaned up, laundry was started, and the eggs were gathered and delivered to Lorna at the general store. To-go cup of hot coffee in hand, Josie felt as if she'd already put in a full day's work.

Life was certainly on a different schedule in Dorset Falls than in New York. Back in the city she would just be getting to the office, after having spent at least an hour on her hair, makeup, and clothes. Today, she'd rolled off the couch, brushed her teeth and splashed some water on her face, and thrown her hair back into a ponytail. She felt a little naked, but it was liberating at the same time.

Josie pulled the list she'd made last night out of her pocket and reviewed. Number one item for getting this shop closed down: Set up computer. She opened her laptop and set it on the counter. She hunted around until she located a phone jack and plugged in. Hoping Cora had an Internet connection (and that somebody had paid the bill for it since she'd been gone), Josie booted up and crossed her fingers. Bingo! She was online—a feat that had proved impossible at the farmhouse, so far. If Cora had installed Internet capabilities at the house, Eb didn't know about it. Or was too ornery to tell her.

Number two, start making an inventory of the store goods. Eb had told her there was a back room on the first floor, as well as an empty apartment upstairs where Cora might have stashed her excess. A glance around told Josie there was only one interior doorway, so that must lead to the storeroom. Taking a deep breath, she opened the door and flipped on the lights.

To her left was a bathroom. Thank goodness. Now she wouldn't have to walk down to Lorna's when the need arose. Beyond that was a large room lined in shelves. Cardboard boxes full of old books, patterns, and various types of yarn were stacked on the shelves. As she moved around the room, her heart sank. This was a huge job, and she had no idea how to put a price on any of the stock. But there was nothing for it but to get down to work.

In one dim corner stood a tower of boxes as tall as she was, all marked CASHMERE in black ink. *Mmm, cashmere sweaters.* So soft, light, and warm. That seemed as good a place to start as any. Pulling the top box off the stack, she set it on the floor. The movement must have disturbed the balance of the stack because it began to teeter. Josie put out her arms to try to steady it, then jumped back as the boxes tumbled over. She landed hard on her bottom on the unforgiving wooden floor.

There was no time to worry about whether she'd broken anything. She was too shocked at what had been uncovered when the tower fell. Scrambling to her feet, she moved closer.

A woman lay atop a bier of open boxes. Face pale and still as that of a statue, her gray head rested on a pillow made of skeins of fluffy yarn. A blue, tightly twisted cord was wrapped around her neck, the tassel end fanned out and situated precisely in the center of her ample bosom.

Josie stifled the urge to scream. She'd met this woman, if only briefly, the day before. Lillian Woodruff. One of the women who'd tried to buy the shop. The one who'd accused Josie of taking advantage of Uncle Eb. Josie ran to the front of the store and punched 911 into the keypad of the phone on the counter. "Send an ambulance to Miss Marple Knits. And hurry."

Chapter 4

Josie's stomach roiled as she disconnected the call and returned, reluctantly, to the storeroom. Could she help the woman? She had no first-aid skills beyond basic peel-and-stick bandages. To her untrained eye, the woman appeared stone dead. Lillian's skin was as gray as her hair, her chest was not rising and falling, and she hadn't so much as twitched. Should Josie cover her up? Start CPR? Mouth-to-mouth? She shuddered, then looked at her watch, a gift from Otto to her last Christmas. How long would it take for someone with medical skills to get here? She shouldn't disturb the crime scene, that much she knew.

The sound of the bells at the front door caused her heart to jump into her throat, but then she breathed a sigh of relief and headed for the front. A uniformed police officer stood there. The woman was petite, with her dark hair pulled back into a rather severe bun. She unzipped her winter jacket and put her gloves in the pockets.

"The ambulance is on its way," she said with efficiency. "I'm Officer Coogan. Take me to the injured person, please."

"Uh, this way." Josie led the way to the back. Officer Coogan scanned the room, then made a beeline for the body. She put her fingertips to the woman's wrist, then looked thoughtful. "No pulse," she said. "I think it's too late, but we'll wait for the EMTs from the fire department to get here to confirm. Looks like Lillian Woodruff."

Josie swallowed the lump that had risen in her throat. The woman was dead. In her storeroom. *Eb's storeroom,* she mentally corrected. What was she supposed to do now? Fashion school had prepared her to design clothing to wear to funerals, not how to behave in the face of death.

Officer Coogan's large brown eyes softened, as she apparently took pity on Josie. "I haven't seen you around town. Are you Eb's niece, the one who's here to take care of him while he recovers?"

Wow. Big surprise. Everyone in town already knows I'm here. Memories of living in Dorset Falls, where everybody knew everyone else's business, came flooding back. "Yeah, I'm Josie Blair."

"Well," the officer said, giving a wry smile. "I'm sure the Visiting Nurses' Association is thrilled you've come."

Josie chuckled softly. She liked this woman, despite her no-nonsense demeanor and the circumstances under which they'd met. Officer Coogan was clearly trying to put her at ease, and it was working. A little.

"Eb's family, and I was the only one available to come."

The officer nodded in approval.

Josie felt her spirits rise as she and Officer Coogan returned to the retail part of the store. Through the expanse of glass in the front windows a set of flashing lights had appeared, and the lights were attached to a big white ambulance with the words Dorset Falls VFD Emergency Services emblazoned on the side.

"Well, Josie. What happened here? Why is Lillian Woodruff

lying in the storeroom with a cord wrapped around her neck? I don't think that's a fashion statement."

Officer Coogan's words echoed Josie's own thoughts. Why *was* Lillian here?

Josie looked the police officer in the eye. "I wish I knew."

"Me too," Officer Coogan said, returning the look. "Because I'm pretty sure she didn't die of natural causes."

Josie gulped. The officer's words confirmed what Josie had already suspected. That cord of blue yarn was wrapped too tightly around Lillian's neck to be anything other than a murder weapon.

Officer Coogan smiled sympathetically. "Why don't you sit down? Is there someone I can call for you?"

"I'll be fine." Josie realized, a bit ruefully, that there *was* no one to call. She only knew a handful of people in Dorset Falls. Uncle Eb couldn't drive until his leg healed. Lorna, with whom she'd barely had time to reconnect, was busy running the general store. And that crabby lady from the Charity Knitters. Diantha, Trey's mom. Well, nobody was likely to show up at the meeting of their mutual admiration society.

Josie sat down on the couch by the front window just as the EMTs rushed in. Officer Coogan met them and led them to the back.

Josie stared outside. Main Street, what she could see of it that wasn't blocked by the ambulance, was deserted. Despite the fact that she was in semirural Connecticut, she would not have been surprised to see a tumbleweed roll down the two-lane road rimmed with empty parking spaces. Of course, what was there to attract people to downtown? The potentially charming brick storefronts were mostly empty, the windows of the shops papered over. She wondered again how Cora had managed to keep Miss Marple Knits in business. Maybe she'd ask Eb if he knew where Cora's shop records were kept. Josie hadn't seen an office or even a desk here.

"Why do I even care?" Josie mused aloud. Her eyes roved over the bins of yarn and the scarves and sweaters hanging in various spots about the room, presumably sample items made from the shop's inventory of fibers. "I'm only here to help Eb and to close up. I'll be gone in a couple of weeks." Why did that make her feel just a little bit sad?

She stood at the window and looked out on Main Street again, thoughtful. Across the road, a narrow wooden door between two empty shops opened a crack. Josie glanced up. The upstairs windows were dark and shaded, without any discernible curtains or houseplants sitting on sills. The door opened farther, and a woman dressed in a drab khaki-colored trench coat stepped out onto the short stoop. She glanced around, stared for a moment at the ambulance, then pulled her unstructured hat firmly down over her head. She walked off briskly in the direction of the general store, the tails of the long coat blowing in the cold February wind.

Josie frowned. If she wasn't mistaken, that was one of the ladies who'd accompanied Lillian here yesterday, looking for a sale on Cora's yarn. What had she been doing over there, in an apparently abandoned building? Not that it was any of Josie's business. In New York, you learned to stay out of other people's affairs, no matter how curious you were, and it seemed like good advice here, too.

"Josie?" Officer Coogan's voice made her jump. "Sorry to startle you. I think it would be best if you went on home now. It's going to be a while before the techs get here to process the scene."

"Process? You mean this is a crime scene?" Officer Coogan nodded. Even though Josie had expected it, the confirmation hit her like a falling anvil in a cartoon. Someone had died at Miss Marple Knits, and it hadn't been an accident.

"You're staying at Eben's, right? If you're all right to drive, go on back there now. I or someone else will get in touch with you. We'll need a statement."

"Me? I got into town yesterday, and I met the . . . dead woman . . . once for about five minutes. What could I possibly know?" She hated the way her voice had risen along with her agitation level.

Officer Coogan put a hand on Josie's shoulder. "We know that. News travels fast in a village this size. But it's procedure. So go on home, make a cup of tea, and wait until we contact you, okay? We'll let you know when you can come back to the shop." Her tone was calm and kind, but it also brooked no opposition.

Josie wrapped the scarf Cora had given her around her neck, then buttoned up her coat and donned her leather gloves. Strange. She felt a little proprietary about this shop, somehow, and didn't want to leave it in the hands of strangers. Not that she wanted to be here when they wheeled out Lillian's body. "Okay," she finally said. "I'm going to stop first at the general store and pick up something for Eb's dinner since I don't know where to buy groceries yet."

"There's a good-sized store in Litchfield, five or so miles south. You can buy pretty much anything there," Officer Coogan offered. "But I'd suggest the chicken potpie or the macaroni and cheese from the g.s."

Josie's stomach rumbled in response. Yankee comfort-food meals and working in the fashion industry were, for the most part, mutually exclusive, at least in public. But goodness, chicken potpie. And she wasn't exactly working in the fashion industry anymore, not until she could convince Otto to give her and her designs one more chance.

"I'll wait for your call," she said, shouldered her bag, and headed out the door.

The general store was blessedly warm. Josie was grateful to be out of the cold wind and unwound her scarf, letting the ends hang loose while she shopped. She picked up a plastic basket and looped the handles over her arm.

Lorna waved her over. "What's going on at Miss Marple? Did Eb fall? I saw the ambulance pull up out front, but couldn't leave the store to see if you needed help."

Josie's heart warmed. She barely knew this woman after so many years, yet Lorna felt like an old friend. Still, Josie debated. Should she say anything? Officer Coogan hadn't given her any instructions. It could hardly hurt to tell—the news would be all over Dorset Falls by sunset anyway.

"No, it's not Eb. He's home doing . . . whatever Eb does. It's Lillian Woodruff."

Lorna's eyebrows shot up. "Lillian? What was she doing at Miss Marple Knits? You're selling the inventory online, right?"

Why did Josie's stomach give a little flip every time she thought about closing up the shop? Dread, most likely, at the size and scope of the job before her. And with a murder investigation underway, who knew when she'd be able to get started in earnest? She might be here in Dorset Falls longer than she'd planned for.

"Lorna, were you and Lillian friends?"

Her friend's mouth fell open. "What do you mean, *were?* And I'd say we're acquaintances, not exactly friends."

Josie caught her lower lip between her teeth. There was no nice way to put it. She dropped her voice. "Lillian's dead. I found her in the storeroom."

Lorna rushed out from behind the counter and wrapped Josie in another hug. "Oh my goodness," Lorna said. "Sit down at one of the tables, and I'll make you some tea. Unless you'd rather have a coffee?" Her face was filled with concern.

"I can't stay long," Josie said. "I should get back to Eb and let him know what's happened, since he owns the shop now. But a cup of tea sounds lovely." Josie sat back and shrugged off her coat and laid it on the chair next to her as Lorna returned to her station.

A shadow passed in front of her, and Josie looked up.

"I just talked to the police officer at Cora's shop. What did you do to Lillian?" The voice was clipped, laced with barely controlled anger, and came out of the hard lips of Diantha Humphries.

Josie stiffened. "What is it you *think* you know, Diantha?" Josie wasn't a teenager afraid of her boyfriend's mother anymore, and she had no intention of letting Diantha bully her. She'd been through enough today.

Diantha's eyes narrowed, and her voice lowered. "I know everything that goes on in my town, Ms. Blair. *Everything*. Whatever it is you're up to, you won't be able to hide it from me for long."

"Well. I guess I'll have to go rework my evil master plan, then, to keep you on your toes." Josie sat back in her chair. "Don't you have anything better to do? I'm sure Trey and his wife have some business you can stick your nose into."

Virtual steam was emitting from Diantha's ears. Her finger shook as she pointed it at Josie. "You've still got an attitude, haven't you? I want you out of this town before you do any more damage. Head on back to New York and stay there," she ordered.

Josie smiled sweetly. "Great! I'll make up the spare room for you out at Eb's so you can take care of him. I'm sure you can handle him and the farm chores too. Do you like chickens?"

Lorna returned with two oversized china mugs with real steam rolling off the tops. "Can I help you, Diantha?" Her voice was innocent as she set down the mugs. "That hemorrhoid cream you special ordered should be in any day now."

"Watch it, Lorna. I'm in no mood to deal with you right now." Diantha turned to Josie. "Don't underestimate me, Ms. Blair." She stormed off in a cloud of perfume—Elizabeth Taylor's White Diamonds, if Josie wasn't mistaken.

Lorna sat down and began to dunk her teabag up and down. "Don't let her get to you. Ever since that old battle-ax got elected to the town council, she thinks she's entitled to run everything her own way."

"I get the strange feeling she still doesn't like me." Josie sipped her tea, let some of the hot liquid roll around on her tongue, and swallowed. "This tea is amazing! What is it?"

Lorna waved her hand in the air. "Oh, it's one of my own special blends. Winterberry."

Josie was impressed. "Well, it's as good as anything I ever tasted in New York. Maybe better."

Lorna beamed. "I do the baking here, too. I'll send you home with some cookies for Eb. He likes my oatmeal raisin. So what happened to Lillian? Did *she* fall?"

Josie took another sip of the tea. It tasted of blueberries and maple with a hint of vanilla. Lorna could make a fortune selling this stuff in the city. Josie leaned forward, seeing no reason not to tell her old-new friend, but not wanting to broadcast the news about Lillian either. "I think she was murdered. The police think so too. They're investigating the shop now."

Lorna's jaw dropped. "Murder?" she whispered. "But who would do such a thing to an old woman? Sure, she had her opinions on things and wasn't shy about letting anyone know what those opinions were, but she wasn't disliked." She dunked her teabag again, then used a spoon to fish it out of the mug. "Not like Diantha. Any number of people in Dorset Falls would have a reason to want her dead."

"I wish I knew," Josie said. "Not only who killed Lillian, and why, but what was she doing in the storeroom of Miss Marple Knits?"

Lorna looked thoughtful. "Were there any signs of a break-in? A struggle?"

"Not that I noticed." Josie's heart gave a little squeeze. "Did Lillian have family? How awful for them, to lose her this way."

"Let's see," Lorna said. "She has a son who lives on the West Coast, and a daughter out toward Boston. Her husband died years ago. The only local relatives I can think of are her brother, Roy Woodruff, and his grandson, Mitch."

Josie reached back into her memory banks. "I don't remember any Woodruffs from when I lived here as a teenager. Of course, I was only here for a couple of years after my father died."

"Mitch would have been a few years ahead of us in school, then he went off to college. Cornell, I think. Agricultural sciences." Lorna set down her cup. "He came back to Dorset Falls a year or so back to help Roy and try to get the farm certified organic and to manage the alpacas. I'm surprised you haven't seen either one of them yet."

Josie drained her teacup. "Why's that?"

"Because the Woodruff farm is right next to the Lloyd farm. Mitch and Roy are your neighbors."

Chapter 5

It was just after noon when Josie's battered Saab rolled to a stop in Eb's driveway. She made her way up the front walk, which she noticed had been freshly shoveled and salted. How had Eb managed that on crutches? Guilt pricked her conscience. The shoveling should have been her job. Not that she was an expert, having had that particular chore performed for her for the last decade in the city. But it wasn't brain surgery.

She transferred her bags to one hand, but before she could turn the knob the door opened, and Jethro came barreling out and off the porch. She barely kept her balance. Fortunately, the bags stayed upright as she entered the sweltering house. It would have been a shame to lose lunch.

Eb's back was toward her as he walked to the table and sat down in a chair. He stretched out his injured leg, then began to fiddle with some kind of fine line attached to a couple of sticks painted a dark green, which matched the outside trim around the windows. He looked up at her through a pair of half-moon reading glasses. "What the hell's going on?" he demanded.

"You mean other than my almost getting run over by your

hellhound?" She had planned to set the bags down on the table while she removed her boots and coat, but the spot she'd cleared on the table was filled up again. There seemed to be a number of contraptions identical to the one Eb was working on, stacked four or five deep. "Let me go put away these groceries and get lunch together, then we can talk. Something . . . happened at the shop."

He stopped playing with the line and looked at her again over the rims of the glasses. "Lunch sounds good," he finally said.

A few minutes later she came back out with two plates, each of which contained a generous slice of chicken potpie. Eb moved the thingies he'd been working on to the top of a stack of magazines and old newspapers. First order of business, Josie thought, was to take a tour of the house and find herself a bedroom. Second was to clear this table so they'd have a place to eat.

Eb dug into his lunch with gusto. Josie was pleased to see that he not only ate the tender chicken, he also ate the carrots, peas, and onions that were dispersed throughout the rich yellow gravy. She mentally shook her head. Why should she care if her great-uncle, whom she barely knew, and who didn't seem to like her much, ate his veggies? He wiped his mouth with a paper napkin. "Now, missy. 'Fess up. Did you set something on fire?"

The bite of chicken she'd just swallowed seemed to stick in her throat, as she remembered Lillian's cold body lying on the boxes of yarn. Was there any sensitive, tactful way to relay the information that someone had died in Cora's store? But Eb wasn't the type who'd appreciate tact.

"I found Lillian Woodruff dead in the back room. I'm pretty sure she was strangled."

Eb's eyebrows drew together as he processed the news. "Wouldn't be the first murder in Dorset Falls," he finally said. "Probably won't be the last." He speared a piece of flaky crust and returned to his meal.

Connecticut Yankees. So warm and fuzzy. Jethro's frantic barking interrupted her thoughts. She rose and went to the window. A faded red pickup truck sat behind her Saab, plumes of blue-gray exhaust rising up from the tailpipe. Jethro was growling at the driver's side door. A tall man with dark hair got out from the other side and approached Jethro, his hand outstretched, palm up. Jethro stopped barking and began to lick the man's hand. The driver's door opened, and an older gentleman got out. He made his way up the front walk, the loose earflaps of his fluorescent orange cap bobbing as he walked.

"Well? Who is it?" Eb said. "Sounds like Woodruff's truck. Engine's knocking. Bad piston."

"I don't know, but they'll be here any minute." The younger man tossed something at Jethro and left him in the driveway, munching happily and wagging his tail. *Brilliant.* Why hadn't she thought to buy dog biscuits?

Josie stepped away from the window. "Should I set a couple more places? There's plenty of potpie left."

Eb looked at her like she'd suddenly materialized out of thin air wearing a sequined top hat and cutaway coat, singing a show tune. "Hell, no," he said.

She was saved the trouble of responding by an insistent banging on the heavy wooden door. Eb nodded, and she opened it.

The older man pushed past Josie. He stood over Eb, who nonchalantly scraped up some gravy from his plate. "What happened to my sister?" the man demanded.

"I could ask you the same question, Roy," Eb said. "Not that a lying bastard like you would be likely to tell the truth."

Josie's mouth hung open. The younger man turned a pair of pale blue eyes toward her and smiled. "You must be Eb's niece." He extended a hand, then thought better of it and wiped his hand on his jeans. "Dog slobber. I don't suppose I could use the kitchen sink and wash up?"

The two old farmers continued to trade barbs. "Can we, um,

leave them alone together? Will they hurt each other?" Josie was genuinely concerned.

The man chuckled. She liked the sound of it. "Yes, and probably not, to answer your questions in order. I think it's been a lot of years since they got into it physically. Mitch Woodruff," he said. "I live on the next farm over with my grandfather."

"Josie Blair," she said, over the escalating argument. "Come on into the kitchen. This way."

"I know the way, thanks," Mitch responded. "I was just here this morning, actually, while you were in town."

Light dawned. "You're the one who filled up the wood box and took care of the front walk, aren't you?"

Mitch grinned and moved to the sink, squirting some dish soap on his hands. "I'd appreciate it if you'd keep that quiet. My grandfather would have a stroke if he knew. I told him I've been working on the sap tubing."

Josie grinned back. "Sap tubing?" She handed Mitch a paper towel.

"For collecting the sap to make maple syrup. We should talk about how that's going to get done this year. Eb can probably handle the boiling itself, but he won't be able to do the collecting."

Josie pursed her lips. "Doesn't maple syrup come from a store? Like eggs." She reached into one of the bags she'd brought back from the general store, then handed him a cookie.

"Eventually," he said. "But it starts out with trees." He took a healthy bite. "You got this from Lorna, didn't you? That woman is one fine baker."

"She's a good friend, too." The thought pleased Josie. She nibbled at her own cookie. It was just the way she liked it, with lots of cinnamon and fat, juicy raisins. "What's the deal with those two?" She nodded toward the dining room, where Eb and Mitch's grandfather were still going at it.

Mitch looked thoughtful. "Honestly, I don't know what started it. They've been bickering for as long as I've known them.

It goes back even further, to their fathers or maybe grandfathers. Our families have been neighbors for more than a hundred years, and they've been fighting about something or other that entire time."

Josie laughed. "You mean, the Lloyds and the Woodruffs, Connecticut versions of the Hatfields and the McCoys?"

"That about sums it up. Sorry about barging in. The police called us about Aunt Lillian, and I couldn't let Gramps come over here without me to run interference. Although I think Eb could hold his own with or without a broken leg."

"Who's winning the feud, do you think?" The whole thing sounded petty and childish. But Josie couldn't help but secretly root for Eb.

"Last month, Roy put a pile of alpaca droppings in the air vents of Eb's Ford. Eb retaliated by somehow getting into Roy's truck and messing with the engine. Not enough to make the truck dangerous, but enough that Roy might break down if we don't get it repaired soon. I'm not sure how Eb managed it, actually."

Josie thought of the camouflage-painted ATV he'd made her ride on out to the barn. Eb might not be able to drive a car or a truck right now, but he could get around if he needed to. She decided to say nothing. "I'm sorry about your aunt," she said, changing the subject.

Mitch smiled sadly. "She was a pip, just like Roy. I'll miss her always telling me what I should think and do. Speaking of Auntie"—he pronounced it *awn-tee,* in the New England way—"I'd better get Roy out of here and down to the hospital morgue so we can identify the body." His eyes were sad. "Her kids, my cousins, won't get here until tomorrow."

Josie nodded. "Mitch? Forgive me if this is a bad time to ask, but you wouldn't happen to know what she was doing in the yarn shop, would you?"

"Not a clue. She's got an entire room of bins and boxes and

shelves full of yarn at home. I can't imagine what she'd want with more." He headed back out to the dining room.

"Gramps. Roy," Mitch said, louder this time. Roy's face was red, contrasting garishly with his bright orange hat. He picked up one of the wooden things Eb had been working on when Josie got home and broke it over his knee, tossing it to the floor before storming outside. Mitch nodded apologetically to Eb, then to Josie, and followed. Jethro was quiet. Mitch probably had a whole pocketful of dog treats.

Eb watched them go. "That was fun. Not that I'm not sorry about Lillian."

Josie bent over and picked up the broken sticks from the hardwood floor. She made a mental note to find out if Eb had a vacuum cleaner. There were some lethal-looking dust bunnies making a warren under the table.

"What is this, anyway, Eb?" She handed him the pieces.

He rolled his eyes. "Missy, you have lived in the city too long. That's a trap." He began to disassemble it, presumably for parts.

Of course. A trap. That explained everything. "Uh, a trap for what?" She hoped it wasn't for small, furry animals. She always felt bad when Coco brought her mice. Not that she wanted them alive in her home, of course.

Eb put his glasses on, then went back to work. "They're for fishing."

Josie inspected one more closely. It didn't look like any fishing pole she'd ever seen, though now she realized it did have something that might have been a reel attached to it. Still, how the thing worked was a mystery. "Getting ready for warm weather? I like trout. Do trout grow here?"

Eb shook his head, then began to laugh. It was a wheezy sound, which Josie attributed to the overheated dry air in the house. Maybe she could order a humidifier online.

When the laughter subsided, Eb said, "Yes, missy, trout

'grow' here. In the lake. These are *ice-fishing* traps. I figured you could come with me this afternoon, and we'll catch dinner."

Did the man not know that he was on crutches and that it was February? The coldest part of winter? He couldn't be serious. And ice fishing? Wasn't that where people sat around a hole all day and waited for a fish to come by and allow itself to be caught? No thanks. She'd rather dump her entire sample-sale collection of Kate Spade bags into the East River and carry her stuff around for eternity in a plastic grocery sack.

"Um, yeah. That sounds like a lot of fun. But the cops told me I was supposed to stay here in case they wanted to come talk to us. And I've got, uh, work to do."

He stared at her out from under those bushy eyebrows, then let out another guffaw. "Just yankin' your chain drive, missy. You don't put your traps in the water in the afternoon. Fish don't bite then. We'll go tomorrow morning, soon as the sun's up."

That gives me less than twenty-four hours to come up with an excuse, she thought. *And it'll need to be a good one.*

"I'll take it," Josie said to herself, surveying the eight-by-ten bedroom at the end of the upstairs hallway. Not only did it have a window overlooking the road and the snow-covered meadow across it, but it contained no clutter, so would be the easiest to clean and make habitable for her short stay here. Eb had told her to take whatever room she wanted. He slept downstairs, and Josie suspected he might not have been up the narrow stairway to the second floor in years. Still, it wasn't as dusty as she would have expected, and there were some touches only a woman or a man with the decorating gene would have thought of.

A watercolor painting showing a pastoral scene hung over the bed, which was flanked by a Victorian-era table with a marble top and a pretty, but more modern lamp. The dresser matched the table, and when she opened the drawers, she found them clean and ready to receive clothes. Josie pulled out a tiny knitted pillow and put it to her nose as an old-fashioned scent wafted up. A lavender sachet. Lovely. She held the sachet in her hand and studied it. Cora had made this, she'd bet on it, and a pang of emotion surprised her. How was it possible that Josie felt such a connection to a woman she'd never met?

She replaced the sachet and closed the drawer, then looked around the room again. It was as though Cora had prepared this room especially for her, right down to the overstuffed armchair in the corner and the little painted bookcase next to it, filled with paperback novels and a couple of knickknacks. Josie shook her head. That was ridiculous. Cora had probably been reclaiming rooms in the house one at a time, like she'd started to do in the kitchen, and she'd chosen to make this into a guest room.

Josie began to pull off the bedding, when she felt a familiar brush against her legs. "Coco!" she said, reaching down to pet the cat's soft black-and-white fur. "Where've you been hiding? Not that I blame you. Jethro scares me too." The cat allowed a few strokes before jumping up into the armchair, turning around a few times, then settling onto the cushion. She tucked her legs up underneath her and stared at Josie intently with her bright green eyes.

"You like it here? I guess I made the right choice." Josie removed the rest of the sheets and blankets from the bed and headed to the washer, which was located in the downstairs bathroom.

An hour and a half later, the room was vacuumed and dusted, and Josie had put her clothes away. On the top shelf of the small closet she'd found a treasure wrapped in an old sheet: a heavily fringed, handmade crocheted bedspread. She laid it out over the clean sheets and blankets, adjusting the sides so they hung evenly, then tucked the top over the pillows.

The lacy white pattern allowed the deep blue of the blanket

underneath to show through, throwing each stitch of the flower motif into relief. Josie examined the bedspread, marveling. How many hours had it taken someone—Cora, or perhaps one of Josie's own long-ago ancestors—to form stitch upon stitch into this magnificent whole?

Josie stood back, admiring her work. Yes, this room would do nicely. Too bad she wouldn't be here long.

Chapter 6

Josie left Coco sleeping in the armchair and dragged the vacuum cleaner back down the stairs. Between bumps on each tread, she heard a woman's voice, which was rising and falling in a musical cadence. Had Eb turned on the television? No, this sounded like a live human. Eb was certainly a popular guy in these parts. There'd been no shortage of visitors today.

She parked the vacuum cleaner at the bottom of the stairs, which opened up into the dining room. Or what she had been assuming was the dining room, since that's where the big table was. Eb sat in his favorite armchair by the window, holding a folded-up newspaper and tapping the eraser of his pencil on his left thigh. He shifted several times in his seat, and looked decidedly uncomfortable. He turned toward Josie with pleading eyes.

A woman with shiny, obviously dyed strawberry-blond hair cut into a neat cap had pulled up a dining chair next to him and was prattling away. She appeared to be in her mid to late sixties, a little younger than Eb, and apparently didn't notice that Josie was now in the room. The well-manicured fingers of one hand grazed the soft flannel of Eb's shirtsleeve. ". . . so I just want you to know that you can call on me for *anything,* Eben."

Josie cleared her throat. The woman stiffened slightly, then turned around. Eb blew out a breath.

"Hello. I'm Josie," she said, extending a hand.

The woman smiled. "Evelyn Graves. I was just dropping off a casserole to Roy Woodruff, and, since I had an extra, I thought I'd drop one off to Eben as well."

Of course. I keep extra casseroles around, too. "That's really nice of you. Where is it, and I'll put it away?"

Evelyn waved her hand. "I've already put it in the freezer. There are heating instructions taped to the foil on top." She cut her eyes toward Eb. "I'll come by in a few days to collect my baking dish."

Eb's face registered a mild degree of panic, which Josie would have found amusing if she hadn't felt just a little sorry for him. Evelyn was clearly on the prowl, and it looked like Eb was the intended prey. Josie looked from the country-clubby Evelyn to the just-plain-country Eb and wondered at the attraction. But Dorset Falls was a small village. Maybe Evelyn didn't have a lot to choose from, or maybe she just liked bachelor farmers. Josie couldn't picture Evelyn ice fishing any more than she could see herself doing it. Maybe she and Evelyn had something in common after all.

"That's a lovely cardigan," Josie said. "Did you make it?"

Evelyn preened. "Yes, dear. This is a traditional Irish fisherman's pattern. I bought the wool from Cora, of course. There's probably still some left in the shop. If you haven't sold everything yet." Josie couldn't quite find fault with the woman's tone, but still it sounded like a mild accusation. What was this woman's problem? Miss Marple Knits was a shop, and shops sold things.

"Well, that's on hold right now while the police investigate," Josie said.

A frown crossed Evelyn's face. "First poor Cora, now Lillian. Of course, at our age you have to be prepared for friends to go suddenly, but it still reminds us of our own mortality. Right, Eben?" He just sat there, his face a stony mask. Evelyn was going to have a tough time romancing him, if that was her plan. And Cora had only been gone six weeks.

Evelyn turned to Josie. "Speaking of Cora, I know you're here to close up her shop. What are you going to do with all the yarn she kept here at the house?"

"Did she keep yarn here? I've only been here a couple of days, and I haven't been through the whole house yet."

Evelyn's mouth hung open, just a little, then she gave a small laugh. "My dear, it's probably just as well you're closing the shop. You know *nothing* about knitters."

Josie stiffened. This woman was somewhere between good-naturedly condescending and downright rude. "What don't I know about knitters?" she said.

Evelyn smiled. "Knitters have stashes *everywhere*. We see beautiful yarn and we buy it, whether or not we have a project in mind for it or time to knit it. We can't help ourselves. Come on," she said. "I know where Cora kept at least some of her hoard."

She headed into the living room without a backward glance at Eb. Apparently yarn was more interesting to her than romance. Eb let out a breath. "Go on, and keep her busy, will ya?"

Josie grinned, then caught up with Evelyn, who was standing in front of a wooden door in the back corner of the living room. Josie had assumed it was a closet, so she was surprised when Evelyn opened the door and led her into a medium-sized room filled with late afternoon sunlight.

Josie let her eyes roam. A golden oak desk with a matching filing cabinet sat in one corner. A comfy-looking pair of mismatched armchairs flanked the window, which looked out over the meadow behind the house. And everywhere she looked, she saw baskets and bins of yarn. Evelyn was scanning the room, a reverent expression on her face.

She turned to Josie. "Of course, this would have been the borning room in the old days."

Josie frowned in confusion, thinking of the period dramas she liked to watch on public television. The costumes were always so gorgeous. "You mean morning room. Like they had in mansions, where the lady of the house wrote her letters and things." Of course, that didn't make sense. This was a farmhouse and gave no appearances of ever having been anything else.

Evelyn shook her head. "No, dear. I said *borning* room, and I meant *borning* room. This is where the lady of the house gave birth—and remember, not so long ago most women had a baby every year or so. It's also where the sick were tended, and where people died."

A shudder ran through Josie. It was kind of nice to think about generations of Lloyd babies being born here. But it was not so nice to think of people dying. Her thoughts skipped back to Lillian, the only dead body she'd ever seen. Yup, Josie had had all the death she could handle.

She forced her brain back to the present. "You say you've been in this room?"

"Of course Cora only lived here a few months before she died." A look of sadness passed over Evelyn's face. "Before she married Eben she had her own house, that big saltbox on Elm Street. Such a beautiful place, built by one of the founders of Dorset Falls. She sold it for a nice profit to some out-of-towners, you know."

Josie didn't know. But she wondered if Cora had been spending the proceeds on keeping her yarn shop afloat. That would explain how she'd been able to stay in business in Dorset Falls, but that money wouldn't have lasted indefinitely. "So you were friends?"

"Well, of course. Cora and I went back a long way. We used

to get together for dinner at my house or hers—either the house in town or later here—before our committee meetings. Put two knitters in a room together and, well, they're going to start knitting." She gave a sad laugh. "You might want to keep the dog out of here. He'll ruin the yarn."

Evelyn bent down and pulled a cherry-red skein out of one of the baskets. She ran her fingers through the strands. "Wool and mohair blend. Very nice. I wonder if there's any more of this?" The woman picked up the basket, parked herself in one of the armchairs, and began to rummage.

Josie watched, fascinated. Evelyn seemed to have forgotten all about her as she methodically pawed through the yarn. *Oh well,* Josie thought. *What can it hurt?* Josie used the opportunity to survey the room again. If Cora had been a superheroine, this would have been her inner sanctum, not a room that Eb appeared to have any presence in at all. Josie made her way to the desk while Evelyn did her thing.

This must have been where Cora had done her paperwork, not at the shop. Josie put her hand on the drawer handle. A pool of unease sloshed in her stomach. This didn't feel right, looking into Cora's personal world. She shook her head. No sense being squeamish, she told herself firmly. Cora was gone. And this was why Josie was there, to help close up Cora's affairs. Eb had given her carte blanche. If Cora had any secrets, they couldn't hurt her now.

Josie glanced up at Evelyn, who was still industriously going through the basket. The woman was focused, that was for sure. She'd pulled out three more skeins of the red yarn and set them on the side table next to her. Finally, she looked up.

"What are you going to do with all this?" She swept her arm around. Her eyes glinted, ever so slightly. A glint Josie had seen before in the eyes of Diantha Humphries. Suddenly, Josie knew why Evelyn had seemed familiar. She was one of the women who had descended on Miss Marple Knits the first day Josie had arrived. Not the one she'd seen coming out of the building across the street earlier today, but definitely one of the women who'd accompanied Lillian Woodruff into the shop looking for a bargain.

In truth, Josie had no idea what to do with all the yarn that surrounded her. She supposed she'd just pack it up and add it to the inventory at the shop, then start looking for a buyer. Darn it. There was that flutter in her stomach again. The potpie she'd eaten for lunch rather than her usual salad, she told herself. Maybe she'd fix something for Eb, but just have a yogurt for dinner.

"Honestly, since I didn't know about this . . . stash, I don't have any plans for it yet. Sell it along with the shop inventory, most likely."

A cloud of disappointment passed over Evelyn's face. "Well, of course you'll do what you—and Eben—see fit." She ran her fingers over the red wool again.

Josie had an idea. Whether it would turn out to be a good idea, or a bad idea, she didn't know. "Say, Evelyn. If you're not too busy, once the police clear me to go back to Miss Marple Knits, maybe you could give me a hand with making an inventory? I can't make any decisions until I know what's there." Having someone to help who knew what she was doing would mean Josie could have this business over and done with quickly. She'd wait for the doctor to clear Eb, then she could hightail it back to New York in time for the spring runway show. Brilliant.

Evelyn looked at Josie appraisingly. "So, you'd like me to help you close up my favorite store in the world, a place where I have many happy memories of knitting together with my friends. That's what you're asking, you know."

Josie hadn't thought about it that way. "Uh, yeah. I guess so. I could really use your expertise, though. And of course, by helping me you're helping Eb." She felt a little guilty, dangling Eb out in front of Evelyn like a crotchety, flannel-wearing carrot. But desperate times called for desperate measures, and Eb had been taking care of himself for a long time. He could handle this.

Evelyn's features softened into a smile. "At my age, it's nice to be needed. And you clearly need me. So yes, you can count me in. I'll call the police chief and find out what's taking so long. I'll have you back at Miss Marple Knits in the morning."

Her confidence was impressive. Whether she could deliver on the promise was another thing. But Josie was certainly going to let her try.

"I'm so glad," Josie said, and meant it. "Why don't you take that red wool? I'm sure Cora would have wanted you to have it."

"Well . . . if you're sure." Evelyn was making a good show of appearing nonchalant, but not quite succeeding. She really, really wanted that yarn.

"I'm sure," Josie said firmly.

"All right then. Look in the drawers of that desk, will you? Cora will have a box of gallon-sized plastic zip bags in there somewhere."

Sure, Josie thought. *I keep those in my desk back at the Haus of Heinrich offices, too. Doesn't everyone?* But obediently she began opening drawers. The third one contained . . . a box of plastic bags. She pulled one out and took it over to Evelyn, who was waiting expectantly with the skeins of wool on her lap.

"I'll wind these into balls when I get home," Evelyn said, placing her loot into the bag and giving it a quick zip.

Josie had to ask. "How did you know she'd have those?"

Evelyn laughed. "Dear, how do you think we keep our projects clean and organized in our purses? Now it's time for me to go. I'll just find Eben and say good-bye. Meet me at the general store tomorrow morning, and we'll get to work."

Evelyn never did say good-bye to Eb, who was hiding out somewhere and was apparently prepared to wait her out. But the next morning she was as good as her word. Josie found her sitting at a table in the back of the general store, sipping from a mug. Half of a toasted, buttered bagel lay on a plate in front of her. Evelyn waved her fingers at Josie and set the mug down. Josie greeted her, then headed for the counter.

Josie handed Lorna the morning's eggs, then unbuttoned her coat and unwound the ocean-blue scarf Cora had given her. "Morning, Josie," Lorna said. "Coffee?"

"Yes, please. Working in a chicken coop in February is cold work."

Lorna laughed. "I never would have pictured a famous New York fashion designer like you managing poultry."

"You and me both," Josie said. "And I'm not famous. I'm not even sure I'm a fashion designer, though I work for one." She looked around the store. That Master of Fine Arts degree Otto had insisted she get—and pay for herself—was dead useless in Dorset Falls.

Lorna handed her a steaming mug. "Cream and sugar are right here. You make drawings of dresses and things, right? So that makes you a fashion designer."

Her words were meant to be encouraging. "I suppose so. But I'm beginning to suspect I'm not a very good one. Lately every design I turn in has something wrong with it." She gave her coffee a stir.

"Well, and of course this is none of my business, and we've barely gotten reacquainted since you've been back. But maybe you're designing the wrong things." Lorna sprayed something, probably disinfectant by the astringent smell of it, on a paper towel and began to wipe down the counter.

Josie hadn't ever thought about it that way. Maybe she was. But there were more pressing things to address now. "Thanks for the coffee, Lorna. I'll probably be in later for lunch. There aren't any restaurants in this town, are there?"

Lorna chuckled. "Businesses don't tend to last long around

here. There's nothing to bring in out-of-towners other than the occasional lost leaf-peeper in the fall. And the locals go to Litchfield or Kent when they want to eat anything fancier than what we've got here at the g.s."

"I've been meaning to ask. How is it that Cora kept the yarn shop going? The old ladies in this town can't have bought enough yarn per month to make the rent, let alone all the other expenses there must have been."

Lorna wiped down another section of counter. "Well, Cora had some money. Her first husband was a Margate—they owned the sweater mill, before they sold out in the sixties to new owners who ran it into the ground within a year. The yarn shop kept her busy, and she didn't live extravagantly."

Josie wondered what a woman like Cora had seen in someone like Eb, but decided it didn't matter as long as they'd been happy for the short time they had had together. Which she assumed they had. Her great-uncle was no Richard Gere, but he had a cranky sort of charm. Maybe Cora had thought of him as a project, same as any ball of yarn in her shop. Something with potential, that could be twisted and turned into something new.

"You'd better get on over to Evelyn." Lorna nodded in Evelyn's direction. Evelyn was clacking away, rhythmically wrapping a cherry-red strand around one needle and pulling it off with the other. "This is her afternoon to babysit her grandson, so she'll need to be home on time."

"Thanks, Lorna," Josie said. "I'll see you later." She made her way to Evelyn's table and set down her coat and coffee. The older woman looked up, then held up her knitting for Josie to see.

"I couldn't wait to use this yarn," she said, grinning. "And it's just as lovely as I thought it would be. I don't remember noticing this brand in the shop. Cora must have been holding out on us."

Josie sipped her coffee. "I saw the crime-scene tape still up across the door of the shop, so I guess we can't get started today."

Evelyn sniffed. "Oh, please. I said I'd get you in there, and I will. So have Lorna give you a to-go cup for that coffee, and let's to-go." She put her work, needles and all, into her oversized purse and snapped it shut. What else was in there? Josie wondered. A Mary Poppins–style magic coatrack?

A few minutes later the pair stood in front of Miss Marple Knits. The bright blue door was crossed with garish yellow crime-scene tape. Evelyn didn't hesitate as she yanked down the tape and opened the door. "Sharla!" she called out, and marched inside, bumping the doorframe with her handbag on thc way in.

Josie hung back for a moment, but when Evelyn didn't come flying out to land on her backside on the sidewalk, curiosity got the better of her. She peeked cautiously inside.

Evelyn stood talking to Officer Coogan, hands on hips with her bag looped over her arm. Officer Coogan looked toward the door. "Come on in, Josie. Party's just getting started."

"Now, Sharla," Evelyn said. "We've got work to do here. So finish up and let us get to it. I'm planning to take Andrew to the library this afternoon."

"He'll like that," Sharla Coogan said. "Just don't fill him full of cookies on the way home, will you? He'll be bouncing off the walls and won't want supper, thanks to you." Her tone was good-natured, and she leaned over and gave Evelyn a light buss on the cheek.

Josie looked from one to the other, mentally calculating the relationship between these two women. "Officer Coogan is your daughter?" Josie shouldn't have been surprised. Dorset Falls was a pretty small town.

"Daughter-in-law. She's married to my son Harrison. But she's like a daughter to me. She'll be making detective soon," Evelyn said, with obvious pride.

"Thanks, Mom." Officer Coogan turned to Josie. "We're just about finished up here. The crime-scene techs have been here most of the night. They'll just take a few more photographs, then you can have your shop back."

Josie chewed her lower lip. "Did they . . . find anything?"

Sharla Coogan assessed her before answering. "They picked up some hairs and lots of fibers." She laughed, waving her arm around the room. "As you can see, there are literally hundreds of different places that fiber could have come from. It's going to take a while to do the analysis. My guess is that most of the fibers are going to originate right in this shop. Anything they find probably won't be any help at all."

"Officer Coogan," Josie said. "I can't stop wondering why Lillian was here." A thought struck her. "She is . . . gone, isn't she?"

Sharla patted her arm sympathetically. "She was taken away yesterday, and is at the funeral home waiting for her children to get here to make the arrangements. The boxes of yarn she was lying on have also been taken away for analysis."

Josie blew out a breath of relief. She'd half thought she'd have to figure out what to do with that stuff herself.

"Yarn?" Evelyn leaned forward. "What yarn?"

Sharla considered for a moment. "Well, I can confirm that Lillian was found in the storeroom lying on some boxes."

"What kind?" Evelyn's eyes had taken on that glint Josie had seen before. Yarn lust.

"Cardboard." Sharla's lips turned up into a barely perceptible smile. She was teasing her mother-in-law.

Evelyn rolled her eyes. "You're hysterical. Now tell me what kind of yarn it was."

"Cashmere," Officer Coogan and Josie said together.

Evelyn nodded in satisfaction. "Perfect. That's how I want to go, too." Evelyn tossed her handbag a few feet, where it landed with a heavy thud on a nearby armchair. "Can the cashmere be saved? It would be a shame to waste it," she said, her voice matter-of-fact.

Officer Coogan and Josie exchanged a look. They seemed to have developed some kind of sympatico in the last few minutes. *That yarn would be covered with . . . death cooties,* Josie thought.

She shuddered thinking about even seeing it again, let alone running it through her fingers and knitting with it. Or even worse, *wearing* something that had been knitted with it.

"Sorry, Mom," Sharla finally said. "It's evidence."

Evelyn shrugged. "Well, it was worth a try. Cashmere is expensive. Now can we get to work?"

"Let me just double-check with the detective in charge. I think you'll probably be able to work out here in the main shop. The storeroom should be almost done." Sharla turned and walked briskly toward the back.

"I like her," Josie said. "You must be proud of her."

Evelyn pursed her lips. "Of course I am. She's a good mother to my grandson and a good wife to my son. But I wish she were a little more forthcoming with information. I have to hear about what's going on in this town on the street, just like everyone else."

Chapter 7

It wasn't long before Officer Coogan returned, followed by a middle-aged man of medium height. He wore his dirt-brown hair clipped short, and his reddish mustache thick and long enough that it covered his top lip. His simple white shirt, regimental striped tie, and dark suit left no doubt that he was a plainclothes detective.

"This is Detective Bruno Potts," Sharla said. "He's in charge of the investigation."

Potts nodded politely to Evelyn. "Mrs. Graves."

"Detective." She nodded back. It was obvious they had some history between them. Josie could only imagine what that might be.

The man stuck out his hand to Josie, and she took it. His grip was firm, but his hand felt . . . unnatural. Her face must have showed her surprise, because he held up his fingers and peeled off a glove, grinning. At least she thought it was a grin, noting that his cheeks moved upward and the wrinkles around his eyes deepened. His teeth were hidden under that soup strainer. "Sorry," he said. "These are clean, don't worry."

She wished she could surreptitiously reach the hand sanitizer she kept in her purse, just in case. "Josie Blair," she said.

"Yes, I know who you are." He pulled a small spiral-bound notebook out of his jacket pocket, along with a ballpoint pen that he clicked on, and began to flip through pages. "Josephine Blair. Great-niece of Eben Lloyd. Eben and your mother's father were brothers."

"That's right." At least, she thought it was. She hadn't actually seen a genealogy chart, but seemed to recall her mother's telling her the relationship.

"I ran out of time yesterday, but I still need to talk to both you and Mr. Lloyd. Would you like to do that now or later?" The words sounded like a question, but Josie was pretty sure the correct answer was "now."

Before she could say anything, Evelyn piped up. "Oh for goodness' sake, Bruno. Leave her alone. She just got into town, and she doesn't know anything. Why don't you stop wasting time and start questioning some real suspects?"

The mustache twitched, and Detective Potts's face went red. He was clearly struggling to hold his temper. "I'm just trying to do my job, Mrs. Graves."

"I think my daughter-in-law here could do a much better job. When are you going to promote her?" Evelyn folded her arms across her sweater-clad chest and stared at him.

The man squirmed. "Dorset Falls has a small police force, Mrs. Graves. You know that from the town budget meetings. There's only room for one detective."

"Hmmph. Maybe it's time for a new one. Stop bothering Josie here, and go find out who killed poor Lillian," she ordered.

"Uh, why don't I go talk to Eben first? I can release the site to you as soon as the techs clear out, which should be any minute now." As if on cue, two people came out of the back room, carrying containers and briefcases that presumably held their equipment and samples. "Finished?" he said to one of the techs. The woman nodded and exited onto the street.

"So where's Eb? I just need to ask him a few questions, that's all."

"Eb's not home," Josie said.

A frown creased the detective's forehead. He consulted his notebook. "Eben's got a broken leg from that car accident he was in. How's he getting around?"

"None of your business," Evelyn said, her eyes narrowing.

"Oh, it's okay." Josie smiled. "He's out in the middle of the lake."

"What?" The detective was clearly confused.

"Ice fishing." Josie had managed to dodge the ice-fishing bullet this morning. She hoped Eb would get it out of his system before he asked her again.

"How's he getting around?"

"His neighbor, Mitch Woodruff, picked him up this morning and took him out." Josie would have to figure out some way to thank Mitch for sparing her. She pictured his tall, lean frame. He'd look nice in a dark green Ralph Lauren pullover. Maybe a friend back in the city could find one for him.

The detective's eyebrows rose. "Woodruff, you say? The dead woman's nephew?"

"Well, yes. He's been helping Eb with some things around the farm—carrying in wood, shoveling, that kind of thing."

Potts wrote something in his little notebook. "So where were *you* between the time you arrived in Dorset Falls and yesterday morning?"

Apparently the questioning had started whether she was ready to talk or not. Evelyn opened her mouth to protest, but Josie held up a hand. "It's fine, Evelyn. I have nothing to hide, and of course Eb and I want to cooperate." She wasn't actually too sure how cooperative Eb would be, but she'd have to deal with that later. "Let's see. I got into town around noon. I went to the chicken coop and got the eggs, then Eb and I came into town to deliver them to the general store. You can verify that with Lorna."

"I will. Then?" The pen was poised above the notebook.

Josie recounted everything she remembered, including Lillian's tirade the afternoon before she died.

"She was fit to be tied," Evelyn added. "Wanted to buy the inventory and take over this shop, said Cora always planned to sell her a share of the business. Complete poppycock."

"You were here?" the detective asked.

Evelyn rolled her eyes. "Of course I was here. How else would I know what she said?"

"Where did you ladies go when you left here?"

"I . . . don't recall. Oh, yes, of course. There was a meeting of the Dorset Falls Charity Knitters Association, which we all attended."

"You'll need to let me know who was at that meeting and where you met." The detective's eyes bored into her face.

"Yes, yes, I'll have to think about it and call you later. My memory's not as good as it used to be."

Interesting. Josie wondered just how often Evelyn played the age card. From what Josie had seen, Evelyn was sharp as a tack. So why was she feeding the detective a heaping helping of . . . poppycock?

"You do that. Miss Blair, I'll be in touch. You can have the store back now." He closed up his notebook and replaced it in his jacket pocket.

When he and Sharla had gone, Evelyn patted Josie's arm. "Don't worry about him, dear. There's a new police chief in town, and he's probably putting pressure on Bruno to get this case solved quickly."

"Do you know him well?" Josie couldn't help but ask.

Evelyn *tsked*. "I was his third-grade teacher. He was a brat then, and he's still a brat. Now let's get to work."

Josie set up her computer on the sales counter and was pleased to find an unsecured wireless signal labeled *Bondgirls* pop up when she checked for networks. Where it was originating from, she had no idea, because she didn't see a router anywhere nearby. But why argue? She opened up a new spreadsheet document and labeled the first column *Type of Yarn*. The second column was *Quantity* and the third was *Value*. "Okay, Evelyn. I'm ready to start."

Evelyn hefted a basket of yarn up onto a table and dumped it out. She began to sort, using some system of her own. Josie was impressed. Evelyn was very efficient. When she finished, the yarn lay in soft heaps of varying sizes, separated by color. "Four skeins of Killarney Irish worsted-weight wool, color natural. Six skeins—"

"Hold on a second. I need another category." Josie added a column titled *Color*, then entered the information Evelyn had given her.

The two worked steadily for a couple of hours, emptying four of the big baskets and one of the cubbies on the wall. Once the yarn was sorted and inventoried, Evelyn placed the skeins into individual plastic bags, of which there seemed to be a more or less endless supply behind the counter. Evelyn hadn't been kidding about knitters and plastic bags.

Josie stood next to Evelyn and surveyed their handiwork, which consisted of rows and rows of bags along one wall.

"Nothing sadder than empty cupboards," Evelyn said. "You sure you can't find a local buyer? I'm going to miss this place."

Josie looked around. "You know something, Evelyn? I think I am too." She shook her head, trying to ward off a swell of emotion that was threatening to wash over her. "Isn't that crazy? A week ago I'd never even been here."

"I don't hold with a lot of woo-woo." Evelyn stared at Josie, her face unreadable. "But Cora put her heart and soul into this place, and friendships were formed around that coffee table." Evelyn inclined her head toward the front window and the couch and chairs. "When a person knits, they put love into every stitch. Knitting is optional, you know."

"Optional?" Josie didn't understand.

Evelyn patted Josie's arm again. "Nobody *has* to knit anymore. Clothing is made in factories now."

"Well, except for couture, of course. That's hand sewn."

The older woman chuckled. "Okay, *most* clothing is made in factories now. The point is, people knit by choice today, not out of necessity. So they do it because they love it. They love the yarn and the physical act of knitting." A smile creased her face and made her look ten years younger. "And they love the people they give their knitted items to. Knitters tend to give most of their projects away."

Josie nodded. She thought she understood. "Positive energy."

"Whatever you want to call it, Cora had that in spades."

Once again Josie's heart gave a little squeeze. Why had she never made time to drive up here and meet Cora? It was only a couple of hours' trip. "Cora made me this," she said, pulling the blue scarf out of the sleeve of her coat, which was hanging over the back of the chair she'd been sitting in. "Isn't it gorgeous?"

Evelyn took the scarf and rubbed it between her fingers, then examined the stitches. "Very nice. I remember her working on this. She said she couldn't wait to meet you someday. Even talked about taking the train into New York some Saturday to take you to lunch."

"Really?" Tears welled up in Josie's eyes.

"Really. Now don't cry. Cora wouldn't have wanted that, and neither do I, honestly." She held up the scarf to Josie's cheek. "This is a very nice hand-dyed alpaca and wool blend, and it looks lovely with your coloring. Why don't I make you a hat to match? I seem to recall that brand of yarn being over here."

She led the way to a cubby closer to the sitting area, then began to paw through the contents. "Hmmm, it's not here. But this is where the alpaca yarns were always kept. I suppose she could have sold out of it."

"That's all right. It was sweet of you to offer."

Her face brightened. "I know! Let's check her records and find out whom she sold it to, then we can see if we can get whoever it was to give up a skein or two."

"Cora kept records of whom she sold yarn to?" Of course, large retailers did it all the time. But it seemed unlikely that Cora had a computerized record-keeping system that sophisticated.

"Yes, of course. In case the customer didn't buy enough to complete the project, then Cora could easily reorder for her. Or him. Of course the dye lots would probably be off, but there are ways to work around that. Now where is that book?" Evelyn began to rummage around behind the counter. "Hmmm, I don't see it. It's a black looseleaf binder with regular old lined paper inside. Nothing fancy. Look for it when you get back to Eben's, will you? She must have taken it home, though I can't think why."

"I will. And thank you for all your help today." Evelyn shrugged into her long, tailored coat, a charcoal-gray herringbone that would never go out of style. Josie pictured a pair of black leather knee-high boots underneath, and a cherry-red scarf accenting the neckline. Perfect. She hoped that was what Evelyn was knitting with the wool she'd given her.

"Not at all. I'm happy to help Eben. And you, of course," she added quickly.

Josie smiled. Evelyn was not exactly subtle. Should she invite Evelyn to dinner? No, Eb would kill her. But it would almost certainly be amusing.

"So I'll meet you back here tomorrow morning around ten?" Evelyn continued.

"I'll see you then." Josie accompanied her to the door.

When Evelyn had left, Josie sat down in one of the armchairs by the front window. She counted the number of baskets and bins that still needed to be sorted, multiplied by the number of hours she and Evelyn had put in today, then wished she hadn't. It might have been better not to know. And of course that number didn't include what Cora had stashed away in the morning-borning room at home, or, even worse, what was still in back.

She looked out the front window at the empty storefront across the street. This little village was so sad, and she was about to make it sadder by closing up one of the only businesses left downtown. Not my problem, she told herself. So why did it feel like it *was* her problem?

Movement caught her eye. She leaned forward in her chair to get a better look. Huh? She'd watched Evelyn walk up Main Street in the direction of the general store only minutes ago. But now Evelyn stood in front of that narrow doorway between the two empty shops. She looked quickly in both directions, then appeared to put a key in the lock and turn the handle before disappearing behind the door.

What was up there? Evelyn was the second woman Josie had seen going upstairs into an apparently abandoned building. Her eyes moved to the rows of windows on the second and third stories of the redbrick building. No movement, and still no other signs of habitation, current or former. *Put that thought out of your head, Josephine,* she told herself. *What business is it of yours?* And even though the answer was clearly *none*, she could easily solve that little mystery by asking Evelyn tomorrow.

Her stomach rumbled. It was well into the afternoon, and she and Evelyn had not stopped for lunch. But it was too close to dinnertime to eat more than a snack. She looked toward the back of the shop. At some point she'd have to face going into the storeroom, where a person had died. But not today.

Chapter 8

Josie picked up cat food and a candy bar at the general store before heading back to Eb's place. She'd decided to walk to the store, which just happened to give her an opportunity to cross the street and look in the unmarked window of the door that the yarn-crazy women of Dorset Falls kept disappearing into. But all she could make out through the frosted glass were the fuzzy outlines of what might have been a stairwell. And of course, the door was locked. Not that she'd really expected it to be open, but it was worth a try.

The Saab's heater was about the only thing that worked well, and Josie had it going full blast, along with the radio, which refused to pick up any stations other than AM. She switched it off.

Since there was still some daylight left, this seemed as good a time as any to take a drive through Dorset Falls. The Saab sputtered as she motored down Main Street, past the small snow-covered town green. The spire of the Congregational church was bright white against the fading blue of the sky, as a ray of remaining sunlight made its last stand for the afternoon. At the stop sign in front of the redbrick town hall, she took a left onto Maple.

Two blocks down, the house was still there. It had been painted a pale green with darker green trim, which seemed a little monochromatic for a proper Victorian color scheme, but was pretty enough. The clapboards had been yellow when she and her mother had rented the house for a couple of years, what seemed like a lifetime ago.

She pulled up and parked in front of it. It wasn't large, or grand, like the houses over on Elm Street, but it was being lovingly tended just the same. The front walk had been shoveled, the edges cut precisely and neatly into the snow. The steeply pitched roof appeared to be new, and a wreath covered in pink and red silk flowers hung on the door, presumably in honor of Valentine's Day next week.

It had been tough, changing high schools in her sophomore year, leaving behind her friends. She'd eventually made a new friend in Lorna, but she'd never felt like she fit in. Dorset Falls was always temporary, just a stopping place. So when graduation came, the city called her, and she'd never looked back. She wondered now if maybe that had been a mistake.

Lost in her musings and distracted by the white noise of the car's heater, she didn't realize someone was at her driver's side window until a gentle tap brought her focus to the present. A woman stood there, her pink puffer coat open despite the cold.

"Can I help you?" she said as Josie rolled down the window. "Do you need directions?" Her face was friendly, framed in dark blond hair that feathered softly. She seemed to be about Josie's age.

"Oh, no," Josie said, feeling her cheeks heat up. "I used to live here, that's all. It looks really nice."

The woman smiled. "How wonderful! I'd invite you in for a

tour, but I'm just on my way to pick up my kids from the bus stop. I'm Gwen Simmons."

"Josie Blair."

Gwen looked thoughtful. "Oh, I know who you are! You're here to close up Miss Marple Knits. Such a shame about Cora. I'm so sorry for your loss."

"I . . . didn't really know her." Every time someone said something sweet about Cora, Josie felt a stab of guilt.

"Well, she was wonderful. And the fastest knitter I've ever seen. I could never keep up with her." Gwen glanced toward the next intersection.

Was everyone in this town a knitter? No wonder Josie had never felt like she belonged here. "I should let you go." A big yellow bus appeared in her rearview.

"There it is. I need to catch my little monsters before they wreak their special brand of havoc on Dorset Falls. I'm downtown three mornings a week to do the books for my husband's gas station and car repair shop. Maybe I'll stop in and say goodbye to Miss Marple."

"Sure," Josie said. "That would be nice." She found she meant it, then chastised herself. No sense getting attached to people when she'd be leaving soon. She rolled up the window and drove off, waving to Gwen as she passed.

Another left turn took her onto Elm. This was where the big houses were, ancient saltboxes that were as old as Dorset Falls itself interspersed with oversized Victorians completely impractical for the small families of the twenty-first century. One of these would have belonged to Cora, though it was impossible to tell which one. Josie alternately watched the road in front of her and glanced at each home as she passed, trying to read the dates on the plaques on some of the historic houses.

Oh, no. No, no, no. Diantha Humphries, the last person she

wanted to see, had emerged from one of the houses and was walking gingerly toward a late-model car that idled in the driveway. Why could Josie not seem to get away from that woman? Diantha got into the car just as Josie passed by. Maybe the—what was it Lorna had called her?—old battle-ax hadn't seen her. Though why should Josie care? She had just as much right to be driving down Elm Street, Dorset Falls, Connecticut, as any other person on the planet.

"You're being ridiculous," Josie said aloud. Maybe if she said it enough times, she'd come to believe it. A glance in the rearview mirror revealed Diantha's taillights. Josie blew out a breath she didn't know she'd been holding. Her old boyfriend's mother was going in the opposite direction.

Ten minutes later she pulled into Eb's driveway. Her car sputtered again as she shut off the ignition. Hmmm. That was a new sound. Of course, the temperature was in the single digits. Miss Bessie didn't like the cold any more than Josie did, apparently.

She found Eb seated in his usual spot, with his daily crossword in progress. He didn't look up as she came in, but filled something in on the newspaper. "Hope you've got something planned for dinner. Got skunked today."

"Skunked?" Josie hoped that didn't mean Jethro had been sprayed. That smell might never come out of anything he touched, and the dog had the run of the house. At least Coco would have enough sense to stay away. Where was Jethro, anyway?

Eb looked up at her, over the tops of his reading glasses. "Means we didn't catch anything." He returned to his puzzle.

Whew. Josie loved to eat fish. In restaurants. Where someone else cooked them. "Oh. Well, I'll figure out something for dinner."

"Yup. Maybe you could figure out how to use the percolator, while you're at it."

"Sure thing." Not. She'd asked Lorna to pick her up an automatic drip coffeemaker next time she went to the big-box store. That percolator thing scared Josie. What if it exploded?

"Your nose is growing, missy. I'll settle for tea."

By the time the water was hot and the tea was steeping, Eb had moved from the crossword on to the Jumble. She set the mug down on the table beside him. "The detective in charge of investigating Lillian's death talked to me today. You'll probably be hearing from him."

Eb marked something on the newspaper, then erased it. "Already did. Thanks for telling him where I was."

Wow. Detective Potts worked fast. "He actually questioned you while you were fishing?"

"I'm an old man on crutches. What was I supposed to do? Strap on some blades and skate away from him? Neighbor Boy told me I should cooperate."

"I'm glad Mitch was there." For whatever reason, he seemed to like Eb.

"Hmmph. Takes after his mother's side of the family, not his idiot grandfather Roy Woodruff." Eb went back to his newspaper and, based on the set of his jaw, was apparently done talking. Well, she could ask Mitch about Eb's encounter with Detective Potts next time she saw him.

"I'll be in Cora's room if you need me. We should get started on her papers." She gauged his reaction. How had he felt about Cora, really?

Eb grunted. That could mean he missed her desperately, or was over her death already. But it was useless to speculate. People grieved in their own ways. She'd give him the benefit of the doubt.

The morning-borning room was lit with oblique late afternoon light, a last hurrah before darkness set in. And once the sun went down in Dorset Falls, she'd found, it got very dark, very fast. Not like the city, where lights turned on and stayed on to keep the darkness at bay. Preemptively, she switched on a lamp and sat down at the desk.

A *meow* sounded from somewhere around Josie's ankles. She looked down to find Coco curled up in one of the bottom desk drawers, lying on some paperwork. "Must have forgotten to close that yesterday," Josie said. "Sorry, girl. You look comfortable for now, but I'll be more careful next time. Wouldn't want the drawer to shut on you accidentally."

She decided to start with the top of the desk. There was a lamp with a stained-glass shade that looked antique on the right-hand corner. Next to that, pens, pencils, and a letter opener stood upright in a coffee mug that said CORA, the name wreathed in flowers. She wondered if it had been specially made for her. Cora wasn't a name anyone gave a daughter anymore, so it didn't seem likely the mug could have been bought in any regular store. Kind of a shame. The name was old-fashioned, but pretty.

A stack of papers sat to the right. Josie picked up the pile and blew on it. A dozen or so soft black hairs floated off into the air before settling to the oriental carpet on the floor. Coco would never make a good criminal. She left too much evidence of where she'd been.

Cora must have paid her bills, but hadn't had the chance to file them away before she died. Invoices from the electric and phone companies, and what appeared to be yarn suppliers, were marked with the handwritten notation "Paid" and clearly pertained to the shop. Josie put those into one pile. There was a bill for an insurance premium, and the rest were bills for the house she was in. The numbers seemed reasonable. Eb had been a bachelor a long time before he married Cora and had been supporting himself. Josie assumed he'd still be able to do so, as long as the feathered ladies out in the chicken coop continued to do business and the pumpkins continued to grow in the fall.

She picked up a manila file folder. The tab was labeled *Historic Preservation Commission*, but the file was empty. Perhaps Cora had been going to reuse or recycle it. Josie set it into a separate pile in case she needed a folder later.

It didn't take long to go through the rest of the paperwork. She looked through the desk drawers and found a checkbook. The register was dutifully noted with each check Cora had written, along with a balance. Josie shut her eyes, and looked at the balance again. Holy Calvin Klein. If Cora's register was up to date, she had several hundred thousand dollars in her checking account.

Josie sat back in the desk chair and whistled. According to Evelyn, Cora had just sold her historic house. It seemed likely this represented the proceeds, and she'd died before she had a chance to put the money into any kind of long-term account. She could have kept Miss Marple Knits going indefinitely with this kind of money, even if the shop ran at a deficit every month.

Did Eb know about this? More important, did Cora have a will? Was Eb the only beneficiary, or were there others? Josie wondered if a lawyer had even been contacted. She wasn't familiar with the laws of Connecticut, but she was pretty sure the estate would have to be probated. Her mother had been here for the funeral. She would know. In fact she'd probably gotten the legal process started for Eb. But Mom was on a cruise ship in the Mediterranean right now, out of cell range.

There was a good chance that Eben Lloyd, Yankee farmer, was now a rich man.

Josie put the checkbook back in the drawer where she'd found it. What else was she supposed to look for? Right. Cora's notebook that recorded her yarn sales. It hadn't been in the desk, so Josie thumbed quickly through the top drawer of the cabinet. The files were neatly organized, which would make this process much easier. The second drawer contained what appeared to be knitting patterns, each encased in a plastic sheet protector, and was divided up into sections. Hats, Mittens/Gloves, Scarves/Shawls, Sweaters, Socks. Socks? People actually still knitted socks? Miscellaneous.

She opened the third, then the fourth drawers. They were crammed with—she should have expected this—yarn. Not just yarn in every conceivable color, but various knitting needles and some other tools she couldn't identify. How many more stashes would Josie find before she went back to New York?

A godawful howl pierced the silence, followed by a barking frenzy. Coco let out a corresponding yowl, then jumped out of the drawer and ran under the skirt of the upholstered armchair. Not that she needed to be afraid. The door was shut, so the beast couldn't get in.

"Jethro!" Eb's voice was commanding, although muffled. "It's just a car going by, ya big dope." About now Eb would be scratching him behind the ears. She should go out and make sure everything was okay. And it was dinnertime for pets and their humans.

Josie reached down to close the bottom drawer of the desk. Tomorrow she might dust and vacuum this room. This was a nice place to work—and it occurred to her that it was time to check in with the Haus of Heinrich before it was too late to get her job back. She peered into the drawer. Yup, she'd need to vacuum the cat hair out of there too. Hmmm. What was that?

She pulled the drawer out as far as it would go. Coco had been lying on an unopened ream of copy paper. But she had also been lying on something soft and blue. Josie reached in and pulled it out. It was a skein of yarn, wound into a ball. And the variegated shades appeared to be a perfect match for the scarf Cora had made her.

Josie did a mental fist pump. A matching hat was on the radar now. She hoped it wouldn't take Evelyn long to make it, once the cat hair had been washed off the yarn. Why, though, Josie wondered, was this yarn all by its lonesome in the drawer when it could have been all comfy and cozy jammed in with the rest of Cora's stash? It seemed odd for some reason. But Josie supposed she'd never know. Perhaps Cora had just tossed it in there, then never had a chance to put it away. Josie pulled out a plastic bag—she was learning—and zipped the yarn inside.

Chapter 9

"Tell me about the Charity Knitters Association," Josie said the next day. "It sounds so official."

Evelyn laughed. "Well . . . it is. A few years ago, Cora dreamed up the idea. I told you that knitters usually give away what they make?" Josie nodded, then booted up her computer. "Eventually, we run out of people to bestow our bounty upon. A person only needs so many scarves and hats and sweaters, no matter how kind the intention behind the gift. Yarn junkies like us need new recipients all the time."

Josie pulled up her inventory document. She hoped they'd make a good dent in the job today. "Junkies," she laughed. "I had another less-nice word in mind."

Evelyn pursed up her lips, then laughed herself. "We call ourselves less nice things too, especially after we've had a glass of wine at our meetings."

"So you're actually registered with the state as a charity?"

Evelyn dumped a basket of yarn on the counter and began to sort. "No, a nonprofit. They're similar though. It was Cora's idea. That way we could get a tax break on the yarn and supplies we bought for our Charity Knitters projects. Not only that, when we went on that knitters' cruise to the Bahamas a few years ago, we got to write it off."

Josie was impressed. "So why would you elect Diantha Humphries as president?" She wanted to clap a hand over her mouth and take it back. Evelyn and Diantha were probably friends.

Evelyn laughed again. "She's not a fan of yours either, from what I hear." The yarn piles in front of her were growing into color-coded mountains. "And we didn't elect her. Cora has always been the president. But when she died, the vice president had to step in. And that was Diantha. By the way," she added, "thank you for not selling Miss Marple Knits to her."

Josie looked up, startled. "You knew about that?"

"Of course, dear. She and Lillian both wanted it. Or said they did."

"I . . . just couldn't. I can't explain it." Josie's computer dinged, indicating she had a new e-mail.

"Cora wouldn't have allowed either one to buy Miss Marple Knits," Evelyn said, her tone firm. "Diantha is too snooty and would drive away any customer who walked through the door. And Lillian, poor thing, had no head for business." Evelyn picked up a ball of yarn. "Ready? Two skeins of organic cotton, ecru."

"Got it." Josie made the notation. "So where do you meet?"

"Three skeins of organic cotton, light blue. We rotate meeting at each others' houses. Although I'm not sure if we'll continue."

Josie looked up. "That would be a shame." Her stomach fluttered.

"It would. We've done quite a bit of good for other people, and had quite a bit of fun doing it. Even Diantha. But with the shop closing, and two of our members dead just a few weeks apart, the Charity Knitters may very well disband. I'm not sure any of our hearts are in it anymore."

Now that they had a rhythm and an established process, the work went quickly. Within a few hours they'd managed to inventory half of the remaining stock in the front room. But by one o'clock, Josie was ready for a break.

"Let's go to the general store for a bowl of soup, my treat," Josie said. "I'm starving."

"Good idea. Why don't you go on ahead and order for me? Whatever you're having will be fine. I need to make a phone call, then I'll be right there."

"Sure. I'll take the key. Just set the lock and shut the door when you leave." Josie saved the document on her computer.

"Oh, I need to go to my car. I left my phone there." Evelyn put on her coat and looped her giant handbag over her arm.

"Then I'll just go to the ladies' room and head to the g.s. I'll lock up."

"Perfect." Evelyn left and walked briskly to her car, a dark red Buick parked just outside Miss Marple Knits.

When Josie passed the car less than ten minutes later, it was empty. Evelyn must have only needed to make a quick call, or perhaps her party hadn't answered. She was probably waiting in the toasty warm general store, so Josie made her way there and went directly to the back counter. There were only a couple of shoppers wandering about, neither of whom was Evelyn.

"Hey, Lorna. What's the soup today?" Josie shoved her gloves into her pockets and ran her fingers through her hair. It didn't seem to help. Strands floated about her head, giving the occasional crackle of static electricity.

Lorna reached under the counter and pulled up a small bottle of hand lotion. "Rub a drop of this between your hands, then smooth your hair down. And you're in luck. We've got creamy tomato bisque, with homemade croutons. Want a bowl?"

Josie's mouth watered as she tamed her hair. "You know I do. Make it two."

"Should I put them in travel containers for you and Eb?"

"No, I'm meeting Evelyn Graves here for lunch. Is she here?"

Lorna looked around. "I haven't seen her." She began to ladle soup into bowls.

Where was Evelyn? She wasn't in her car, she wasn't here, and every storefront on the block between the yarn shop and here was closed, except for the insurance agency. She could have popped in to pay her insurance premium, but there was one other interesting possibility.

"It's a shame all these little shops along Main Street aren't open," Josie ventured.

Lorna frowned. "Yeah, anybody who's tried starting a new business here in recent years has failed. The town's too small to support any more than what we've got, and most everyone works and shops somewhere else." She swirled some olive oil on the surface of the soup, then sprinkled buttery grilled cubes of bread on top.

"So what's upstairs, over the shops? I haven't been to the upper levels over Miss Marple Knits yet. I'm not even sure where the stairway is." She glanced toward the front door. Still no sign of Evelyn.

Lorna looked thoughtful. "They're all different spaces, though I've only seen a couple. We use the upstairs here for storage. In the old days I think it was used for additional retail space, plus apartments. But as far as I know none of the spaces are occupied now. Why do you ask?" She handed the bowls to Josie.

"Oh, no reason. Just curious." The front door opened, and Evelyn came in, her face red. Was she cold? Or had she been in a hurry to get here after going on some mysterious mission to the upstairs floors of a reportedly abandoned building? Josie could just come right out and ask, but it wasn't really any of her business. If Evelyn wanted Josie to know what she was doing, she would have told her. But, darn it, Josie was curious. She took the tray from Lorna and made her way to a table.

Evelyn shrugged off her coat, parked herself at the table, and dug into her soup. She nodded in appreciation. "Delicious. Lorna, you can be my private chef anytime," she called toward the back.

Lorna laughed and came out from behind the counter, carrying another tray containing glasses, bottled water, and a small dish of sliced lemon. "I may have to take you up on that. Dougie's been talking about shutting down the homemade food service here and switching to premade sandwiches and hotdogs on rollers."

"What?" Evelyn's face went red again, closely matching the tomato soup. "Douglas Brewster may have ancestors who go back to the *Mayflower*, but his brains don't stretch from one ear to the other." She gave her soup a violent stir that caused some of it to slop over onto the saucer underneath. "Imagine trying to turn this place into a convenience store. Next he'll be digging up Main Street to put in gas pumps. Where is he so I can give him a piece of my mind?"

"He's over at the town hall, preparing the agenda for the next town council meeting."

A woman sat down at the table and hung the straps of her bag over the back of the empty chair beside her.

"Josie," Evelyn said. "Have you met Helen Crawford? Helen, this is Eben's niece."

The two older women exchanged a look. Impossible to say what it meant.

"You want something to eat, Helen?" Lorna called out.

Helen shook her head, but her heavily sprayed pale blond hair didn't move at all. She looked at her watch. "Evvy, have you forgotten about our date tonight? Don't you need time to get ready?"

Evelyn dipped her spoon into her bowl. "Plenty of time. The limo doesn't get here for another two hours."

Josie recognized Helen, though this was the first time they'd been introduced. She'd been in the shop with Lillian the other day. And she was the other woman Josie had seen across the street from Miss Marple Knits, entering the door between storefronts.

Helen harrumphed. "You're not going dressed like that, are you? Aren't you going to put on something more glamorous?"

The mystery of what kind of date they were scheduled for was solved when Evelyn responded. "I just need to change into my red beaded jacket and silk shell, then I'm all set." She looked at Josie. "Tony Bennett is playing at Mohegan Sun tonight. The Charity Knitters are having a meeting in the car on the way there. So it's tax deductible."

Josie had heard of Mohegan Sun, and its counterpart, Foxwoods. Her mother had taken bus trips to the casinos more than once. "Evelyn, you should have told me you had plans tonight. No need for you to come back to the shop this afternoon, or even tomorrow if you're tired from your late evening. You've already done so much."

"Nonsense," Evelyn said. "I wouldn't help if I didn't want to. Cora was a good friend." She sipped at her sparkling water. "We bought these tickets months ago, before Cora and Lillian died, so there are a couple extra. You're welcome to come along."

"That's right," Helen piped up. "Please don't think we're being disrespectful by going tonight. We're planning to celebrate the lives of Cora and Lillian."

Josie hadn't thought any such thing. She hoped when it was her time to go, her friends would be having fun in her memory, rather than grieving. The offer was tempting. Wasn't Tony Bennett that old-timey singer who did some performing with Lady

Gaga? Staying up past ten o'clock and seeing some bright lights and being surrounded by lots of people sounded pretty good.

"Of course," Evelyn added. "Diantha will be there."

That settled it. No way was Josie riding a couple of hours, or however far away the casino was, in close quarters with Diantha Humphries. "Thanks for the offer," she said. "But Eb needs me."

Helen nodded in approval. "Very good. You're here to take care of dear Eben, so that's what you should do." She looked at her watch again and turned to Evelyn. "I'll expect you at four o'clock at my house. Don't be late. I asked the limo company to send Rodrigo." Her eyes went dreamy. "He's dishy." She hefted her purse and left.

"Rodrigo *is* dishy," Evelyn said. "It would be worth the trip for you just to see him." She dabbed at her lips with her napkin, then folded it up and placed it inside her empty bowl. "If you really can spare me, I think I will go home and take a short nap. It'll be a late night."

"Don't be silly. Go on. Send me a picture of Rodrigo."

The wind picked up as Josie made her way back to Miss Marple Knits a few minutes later. She pulled her scarf tighter around her neck and hunched her shoulders, but she was still chilled to the bone when she unlocked the door and went inside. More than half of the cubbies were empty, and if the place had felt empty and forlorn the first time she'd entered it a few days ago, it was downright depressing now. The sooner she got this job finished, the better.

Josie brought her laptop over from the sales counter and sat down on the couch. Her e-mail in-box was crowded, so she deleted all the obvious junk, then clicked. She felt a little surge of adrenaline. Monica, one of the sales staff at the Haus of Heinrich, had responded to her query. *Putting out feelers in yarn stores throughout Brooklyn and Manhattan. Will let you know if anyone interested in contents. Have fun in the sticks.*

Monica. If anyone could find a buyer for the inventory of Miss Marple Knits, it was Monica.

There were several messages from Jennifer, Otto's other assistant, begging her to make up to Otto and come back. *He's refusing to hire anyone to replace you, so I know this is just temporary. Please. I stink at writing the blog, let alone the magazine. I'm dying here.* Josie thought about not responding, but finally sent off an answer. *Can't leave yet. Not sure I want to be unfired.* That might or might not get back to Otto—Jennifer was fairly new at the company, and it wasn't clear where her loyalties lay. But it wouldn't hurt to play a little bit hard to get.

What was this? She felt her eyes widen in surprise. There was an e-mail from Otto himself. *Don't be an idiot. Send me some decent designs for the fall collection and you can come back.*

Her heart soared. Yes! Apparently absence made the heart grow fonder, because he wanted her back. Jobs in the fashion industry were tough to get, even tougher to keep, as she well knew. Not that she intended to stay there forever, especially after Otto had put the moves on her in the restaurant the other night. But she had those pesky student loans to pay, as well as rent on her apartment. And she needed a steady cash flow to feed her shameful designer handbag habit. So until she could secure a spot at another fashion company, the Haus of Heinrich it was.

Still, Josie didn't want to seem too eager. She decided to let him stew like a pot of hasenpfeffer for a while. It wasn't like she could leave right now anyway. She closed the lid on her laptop and set it next to her on the couch, then texted her mother with a request that she call when she got somewhere with cell service.

Inhale. Exhale. No more putting it off. It was time to revisit the storeroom.

The wall switch made an audible click as the overhead light

came to life a microsecond later. It was one of those fluorescent fixtures that took a while to warm up, and it was emitting a low buzzing noise that was faintly ominous, like some horror movie killer bee. But there was enough light to see that Lillian was, in fact, gone, and that the boxes she'd been lying on had been taken away, just as Detective Potts had said. That was a relief.

What was not a relief were the boxes and bins that lined the metal shelving units around the room. The Inventory Fairies had not come, and it would take days to get through all this. And now her design career was presumably back on. She needed time to get working on a set of sketches, and she needed them done fairly quickly. Could she hire someone to finish the inventory? The only skills needed were the abilities to sort, count, and record. She couldn't continue to impose on Evelyn for a job of this size. Vaguely, Josie wondered why Evelyn hadn't offered to take over the shop. The other ladies of the Charity Knitters Association all seemed to want it.

A knot formed in Josie's stomach, and she closed her eyes. She could still see Lillian lying there, like an elderly mummy with her arms crossed over her chest and the toes of her sensible shoes pointing up. The cord wrapped around her neck seemed to glow in Josie's memory, emitting a weak blue light. Something about the cord. What was it?

Her eyes flew open. That cord had been made of yarn. Blue, variegated yarn in the colors of the ocean. The same yarn that the scarf Cora had made her was knitted from and the same yarn that she'd pulled out of Cora's desk drawer last night. Josie would bet on it.

Chapter 10

But what was Josie going to do about it? Did she *need* to do anything about it? There could be any number of explanations, including the simple, obvious fact that Cora had owned a yarn shop. A shop that *sold* yarn. And Cora could have sold that yarn to anyone in town, or even the occasional out-of-town customer. There must have been at least a few of those.

Josie swallowed hard. Lillian had been murdered, ostensibly having been strangled with some kind of twisted cord made of that distinctive blue yarn. It didn't necessarily follow that the yarn had come from Miss Marple Knits. Unless it was some kind of exclusive product, anyone could have ordered it directly from the manufacturer and had it delivered to her home. Or *his* home. She supposed there were some men out there who knitted.

It could very well be coincidence. But it was a big coincidence.

She could call Detective Potts, or Sharla Coogan. What would she tell them, exactly? That the murder weapon, which they had in their possession, was made of fiber that might have come from Miss Marple Knits? Since this was the only yarn shop for miles around, as far as Josie knew, it stood to reason they'd already be investigating that angle, vague though it was.

But there was one concrete thing that might help. Cora's notebook. If Cora had sold some of that yarn and had recorded the purchaser—well, it still didn't prove anything. Cora had left some of the yarn out at the farmhouse, and she clearly wasn't the killer since she had died weeks before Lillian.

But it might lead the police to evidence. Josie would redouble her efforts to find the notebook, and, as soon as she did, she'd turn it over to Sharla Coogan. Maybe it would help advance Sharla's career.

If I were Cora, where would I put my sales notebook? Josie scanned the storeroom. Probably not back here. She shuddered. It was dim and creepy. And the crime-scene techs had presumably been all over this space. If they'd found something that listed sales, they would have taken it as evidence.

Same went for the front of the shop. Still, it wouldn't hurt to take another look around out there.

An hour later, Josie put her hands on her hips and surveyed the room. She'd checked everywhere she could think of for a secret or not-so-secret hiding place, even behind the framed movie still of some ancient white-haired actress playing Miss Jane Marple and knitting away. *Skunked.*

Josie checked her watch. Definitely time to get home and feed Eb and the animals, and to make sure there was enough wood carried in for the night. She couldn't just assume that Mitch Woodruff would come over every day and do the heavy lifting. Though it had certainly been nice up to this point, she had to admit.

Her eyes roamed over the shop. What a waste. Even with its contents bagged up, the place still felt somehow inviting, as though it was waiting for its next owner to come in and take over. *You could run this shop yourself.* Where had that thought come from? Josie shook her head. There were about four million and six reasons why she needed to finish up and put this shop behind her, not the least of which was that she had a job in Manhattan—or would have, once Otto gave it back to her—and an apartment waiting for her back in Brooklyn. The city was home. Not this godforsaken town where you couldn't even buy a pair of underwear. She knew. She'd checked at the g.s. when Eb asked her to when she first got here. Lorna had just laughed. "Eb cracks me up," she'd said, and gone back to her work behind the counter.

So why did Josie feel a pull every time she was here? She'd never known Cora, so it couldn't be nostalgia. Cora's ghost? Josie wrinkled her nose. *Pretty sure that's not it,* she thought.

And then, it hit her. Potential. That's what she was feeling. This storefront could showcase anything, from futons to fishing gear. The lack of a customer base in Dorset Falls wasn't necessarily a handicap in the twenty-first century. Someone with a little vision could easily run an online shop. There was plenty of room in the storeroom, and presumably upstairs, to house inventory. She hadn't seen it yet, but there must be a post office in town, and the other overnight delivery companies must have Dorset Falls on their routes. It wasn't *that* far out of the way.

She shook her head. This was crazy talk. If anybody had wanted to open any kind of shop here, they'd already have done it. A person would have his or her pick of locations along Main Street. They were almost all empty. Whoever owned these buildings would probably kill to get a tenant.

Her guts rolled. Seriously poor word choice. A woman had died here, only a couple of days ago.

"Time to go, Josephine," she said aloud. If she stayed much longer she'd have nightmares later.

Her car's ignition made a grinding noise when she turned the key. It started on the next try, but even with her mostly nonexistent knowledge of car mechanics, she knew something was wrong. *Great,* she thought, checking her watch. Well, Eb could take care of Jethro and Coco, and her great-uncle was hardly likely to starve if she took a detour on the way home.

Josie pulled into a parking lot two streets over from Main. Rusty's Car Repair was located in a low building with a gently-peaked roof. She was relieved. The car had held out until she got here.

A very tall man stood when she walked in. "Can I help you?" His name tag said RUSTY, and, with his head of thick, bright coppery hair, it was easy to see where the nickname had come from. Unless it was from the mass of snow-covered, probably junk cars she could see through the window behind him.

Josie was five foot six—not tall nor striking enough to model, which was why she'd ended up in fashion design—but she had to crane her neck to look into his face to reply. Man, this guy was tall. He would have had to special order his wardrobe, no question.

"My car has a problem," Josie said.

He raised his eyebrows. "That's usually why people bring them in," he said, then broke into a smile that showed a lot of teeth. He was handsome in a rugged way, like the lumberjack on those paper-towel wrappers. Not the kind of man she ever encountered in the fashion business.

Josie smiled back. "The ignition is a little wonky, and the engine is making a funny noise."

Rusty glanced at the large utilitarian clock on the wall to his left. "I can't look at it today, sorry. My kids have swimming lessons, and it's my turn to take them."

"Oh, are you Gwen's husband?" she asked. "I met her. When I was a teenager I lived in your house for a couple of years."

"She mentioned you. You're staying with Eb Lloyd, right? He and Roy Woodruff keep me in business, always pranking each other's trucks."

At least someone can stay in business in this town, she thought. "Can you at least tell me if it's safe to drive? I have to get back out to Eb's."

He stroked his chin, which was covered in a thick stubble a shade lighter than his hair, then tapped something into his computer keyboard with his enormous fingers. "I open early tomorrow. I can squeeze you in if you can leave it overnight so it'll be here when I get here in the morning."

Great. How was she supposed to get home? Eb couldn't drive, and Evelyn was getting ready for her night on the town. She didn't know what time Lorna got off work. She'd bet her only pair of Jimmy Choos that Dorset Falls did not have a taxi. "I guess I'll have to chance it," she said reluctantly. "I don't have a ride home, unless you've got a loaner?"

The door opened, and a man walked up to the counter and stood beside her.

"Mitch," Rusty said.

"Hey, Rusty. Hi, Josie," he said, giving her a smile. "I was driving past and saw your car parked out front. Everything okay?"

Josie breathed a sigh of relief. "Can I catch a ride home with you so I can leave my car here overnight? Tomorrow I'll take Eb's truck."

Mitch raised an eyebrow. "Can you drive a standard transmission?"

Seriously? There were still vehicles with clutches and stick shifts? "I'll figure it out," she said with more confidence than she felt.

"I'll come over in the morning after chores and give you a quick lesson. It's not hard once you get the hang of it."

I hope that's true. Still, she reasoned, if she could manage to survive in New York, she could manage to make a piece of machinery go. Maybe.

Josie placed her keys on the counter and slid them toward

Rusty. "You give free estimates, right?" Women—and men—got taken advantage of all the time, and she wasn't exactly made of money.

"There's a fifty-dollar diagnostic fee, but I won't do any work until you give me the go-ahead."

"Fair enough." She turned to Mitch. "Ready when you are, oh knight in shining armor."

He grinned. "Your steed awaits, milady."

Mitch's steed turned out to be a shiny black SUV with cushy leather seats. Josie sank back and allowed herself to relax as the countryside rolled by. Ten minutes and some comfortable conversation later, Mitch slowed the vehicle.

"I took a different route so I could show you my farm," he said. "You probably come back from town from the other direction, so you wouldn't normally see it."

Josie nodded. They passed a couple of ramshackle buildings, at least one of which was a barn made of dark, unpainted wood. A flat area near one of the barns was ringed by a wooden fence. "Oh my goodness!" she said. "Are those llamas?" A couple of dozen fluffy animals in various shades of white, cream, fawn, and gray stood in a huddle inside the enclosure.

"Alpacas," Mitch replied. "Cousins to llamas. Since I came back to Dorset Falls I've been slowly building my grandfather's herd." He pulled in to a driveway that wrapped around one of the barns, then rolled to a stop in front of the pen.

Josie leaned forward for a better look. "They are adorable! Look at those ugly-cute faces sticking out from under their big fluffy pom-poms." She turned toward Mitch. "So this is where alpaca wool comes from. I've inventoried a lot of it in the last couple of days."

"Wool comes from sheep. The sheared alpaca coats are called fiber."

"They look pretty . . . full. When do they get sheared?" She had a sudden urge to see the process and to feel some of that fiber between her fingers. Time to nip those urges in the bud. Unless these creatures were being stripped naked in the next couple of weeks, she'd be long gone.

"We shear in the spring. That's why their coats are so thick right now. See Lulubelle, over there?" He pointed toward a fawn-colored animal standing slightly apart from the herd. Lulubelle seemed enormous, a perfectly round ball of fluff supported by skinny legs.

"She's pretty." Josie mused that if she stuck her hand into that coat, her arm might disappear up to the shoulder.

"She's also pregnant. She's been pregnant for eleven months, so her cria should be born anytime."

"Cria?"

"That's what the babies are called."

Josie's heart swelled. "I'd love to see a cria. Though how it could be any cuter than these guys, I don't know."

"Well, trust me, it can. If the baby comes before you go back to the city, I'll let you know, and you can come see him or her." He put his SUV in reverse and performed an expert three-point turn, giving Josie one more look at the animals. "And now I should get you back to Eb's. If he's like Gramps, he'll be wanting his dinner."

When they arrived at the Lloyd farm a few minutes later, Mitch parked and turned to Josie. "I left enough firewood in the box by the stove for tonight. In the morning I'll swing by and bring in some more."

"You don't have to do that," Josie said. She felt a little pang of guilt.

"It's no trouble. Eb's a great old guy. Not that my grandfather would admit it."

Josie chuckled. "Those two are something. I almost feel like we should stage an intervention. Or get them into couples' therapy, maybe."

"They keep each other going, and it's mostly harmless."

"Mitch," Josie said, reaching for the door handle, "why don't you come over for breakfast tomorrow so I can thank you for all your help? I'm not a great cook, but I can manage scrambled eggs and toast." She picked up her handbag and opened the door into the cold. "Bring Roy if you want." The offer had to be made, she supposed.

Mitch let out a rich laugh. "What a way to start the day. Roy and Eb sitting across the breakfast table from each other. Don't count on Roy, but I'll be over as soon as I take care of the animals, and I'll give you a ride to Miss Marple Knits so you don't have to drive Eb's truck. You can never be sure Gramps hasn't been tinkering with it."

Eb wasn't in his usual spot in the velour armchair by the front window, but his newspaper, folded out to the crossword puzzle, lay on the floor. "Unc, I'm home," she called, but there was no answer. She hung her coat on the rack and left her boots on the mat on the floor, then bent to pick up the paper. A couple of black cat hairs floated to the carpet. Coco must have knocked the paper off the worn arm of the recliner. Josie picked it up and added it to the stack on the dining room table.

What had she been thinking? She'd invited Mitch for breakfast, but where would they eat? There was nothing for it. The table would have to be cleared by morning. In a way she didn't care to analyze too closely, she was rather looking forward to it. There was always something satisfying about cleaning up and clearing a space. Based on the amount of paper and other detritus—Eb had removed his fishing traps, at least—this promised to be a very satisfying job.

Josie heard movement in the kitchen. Eb had thumped through the back door, banging a crutch on the jamb. "'Bout time you got home," he growled. "I'm hungry."

"Me too," she said. "Then after dinner we've got work to do."

Dinner, bless Evelyn's heart, was a casserole labeled SPANISH RICE. It consisted of white rice bathed in tomato sauce, mixed with lots of ground beef and chopped green peppers. A layer of cheese covered the top and bubbled as Josie pulled the vintage Pyrex dish out of the oven. Josie's stomach growled. She wasn't sure what was Spanish about this dish, because the tomato sauce was clearly Italian and probably came from a glass jar, but it didn't matter. It was delicious. She never ate like this in New York, where she was often surrounded by svelte models and waif-like interns, both male and female, who would rather run naked through Times Square than let a carbohydrate pass their lips. But, man, she had to admit, this dinner tasted good. She even had a second helping.

Chapter 11

Josie stared at the paper in her hand, then reread it. *What the heck?*

After cleaning up from dinner, scooping the litter box, and feeding Coco—she left feeding Jethro to Eb, who was now settled in the living room watching a reality fishing show and occasionally making snorts of disgust at the screen—she had sat down and gone to work in earnest on the stacks that covered most of the dining room table.

Outdated catalogs and assorted junk mail went into a cardboard box without a further look. Eb either had no bills, which seemed unlikely, or he had a system for taking care of them, because she didn't find any, nor any overdue notices.

When she moved on to the newspapers, she paused. Each issue of the *Dorset Falls Tribune* was folded out to Eb's word puzzles, except for one. That one was folded to the notices of public hearing.

And one particular notice was circled in pencil, Eb's writing utensil of choice.

> Notice of Public Hearing. On application of Tristan "Trey" Humphries III, the Dorset Falls Planning and Zoning Committee will hold a public hearing on February 10, regarding property located at 13 Main Street. For more information contact the town clerk.

Miss Marple Knits was located at 13 Main Street. She'd seen the numbers painted on the window of the front door.

Why would Trey, her high school boyfriend, be applying to the planning and zoning committee about Miss Marple Knits?

Something was off. She felt her brow crease into a furrow as she made her way to the living room. "Eb? What's this about?"

Her great-uncle didn't look up from his recliner, which was a match to the one in the dining room. "Wait till the commercial, missy. Lemme see if they land this tuna."

Josie parked herself on the couch to wait. She read the notice again. Nope, no idea came to her. She'd have to wait for the fish to either be caught or lost.

Finally, the show went to commercial, and Eb turned toward her. He didn't talk, just raised an eyebrow.

Josie showed him the newspaper and pointed to the circled notice. "What's this about?"

Eb squinted. "Humphries owns the building. He must want to do something with it."

Josie's mouth dropped open. "Diantha Humphries?"

Eb shook his head.

"You mean *Trey* Humphries is our landlord?" It took her a moment to realize she'd said the word "our." "Your landlord?" she amended.

"Not for much longer. Once you get that shop closed up, he can do what he wants with it."

A knot formed in Josie's stomach. What she knew about zoning was analogous to what she knew about chickens and alpacas and knitting—not much. But this must mean Trey was planning to change the use of the building to something other than a storefront. *None of your business, Josephine,* she told herself. That seemed to be her mantra since she'd returned to Dorset Falls. But the knot didn't go away. If anything, it twisted tighter. What if he made big alterations that changed the character of the building? It *wasn't* her business, in any sense of the word. But that would be awful.

"What's he planning to do?" She almost wished she could take back the question. Maybe it would be better not to know.

Eb's brows drew together, then apart, in a sort of hairy mating dance. "Don't know. Not my place to argue even if I did." He turned back to the show, where a heavily bearded man in a pair of chest-high overalls was straining mightily against a fishing rod that was bent nearly double.

Josie sat back. "Didn't he have to notify you or something? I mean, you might have wanted to keep the shop open. Miss Marple Knits is yours now."

Eb let out a snort, which was the closest thing to a laugh she'd ever heard from him. "Do I look like the kind of fella who owns a yarn shop? That place was Cora's, not mine. Now leave me be."

Leave him be. Yeah, that about summed it up. Josie didn't belong in Dorset Falls, had no intention of staying, and needed to finish the job she'd come here to do so she could go home. There was no sense getting involved in things out of her control. But she couldn't help but wish that 13 Main Street had been owned by anyone other than a member of the Humphries family.

Josie returned to the dining room. At least she could finish this job. Soon the surface of the table shone dully up at her. Josie was surprised to find a pretty oak table underneath all the detritus. She ran a damp dishcloth over the top and stood back to admire her work, satisfied. Some placemats would have been nice. There were probably some around here, but she didn't feel much like hunting for them. Asking Eb was out of the question. Her great-uncle was way too prickly tonight. She hauled all the boxes of paper trash out to the back door. Tomorrow, she'd ask Mitch about recycling or at least responsible trash disposal. There was a rusty oil drum in the backyard that she suspected Eb used for burning, but that didn't seem like the right thing to do.

Her great-uncle didn't bother to acknowledge her as she passed him on her way to the morning-borning room. She shut the door, sat down, and reread the zoning notice, tapping a pencil on the desk. Why was this bothering her so much? Was it because Trey Humphries was involved? She hadn't thought about Trey in years. They'd only dated for a few months, and then he'd moved on to some cheerleader. She didn't recall having been particularly broken up about it.

Or was this about Diantha? Maybe she really did want to open a yarn shop, although the odious woman would have to hire someone to work behind the counter. With her personality, she'd never make it in sales.

But if Diantha wanted to open a yarn shop, there'd be no need for a zoning change, which brought Josie back to square one. She wondered if Mitch or Lorna might know something about it. There was a good chance Evelyn might. Tomorrow Josie would ask around, and then maybe she could get it out of her head.

She checked the little clock on the front right corner of the desk. Its dark case had a warm sheen. The clock was probably an antique. Josie reached out and ran her fingers along the wood. So much nicer, Josie thought, than a digital clock with a plastic case. When she squinted, she could just make out the words SETH THOMAS written in black letters on the face. It was close to eight o'clock. Just enough time before bed to start sketching out some preliminary designs for Otto's fall ready-to-wear collection. These had to be stellar, her best work to date, if she wanted to get her job back. She put a pencil to a notepad she found in the desk and began to sketch.

Two hours later, she threw the pencil down in frustration. The floor was littered with crumpled balls of paper, and the pad was empty.

Tears spilled out onto her arms as she lay her head on them on the desk, leaving cold, wet trails of failure. This was never going to work.

Josie didn't feel much better when she woke up after a fitful night's sleep. Her stomach was still in a knot, and her head ached. If she'd been home in New York, she would have called in sick and stayed in bed snuggling with Coco, if the cat would allow it, and watching movies all day. Around lunchtime, she'd call for Chinese takeout and eat it while still wearing her pajamas.

But she wasn't in New York. She was in Dorset Falls, Connecticut, she was late, and she had responsibilities, whether she wanted them or not. She hauled herself out of bed, wincing as pain shot through her head at the bright morning light coming in through the lace curtain, and got herself dressed. Mercifully, the medicine cabinet in the upstairs bathroom contained a bottle of aspirin and some small paper cups. Heedless of the possible damage to her kidneys and liver, she took three pills and headed downstairs.

Eb was sitting at the newly cleared dining room table, with a cup of coffee and the paper in front of him. Josie frowned. Had the old man been holding out on her? Coffee didn't just magically appear.

Or did it? Mitch Woodruff came out of the kitchen, holding two steaming mugs. He smiled when he saw her. "Eb said you were sleeping late, so I took the liberty of starting breakfast. I went out and collected up the eggs, too."

A strange mixture of guilt and relief washed over Josie. She took the cup Mitch handed her and swallowed the hot liquid gratefully. Mitch didn't comment on the puffy purple circles under her eyes, or the fact that she hadn't even combed her hair, but had just run her fingers through it and smoothed it back with a headband.

Eb, however, showed no such restraint. "You look like hell," he said, and went back to the paper.

Josie didn't argue. Her great-uncle was right. She turned to Mitch. "Roy didn't want breakfast?"

Mitch laughed, and little crinkles appeared around his blue eyes. "He said he'd rather starve."

"Hmmph." Eb's face darkened. "Nothing would make me happier. Why do I smell bacon and there's none in front of me?"

Mitch laughed again. "Coming right up. Josie, I can get this. Why don't you sit down and let that coffee start working?"

She started to protest, then sat down. It was nice to have someone do something for her, just because he wanted to. "Thanks," she said simply.

"No problem." She watched as he returned to the kitchen, then closed her eyes, willing the headache to subside.

When she opened her eyes again, Mitch was setting a plate of hot eggs and bacon in front of her. Triangles of buttered toast towered on a plate in the middle of the table. She waited for Mitch to sit down, then forked up a yellow chunk of scrambled eggs and a piece of bacon. Heaven.

"Where'd you learn to cook?" Josie asked.

"My mother trained me right," Mitch said. "And when a couple of bachelor farmers live together, somebody's got to do it. Trust me, I'm the better choice."

Eb snorted, then went back to his breakfast.

Mitch dropped her off at the general store an hour later, where she made the egg delivery; then she walked to Miss Marple Knits. By noon Evelyn had still not shown up, probably exhausted from her night at the casino, so Josie decided to take a break from her solo inventorying. The relatively mindless task had helped her avoid thinking too much about the failed sketches last night and what that meant for her future. The day was bright and, for the first time since she'd arrived in town, above freezing. Now that her headache had subsided, she could enjoy the warmth of the sun on her face as she made her way the two blocks to Rusty's Car Repair.

No one was behind the counter when she arrived, so she sat down to wait. A woman sat in a chair nearby, reading a magazine. The woman did a double take as she looked up at Josie, then glared, her eyes narrowing.

Josie was surprised. She'd only been in town a few days, and there seemed to be an inordinate number of strangers who had some beef with her. Well, no time like the present to find out what *this* woman's problem was. "Hello," Josie said sweetly. "Waiting for your car?"

The woman folded her magazine closed and dropped it on the table between the chairs. She reached into her purse and pulled out a pair of knitting needles attached to some peach-colored yarn. "What I'm waiting for," she said, stabbing one needle through the loops on the other and wrapping the yarn around, "is for you to tell me when you'll be finished closing up that shop."

Josie was taken aback by the woman's sharp tone, but quickly recovered. She was learning that New Yorkers had nothing on the people of this small town when it came to rudeness. "How nice of you to be concerned. Have we met?"

The woman looked up and continued to knit, rather violently. Her fingers flew with a practiced rhythm. Josie was fascinated, in spite of herself. The woman never took her eyes off Josie. "You can stay away from my husband." Her mouth opened for her to speak again, but she was interrupted.

"Courtney?" Rusty's deep voice rumbled around the room

as he emerged from the side door that led into the working part of the garage. "Trey's car is all set."

Courtney. Could this blonde with expensive-looking highlights be Trey's wife? Josie took a closer look. The woman's face softened as she looked at Rusty. "Thanks so much for squeezing me in," she purred.

Rusty was unreadable. He towered over the petite Courtney, who was looking up at him from under her lashes.

"No problem, Courtney. I put a sticker on the windshield. No need to get that oil changed again for at least another three months."

Courtney reached into her purse and pulled out a wallet. "What about the tires? Did you check those?" She handed him her credit card. "I can come back."

Rusty swiped the card across the machine and handed it back to her. "Yes, the tires are fine. And so is every other system in Trey's car. And your car. And your mother-in-law's car."

"Oh. Well, good. So, I guess I'll go over to the general store for lunch." There was a significant pause, while she waited for him to take the bait.

"Meeting up with Trey?" he asked innocently.

Josie had a good view of Courtney's profile. The woman's lips pursed. "I'll see you later, Rusty," she said, and turned to Josie. "Remember what I said," she hissed under her breath.

"Sure thing, Court. You have my word." It was debatable whom Josie liked less, Courtney or Courtney's mother-in-law, Diantha. *I'll bet they have some really fun holiday dinners,* she thought, stifling a laugh.

Courtney glared, then left. Rusty relaxed, blowing out a long breath. "Thank God she's gone. In the last two months she's been in here every week. And there's nothing wrong with any one of their cars."

Josie grinned. "She's a charmer. I came in to see if you'd had a chance to look at the Saab?"

Rusty made a few keystrokes at his computer. "Nothing serious, for a car that age. I tightened up the steering column and gave you a new set of spark plugs. That should take care of it." He handed her the invoice that spat out of the printer. "I only charged you for an hour of labor and the parts were inexpensive, so I didn't bother to call you for authorization. Hope that's okay."

Josie looked at the total. It was half of what she would have expected to pay in New York, assuming she could have even found a mechanic. She gave him her card. "Thanks," she said, relieved.

"You bet. That car will run for a long time if you keep it maintained." He handed her the receipt and a pen. "There's a box of yarn in the trunk."

Josie scribbled her signature, then looked up. "Yarn?" She was sure she hadn't been carrying around any yarn. There was enough of that at Eb's and at Miss Marple Knits.

"It was Cora's. After the accident, the car was towed here so the appraiser could look at it. The car was a total loss, so I bought it from the insurance company for parts."

"And the yarn wasn't . . . damaged?" Josie's stomach knotted up again.

"The yarn was in the trunk." Rusty looked sympathetic. "They went off the road and hit a tree head-on. Her air bag didn't deploy, but Eb's did, which is why he survived."

Josie swallowed. She felt sick that she'd never asked how the accident happened. Poor Cora. And poor Eb. Imagine the survivor's guilt her great-uncle must feel.

"Do they know what caused the accident?" Did she really want to know? "Eb doesn't talk much."

Rusty's smile indicated that he wasn't surprised. "The police think she skidded on a patch of ice and lost control of the car."

Josie wondered vaguely why Eb hadn't been operating the

vehicle. He was old-fashioned, not the kind of man she'd expect would let his wife drive him around.

"I'm sorry," Rusty continued. "I thought you knew."

"I'm fine." Not really. She felt awful for Cora, and for Eb. "Uh, I should be going. Thanks, Rusty." She wrapped Cora's scarf around her neck and shouldered her purse.

"You bet. And I'm sorry about Cora. The car's parked in the side lot. Come this way."

Josie followed him out the back door and around the side of the building. Rusty let her into the car. He pointed to the center console. "I found this set of keys in Cora's car. Eb never came to pick them up when I called him. Not that we need an ignition key anymore. I parted out what I could, then sold the car for scrap metal. It's been crushed by now."

Josie gulped, then turned on the ignition. "That's probably for the best," she finally said. "Thanks, Rusty."

The Saab seemed to be running correctly again, but she decided to take it for a test drive around town to make sure. After a couple of circuits around downtown and the adjoining blocks, she was satisfied the car wasn't going to break down.

As she passed the town hall for the second time, a thought occurred to her. She'd forgotten to ask Mitch this morning about Trey's application to the zoning commission. But that was all right. She could go directly to the source. She stopped at the stop sign in front of the building, took a right, and pulled into the parking lot.

The Dorset Falls town hall was an imposing redbrick building built in the Federal style. Whether it actually dated back to Connecticut's colonial period, she didn't know, but it had clearly been around for a while. The steps were made of some kind of hard white rock speckled with black dots, worn in the center from decades, maybe centuries, of townspeople coming and going. She stepped under the white wooden portico and through a set of tall, very heavy doors.

Inside, the walls were covered in raised panels of dark oak. The space was saved from being oppressive by a line of white-shaded chandeliers that lit it. High ceilings made her want to shout something and see if she got an echo.

About twenty feet or so across the polished floor Josie spotted an easel. TOWN CLERK, 2ND FLOOR. She made her way up the stairwell.

The town clerk's office occupied a fairly large space. A woman at the counter said, "Can I help you?"

"I hope so. I'd like to look at the application of Trey Humphries regarding 13 Main Street."

The woman eyed Josie through the top half of her bifocals. "Are you a town resident?" She set down the file she'd been working on. Wow. Was that an actual typewriter? Josie couldn't remember the last time she'd seen one of those. The woman's name plate next to it read MARIAN MURPHY.

"Does it matter? Isn't the application a matter of public record? I saw the notice in the paper."

Marian pursed her lips. "Yes, it's public record. But we like to know who's looking at our applications. Sign here, please." Her voice was frosty, but she handed Josie a clipboard, which Josie signed. "Just have a seat over at that table, and I'll bring you the file."

While she waited, Josie looked around. The space was utilitarian and 1980s modern, in stark contrast to the more ostentatious lower lobby. Her eyes landed on a series of photographs in dark frames. Ugh. One was labeled DIANTHA HUMPHRIES, COUNCILWOMAN. For the love of Prada, could she not get away from this woman? Diantha's haughty stare seemed to bore into Josie's skull. The frame next to her was occupied by a photo labeled DOUGLAS BREWSTER, MAYOR. Where had she heard that name before? Oh, right. Lorna had been talking about him the other day. He owned the general store. He was also, apparently, the mayor of Dorset Falls.

Ms. Murphy returned and set a bound document in front of Josie. "Bring it to the counter when you're finished," she said crisply.

Well, Josie thought, if I had to work in any kind of proximity to Diantha, I'd be cranky too. "Thanks," she said, and flipped open the cover to the title page.

Application for Demolition and Construction Permits
Regarding Premises Located at 13 Main Street,
Dorset Falls, Connecticut.

Chapter 12

No. Trey couldn't be planning to demolish the building that housed Miss Marple Knits. How would such a thing even be possible? As far as she knew, number thirteen Main Street was attached to number fifteen Main Street. She supposed a construction company that knew what it was doing could accomplish the feat. But why?

Heart in her throat, she began to read.

Redevelopment. Opportunity for growth. Benefits to community. The application went on for pages. She turned to the next tabbed section, and her heart sank. A full color drawing stared up at her. She'd seen this building before, in any number of towns and cities and on television commercials.

Trey wanted to demolish Miss Marple Knits and put up a fast-food restaurant.

Josie sat back in her seat, stunned. She closed her eyes, picturing the giant illuminated spatula that identified every Simon the Fryman chicken franchise across the country. It didn't matter that downtown Dorset Falls was full of empty storefronts. Any charm, any small-town appeal it had would be ruined forever.

And yet, she asked herself, why did she care? This wasn't her town. She had no right to be incensed on its behalf. If the people who lived here didn't mind, why should she? But did they even know about it? Who actually read those notices in the newspaper, anyway? Yet she would have thought something like this could not be kept secret in a town this size.

On the other hand, it wasn't like Dorset Falls didn't need jobs. Working the cash register or fry-o-lator at a fast-food restaurant wasn't glamorous, but it was honest, paying work, something that appeared to be pretty tough to come by here.

Still, why did the restaurant have to be built downtown? Why couldn't it be built a few streets over, on the connector road out of town?

Josie had a pretty good idea why. Because Trey Humphries had a piece of property that was no longer going to be producing rent once Miss Marple went out of business, and he was going to be stuck with both upkeep and probably a mortgage. Bulldozing the building and selling or leasing to a national company would mean Trey would not only be out from under the building, he'd probably stand to make a pretty penny on the transaction.

Josie looked at the picture of Diantha. Trey Humphries's mother was on the town council. Could Diantha be involved? Of course, Josie had no proof of any dishonesty or nepotism on Diantha's part, but Josie wouldn't put it past her.

She closed up the application notebook. She'd seen enough.

Ms. Murphy took it from her and stowed it away efficiently under the counter. "Are you finished? We close early today, and I'd like to get home."

"I'll be going, thank you." Josie took a few steps toward the door, then turned back to the clerk. "When's the hearing on this application?"

The woman eyed her. "At the next council meeting. It's expected to pass, but the town bylaws require the formality of a hearing."

"Do the citizens of Dorset Falls get a chance to voice their opinions?"

"Are *you* a citizen of Dorset Falls?" Ms. Murphy's tone was frosty again. Josie felt her hackles rise.

"Does it matter? You could tell me, or I can ask you to get me the bylaws so I can look it up myself. And that"—Josie glanced up at the big round clock on the wall—"might take some time."

The woman huffed out a breath. "Fine. Yes, townspeople can speak at the meeting, but only if they have an actual legal residence in Dorset Falls. Which I'm assuming you don't." She shoved a piece of paper at Josie. "Here's the agenda."

Josie folded up the paper and put it in her pocket. She thought about reading it right there, just to annoy the woman a little more, but decided against it. You could always catch more flies with honey than with vinegar. "Thanks. You've been great."

Ms. Murphy pursed her lips, but nodded. Yeah, the woman was clearly suffering from Diantha-induced crankiness.

Her car started right up, and Josie sat inside, waiting for it to warm up a little. She pulled out the agenda. The department of public works was asking for more money for snow removal. Various committees and commissions had vacancies that needed filling. Trey's application was the last item on the list. Insurance, probably, that fewer Dorset Falls residents would stay till the very end to voice their opinions.

Should she go to the meeting? There didn't seem to be much point. It wasn't like she'd be allowed to speak, and who would pay attention to her, an outsider, anyway? Going just to listen would probably just make her sad, or angry, or both. She pulled out of the parking lot and drove back to Miss Marple Knits, parking in front of the building. Evelyn's Buick was parked in the space ahead of her, but the car appeared to be empty.

Josie put her hand on the bright blue door of the yarn shop. The wood was cold and solid beneath her bare fingers. It had been here long before Josie was born, probably long before Eb or Cora had been born. If what the clerk at the town hall had said was true, it wouldn't be here much longer. Josie's heart squeezed as she went inside. In a few months, if Trey and Diantha had their way, this spot would no longer have the warm, earthy scent of yarn, but the greasy smell of fried chicken.

And there wasn't a darn thing Josie could do about it.

Evelyn blew in a few minutes later. "Sorry I didn't get here until now. It was a late night."

Josie shook off her depressing thoughts and grinned. "We still have a couple of hours, if you have the time. Did you win?" She set up her laptop and called up the inventory document, which was now several pages long.

Evelyn got right to work. They were nearly finished with the yarn and knitting paraphernalia in the formerly public part of the store. She began to sort. "I was up thirty dollars at the end of the night. I'm strictly a slots girl. Helen and Courtney broke even. Diantha wouldn't admit it, but she was grouchy on the way home so she must have lost a few bucks. We're none of us big gamblers."

Josie was perversely pleased that Diantha hadn't won. Wait, what had Evelyn said? "Courtney Humphries?" Josie shouldn't have been surprised that Courtney was part of the Charity Knitters. She'd been knitting up a storm at Rusty's car repair shop.

"Yes. She and Diantha are thick as thieves. Diantha likes her daughter-in-law better than her own son." Evelyn made quick work of the skeins in front of her, and began to call out the brand and color. Josie made the appropriate notations.

"I saw Courtney this morning," Josie said, typing away. "At the car shop."

Evelyn stopped what she was doing and looked up. "Oh?"

"Yeah, she seems to have a little, uh, thing for Rusty."

Evelyn went back to her sorting. "That's the rumor around town."

"Well, I don't think Rusty has a thing for her. Unless he put on a very convincing show for me."

"The verdict is still out on that one," Evelyn said.

Before Josie could respond, the bells over the shop door rang. Her teeth clenched.

Diantha.

But not just Diantha. Following behind her like a faithful lapdog was Trey Humphries. Josie hadn't seen him in a decade, and he had more weight and less hair, but there was no mistaking him.

She steeled herself, glad Evelyn was there for moral support.

"Can I help you?" Josie said. "Hi, Trey. It's been a long time."

Trey shoved his hands in his pockets. "Hi, Josie." He was clearly uncomfortable.

Diantha glared at her. "I don't appreciate your spying on me," she snapped.

From the corner of her eye, Josie saw Evelyn stiffen. "What are you talking about?" Josie said. "Why would I spy on you? No offense, but you're just not that interesting to me." Take that, Dragon Lady.

Diantha's eyes narrowed to tiny slits. She shoved a finger toward Josie. "I saw you driving past my house the other day. It's bad enough you won't sell me the shop. You have to drive by and rub it in my face?"

"Settle down, Diantha. Remember your blood pressure," Evelyn said.

Diantha's head spun toward Evelyn. "You stay out of this."

"Don't tell me what to do," Evelyn said, her demeanor calm.

"Frankly," Josie said, "I'm not quite sure why you offered

to buy the shop in the first place. I went by the town hall today. If Trey here gets his wish and tears down this building, you'd have to open the yarn shop in a different place."

Diantha's face flushed. "I saw your name on the sign-in sheet. And that's another thing," she spat out. "What business is it of yours what happens in this town? You're only temporary. You don't belong here."

Josie turned to Trey, who stood there like a limp fish. Seriously, what had Josie ever seen in him?

"Give it to her," Diantha ordered.

Trey obediently reached inside his wool topcoat and pulled out a folded piece of paper, which he handed to Josie.

Josie frowned. "What's this?" She opened it and read the subject line. *Notice to Quit*. Quit what?

"That's your formal notice to vacate the premises," Diantha said triumphantly. "You have seven days."

Seven days? Cora had had this shop open for a couple of decades. Did Diantha know how much stuff was in the building? Josie looked at Trey, who was seriously studying something in the vicinity of his shoes. Wuss.

"That doesn't seem legal. I think I'll have my lawyer check this," Josie bluffed. She didn't even know who Eb's or Cora's lawyer was—her mother was handling that—but Josie intended to find out. Josie might not be able to speak at the town meeting, but she might be able to throw a monkey wrench into Trey's—make that Diantha's—plans.

Diantha bristled. "You do that. Trey's lease with Cora was ironclad. The lease is binding on her heirs, and that would be Eben Lloyd."

Josie looked at the paper in her hands again. There was a paragraph, presumably quoted from the lease, that gave the landlord the right to terminate the lease upon seven days' notice.

Truth was, Josie was hoping to be done here in less than seven days. But she certainly wasn't going to say that to Diantha or Trey.

Josie looked Diantha in the eye. "Nice way to treat a friend, Di. I'm sure Cora would be pleased at how you're handling this."

Diantha's face purpled. "This has nothing to do with friendship. This is business. And you're interfering with mine. Just get it done and get out."

"That's enough," Evelyn said. "You've said what you came here to say. The two of you can be on your way now."

Diantha turned to Evelyn. "I told you to stay out of it, and I meant it. I'll see you at the Charity Knitters meeting tonight. Seven o'clock, my house." She stormed out the front door. Trey followed without saying good-bye.

"Whew," Josie said. "That was . . . fun." She felt her shoulders relax.

Evelyn was nonplussed. "Speaking of fun, I wish I could be a fly on the wall of her house tonight."

"Really, why?" Personally, Josie wanted to stay as far away from the woman as possible.

"Because," Evelyn said with obvious glee, "Helen and I have already decided we're not going! So she'll have a lovely meeting with just Courtney. She'll pop a cork. *And* she'll have cooked and cleaned all day for nothing."

Josie was impressed. "Not bad. But what about the Charity Knitters as a whole?"

Evelyn's face clouded over with sadness, and if she'd been closer, Josie would have given her a very non-New-Yorky hug.

"Cora was the heart and the brains of the group. She was the one who found the charities for us to donate to, and who kept us organized and moving. We can't get Diantha out of office until November, when we have our elections." Josie pushed the box of tissues along the counter in case Evelyn needed one.

"But Courtney will vote for Diantha as president, and of course Diantha will vote for herself. Helen and I will vote against her, but with only four of us in the group, we'll be at a stalemate. We won't be able to elect a president, which means we'll have to dissolve."

Josie's stomach gave its characteristic flip. First the shop having to close, then the Charity Knitters folding—all of Cora's life work seemed to be dissolving away. The tissue she put to her own eyes dampened. "I'm so sorry," she finally said. "I know that group meant something to you."

Evelyn shook her head, as if willing herself back to the present. "Seasons change, and people die. It was naïve of us to think that we'd all go on forever." She stuck her hands back into the pile of yarn, and Josie saw her shoulders relax, as if the fiber calmed her. "Still, I will miss getting together and talking and knitting. I guess Helen and I can still do it, of course, but there's an energy a group puts out that we'll be missing."

"You know," Josie said, thoughtful, "the chairs and couch are still here. Why don't we see if Helen can come over tonight? I'll get some coffee from the g.s., and you two can have a knitting session here. If you don't mind my hanging around, that is."

Evelyn looked pleased. "That is a lovely idea. And we'll sit right here in the front window with the lights on, just in case Diantha or Courtney drives by. Cora would approve."

"Super. Seven o'clock." Josie would go home for a while and get Eb settled, then come back. If downtown Dorset Falls was a ghost town during the day, what would it be like at night? Well, she supposed she'd find out.

Eb just shrugged when she told him she was going back out. "Been a bachelor most of my life. Got my dog and my workshop. Don't need you."

She blew him a kiss. "I love you more than I can say, Unc."

"Go on. Get out." He picked up the remote control and began to flip through the channels.

"I won't be late. I'm just going to the shop for a while with Helen and Evelyn."

His brow furrowed. "Good. If those two are in town, they're not bothering me. Stay as late as you want."

Her tires crunched on the frozen dirt of the driveway as she backed out and into the road. The ink-black sky was full of stars, and the moon was huge, like a big silvery medallion on the chest of a celestial Bee Gee. Other than the sound of the engine, there was silence. Josie had to admit, it was peaceful. The city was never quiet. Something or someone was always in motion.

As she rolled along toward town, her thoughts turned back to Trey and Diantha and the eviction notice. What was the point? It was no secret she was packing up the contents of Miss Marple Knits with the intent of closing up the business. There was no need for any formal proceedings. Eb had no reason to delay vacating the premises. So what was Trey's hurry? He needed the variance, or the permits, or whatever exactly it was that he was looking for at the upcoming town meeting. But Marian at the town hall had said the application would most likely be approved, and with his mother and Dougie Brewster on the town council, there didn't seem to be any obstacles. The ground was still frozen and covered with a foot of snow, so it didn't seem likely that any demolition or subsequent construction was going to get done before spring.

The most obvious explanation was that Diantha was pulling the strings and manipulating her spineless son. Diantha didn't like Josie, that much was clear. Did she think she could force Josie out of town by putting on some legal pressure? Diantha seemed to think that Josie still had designs on Trey, which was laughable. Not in a million years would she come between Trey and the delightful Courtney.

Still, it seemed like overkill. Josie would be finished and gone, soon enough.

Josie gulped. Overkill. How had Lillian gotten into the yarn shop? And who had killed her? If the police had a suspect, it wasn't common knowledge around town yet—or at least Josie hadn't heard, and she had to think Evelyn would have told her if she knew.

Josie pulled up in front of Miss Marple Knits. All the shops on Main Street were dark. Streetlights cast an eerie yellow glow over the empty sidewalks as a faint sense of foreboding washed over her. She really, really did not want to go into the dark building alone, so she decided to wait for the ladies. With the radio turned up, she made sure the car doors were locked—carjacking seemed unlikely in Dorset Falls, but then so did murder—and leaned back in her seat to wait.

Suddenly, a glimmer of light registered in the corner of her eye. She turned toward it, then sat up straight. It wasn't a car's headlight, as she'd thought. This came from up high. Josie stared. A sliver of illumination shone from one of the third floor windows in the vacant building across the street. The light blinked out for a moment, then reappeared, as if someone had walked past the shaded window.

Neck craned, Josie scanned Main Street. Not a car or another person in sight.

The apprehension she'd felt moments earlier was replaced by curiosity. What was going on up there?

Josie put the car into drive and pulled out. Where else could someone park? She drove down to the g.s. on the corner and around the back, but the building was dark and the parking lot was empty. She circled around and crossed Main Street again, this time continuing on past the block that faced Miss Marple Knits. She slowed and pulled into a narrow alley behind the building. No lights were visible on the second or third floors from this direction.

Parked in the alley was a car. Not just any car. If she wasn't very much mistaken, she was looking at a Buick. The license plate read KNTTR-1. *Evelyn.*

Chapter 13

Josie backed out onto the street and returned to the spot in front of the yarn shop. What was going on? What could Evelyn possibly be doing up there? There was one way to find out. Josie would come right out and ask.

Before she could think any further, a car pulled in to the spot in front of her. A woman got out and made her way toward the shop. Helen waved, and Josie shut off the engine and met her at the door, feeling a sense of relief. Why, she couldn't say. Helen had a secret too. Josie had seen Helen go up those stairs across the street a few days ago.

"Hello, Josie," Helen said. "It's certainly nippy tonight, isn't it?"

Josie put her key in the lock and turned. The big door swung open, and she flipped on the lights as fast as she could. "Sure is. Glad you could come. I hope you don't mind that I invited Lorna."

Helen glanced at her watch. "No, of course not. I've been dying to bring her over to the Dark Side. Get her knitting, you know? Though we're going to have to start buying our yarn somewhere else, now that Cora's gone. But don't feel bad about that, dear."

"I don't." Well, maybe she did. She glanced around. The couch and chairs sat like a friendly oasis in the midst of the bare walls and piles of bagged inventory. "Let's sit and wait for Evelyn and Lorna."

Helen parked herself in one of the wingback chairs, reached into her purse, and pulled out an enormous piece of knitting. The stitches were on a flexible cable of some kind that had two pointy ends. Interesting. She pulled out a few feet of yarn and began to knit.

"What's that you're making?" Josie asked.

"Afghan," Helen replied. "It's just a simple basketweave pattern. Sometimes you don't want to do anything complicated. I could practically knit this in my sleep."

Josie laughed. "Well, you could cover your whole body with it while you're making it, that's for sure. I've never seen a knitting needle like that."

Helen held it out so Josie could get a better look. "This is a circular needle. We use them for knitting big projects, or for knitting in the round. You've got some hanging on the wall over there." She indicated the wall of tools and implements that hadn't yet been counted and logged.

The shop bells jingled. Lorna came in carrying a tote bag. Was there knitting in there? Josie had invited Lorna as much for the fact that she didn't want to be the only nonknitter in the room as for the fact of their reestablished friendship. But Lorna set the bag on the floor, reached into it, and pulled out a bottle of white wine and a short stack of plastic cups that she put on the coffee table. Her bag of tricks also contained a plastic-wrapped platter of cheese and crackers. Not a knitting needle or a strand of yarn in sight, bless her.

"Hope you don't mind I brought us a snack," she said.

"Are you kidding? Just toss your coat on the counter, and

let's dig in." Not that she should have been hungry. There was still casserole left at Eb's house even though Josie hadn't been stingy with the portions at dinner. It seemed to regenerate itself every time she took a spoonful. They'd barely made a dent in it.

The door blew open, and Evelyn appeared. She smoothed down her hair, then came and sat down. "Sorry I'm late," she said.

Josie studied her, not sure what she was expecting to see. Guilt written across Evelyn's forehead? But guilt for what? Sure, Evelyn seemed to be sneaking around, but there was no evidence she'd done anything wrong.

"Babysitting again?" Helen asked.

Babysitting? In an abandoned building? Not likely.

Evelyn nodded. "Harrison is working late, and Sharla needed to run out to the store. I got here as soon as I could." Her face was all innocence.

"Well, I'm glad you're here now," Josie said, taking a cracker and topping it with a slice of yellow cheese. She decided to go for it. "You know something? I just saw the strangest thing."

"Do tell," Lorna said. She put her wineglass to her lips and took a sip.

"Those buildings across the street? I saw a light in one of the windows on the third floor." She stole a glance at Evelyn, who was looking down and reaching into her purse. Impossible to tell if she'd reacted.

"Just now?" Lorna asked, leaning forward slightly. "Are you sure you didn't see a reflection from the streetlamps, or a car's headlights? That building was a ladies' dress shop, I think, years ago, and I have no idea what was on the upper floors, but it's been closed up for years."

Evelyn continued to rummage in her purse, finally extracting her knitting. She got right to work, staring down at the cherry-red piece that had grown in length since the last time Josie had seen it. "Yes," Evelyn said, without looking up. "That was Beatrice Ryder's dress shop in the sixties. I'm not sure who owns the building now." She looked into Josie's eyes. "But I *am* sure you must be mistaken about that light. That place has been closed up tight since Nixon was in office." She went back to her knitting.

Helen was also knitting away, and also avoiding looking at Josie. Interesting. Should Josie confront them? They were deliberately lying. She'd seen both of them on separate occasions enter the building through the wooden door fronting Main Street, after checking to make sure the coast was clear. But did she have any right to interrogate them? She barely knew these ladies. They didn't owe her an explanation for anything.

Yet, these past few days working with Evelyn, Josie had felt that they were developing a friendship. So it hurt a little that Evelyn was not telling her the truth.

Her thoughts were interrupted by the door's opening yet again, causing another blast of cold air to circulate around the room. Who could this be? All of her invited guests were here.

Diantha barged into the shop, followed by Courtney. Diantha's face was red, presumably from the cold, but two little circles of white dotted her cheeks. "Well, isn't this cozy? I suppose you forgot about the Charity Knitters meeting at my house? The one that started half an hour ago?" Courtney just stood there, glaring at Josie.

Evelyn spoke up. "Oh, we didn't forget. We just didn't come." She knitted a few stitches, then pulled up some more yarn from the skein.

Diantha purpled. This couldn't be good for her blood pressure, Josie thought, remembering Evelyn's earlier words about Diantha's health. Josie hoped there wouldn't be another death in the shop.

"What," Diantha said through clenched teeth, "about the orphans in Uzbekistan? Just when are those hats going to get knitted?"

"Diantha, you know we sent three dozen hats six months ago. Those orphans' heads are plenty warm. Helen and I have moved on to catnip mouse toys for the pet shelter in Hartford."

Diantha went rigid. "The president of the Dorset Falls Charity Knitters Association chooses the projects. And I"—she jabbed a thumb toward her chest—"am the president."

"Hail to the chief," Helen muttered. Josie stifled a giggle.

Diantha turned toward her. "This is all your doing. I want you out of here. Tomorrow." Her hands were fisted on her hips.

"Doesn't Trey own this building?" Josie said evenly. "The eviction notice said seven days, and I will have this building vacated in seven days. You wouldn't want me to take Trey to court for an unlawful eviction, would you?"

Diantha opened her mouth, but nothing came out. Courtney, though, finally found her voice. "You do that, and we'll countersue for . . . we'll countersue. Mark my words."

"Marked." Josie sat back on the couch.

"Now run along, you two," Evelyn said. "We'll let you know when the mice are ready, then you can deliver them. Oh, that reminds me. Lorna, can you order us some catnip through the g.s.?"

Lorna smiled and nodded. "Sure. Anything for the cats."

Diantha stormed off, Courtney following close and slamming the door behind them.

The four women exchanged looks. Josie began to giggle. Soon they were all laughing. "Well," Evelyn said, wiping her eyes with a tissue she pulled from the sleeve of her sweater. "That was fun."

Josie had to agree.

It was nearly ten o'clock when Evelyn and Helen finally put away their knitting. Josie had watched, fascinated. These two had been knitting for hours straight, with only a bathroom break. Didn't their fingers get tired?

"This has been lovely," Helen said to Josie. "A last hurrah for Miss Marple Knits. I feel like Cora was with us, somehow."

"I agree," Evelyn said. "This was almost like old times. Not that they were necessarily better." She rearranged an errant knitting needle that was sticking up from the opening of her bag, then gave the bag a zip. "It's nice to have some younger people with us." She rose and donned her coat.

"What about Courtney?" Lorna smiled. "She's about our age."

Helen gave a little sniff and put on her coat, wrapping a long purple scarf around her neck. "Courtney is Diantha's Mini-Me. She doesn't count. Now, Josie." She enveloped Josie in a warm hug. A faint scent of roses reached Josie's nose. "This has been lovely. Thank you."

Josie returned the hug, then let the older woman go. "You're welcome."

"Same goes for me," Evelyn said, her tone more businesslike. She'd seemed a little distant tonight. Josie had to wonder if it had something to do with Josie's mentioning the building across the street. "I'll see you in the morning. We need to get this place packed up so you can be out of here in plenty of time. I'd hate to give Diantha and her wishy-washy son any ammunition against you." She and Helen left.

Josie stood in the doorway and watched Helen and Evelyn get safely into their cars. The light, whatever it had been, was no longer shining from the upstairs window. Not that that was surprising. Evelyn had no doubt shut it off before she came here. The sound of the ladies' cars faded off into the distance. No sound of them circling back reached her ears. So she came back inside.

Lorna had cleared the bottle, plates, and cups and had rearranged the stacks of knitting magazines on the table. "This was fun. Thanks for inviting me."

"I loved having you. Thank *you* for the snacks. I guess I'm not a natural hostess or I'd have thought of that myself."

"Not a problem." Lorna put her empty tray into a plastic grocery sack and stuffed it into her bag. "Are you going to need help finishing here? I've got a day off this week, and I don't have anything planned."

Josie smiled. "I may take you up on that. Do you have a big car? Or a truck? I'm probably going to have to transport all this stuff out to Eb's house to store. Not that I know where I'm going to put it." Well, she supposed she could clean out one or two of the other bedrooms. Although the stuff in those rooms would have to go somewhere to make room for the new stuff. It made her brain hurt just a little to think about it. "Come on. Time to go home before we turn into pumpkins."

After locking up, Josie watched Lorna drive away. Her car would be useless for moving all this stuff. It was a tiny, boxy little thing.

Josie started up her Saab and pulled out. Although she knew it was probably pointless—if Evelyn and Helen had any sense, they wouldn't go upstairs in the abandoned building tonight—it couldn't hurt to have a look around. Main Street was empty of cars. The parking lot behind the g.s. was empty, as was the alley behind the abandoned building. Nope. They'd gone home, which she should be doing too.

The countryside rolled by as she motored down the Irish Settlement Road. An animal the size of a small dog with a long, bushy tail ran out in front of her, and she tapped her brakes. She skidded a bit, but was able to keep the vehicle under control. The fox made it across the road safely. Why, Josie wondered, was it out of its den? Didn't they hibernate? Perhaps it was a sign that spring might finally come to Connecticut after all. She just hoped the creature would stay away from the hens at Eb's farm.

Her heart rate had barely returned to normal when she noticed lights in her rearview mirror. Returning her eyes to the road ahead, she was surprised when the lights behind her flashed brighter in the mirror. They drew closer. A glance at her speedometer showed that she was traveling about thirty-five miles per hour, which seemed reasonable on a country road in the middle of winter. The car following was quickly closing the gap, and clearly in a hurry.

Well, if whoever it was wanted to crack him or herself up, there was nothing she could do about it. But she could move out of the way.

Unfortunately, there didn't seem to be a place to go. The road was barely two lanes here, made narrower by snow plowed up along the edges. She could pull over, but not far, and there was a good chance whoever it was would slam right into the back of her.

Her heart rate began to tick up again. Were there any driveways or crossroads along this stretch? Eb's driveway was at least a mile ahead. Roy's farm was beyond that. The lights drew closer.

Keep your eyes on the road. Not behind you. Look for a place to turn off. But she was finding it hard to heed her own advice. *Slow down, you idiot,* she willed the speeding car. Should she increase her own speed? That would prevent the car from gaining on her so fast. Terrible idea. The bulk of the driving she'd done over the last decade had been in the city. She wasn't an experienced winter driver. Her speedometer held steady at thirty-five.

Breathe. Keep calm. Good advice, but hard to implement when the headlights behind her, set on bright, were now reflecting into her mirror and into her eyes. She blinked, attempting to regain her night vision. The car was only a few feet behind her now. Desperately she searched for a place to pull off, but now, instead of snowbanks lining the road, a ditch several feet deep appeared off the edge.

Hands shaking, she forced her fingers to grip the wheel. This was crazy. The driver was crazy. Eb's farm couldn't be far now.

The car maintained a steady distance of a few feet for a quarter of a mile or so. Josie forced her eyes to remain on the road. If the person was going to ram her, the person was going to ram her. It was completely out of her control.

Heart beating hard, she felt a drip of sweat form on her forehead and start to run down the bridge of her nose and onto a cheek. She didn't dare take her hands off the wheel to wipe it away.

The car edged even closer. The bumpers must be close to touching. Suddenly, the lights receded, but only for a moment. The car then moved up alongside her so that its passenger door was mere inches from her driver's side. She glanced over, but couldn't make out who was in the car. It was too dark, and her eyes were still not fully adjusted again. The car drove alongside her. Involuntarily, she turned her wheel slightly to the right in an attempt to increase the distance. The car kept pace with her, driving on the wrong side of the road.

She couldn't go any farther to her right. If her wheels hit the gravel on the side of the road, she'd be off in that ditch. It might not be deep enough to kill her, but she'd be hurt.

Up ahead, she saw the lidded sap bucket that served as Eb's mailbox. *Just hold it steady. You're almost there.* With a surge of adrenaline, she let off the gas to slow her vehicle. The other car shot ahead and drove off into the night. Impossible to tell the color, and she was too rattled to register the make or the model. *Dark,* she thought. It was bigger and taller than her Saab. An SUV maybe. She rolled to a stop in Eb's driveway.

Her breath came in ragged gasps as she willed herself to calm down.

What had just happened?

Chapter 14

Josie lay awake the next morning. Coco had slept on her lower legs most of the night, which was the only thing that had prevented Josie from tossing and turning. Now her eyes were gritty, and she felt drained. The last thing she wanted to do was get up, unless today's itinerary included packing up her car and driving back to New York. If she left now, she could be home in time for a chocolate croissant and espresso at Parisia, her favorite French café.

She thought of Eb downstairs, who'd been snoring away when she'd finally worked up enough courage to get out of her car and come inside last night. She'd made sure all the doors and windows were locked, and checked to be sure Jethro and Coco were in the house. There was no reason to think that the car that had almost run her off the road was threatening her specifically. It was probably some teenager with more guts than brains out tearing around on a country road. She felt safe enough in the house. Jethro was better than any burglar alarm.

But still, Josie couldn't help but wonder. Since she'd been in town she'd made some enemies without even trying, it seemed.

Could it have been Diantha? It didn't seem like her style. Courtney or Trey? But why? No, she was doing what they wanted, which was closing up the shop so they could bulldoze it into rubble.

A thought occurred to her as she got dressed. One she liked even less than what she'd been pondering before. Evelyn? Or even the more mild-mannered Helen? Josie knew they were hiding something, but was it big enough that they'd make an attempt on her life to keep her from digging any deeper?

She came to a decision. She'd report the incident to the police. If nothing came of it, so much the better. It would mean the driver really had been some teenager and there wasn't anything sinister going on.

She pulled Sharla Coogan's card from her wallet and punched the number into her cell phone. Sharla didn't pick up, so Josie left a message asking Sharla to meet her at the shop if she had a chance this afternoon.

Maybe Sharla would reveal some information about the murder investigation. Even better, Evelyn would be there when Sharla arrived. Josie would watch her reaction when Josie told the story of her brush with death last night. If Evelyn was responsible, she might give herself away.

Satisfied she was doing everything she could, Josie got through her morning chores in record time. Eb declared his intention of spending the day in his workshop, which was a space attached to the back of the house. She made him a sandwich on the wheat bread he liked and left it wrapped in the fridge, alongside an apple and a bottle of cola, and headed out to start the second leg of her day.

Mitch was pulling into the driveway just as she got to her car. "Hey," he said, giving her a grin. "I was just coming to talk to Eb. It's going to be above freezing the next few days, which means the sap will be running."

Josie grinned back. "Running where?"

He chuckled. "From the sugar maples, through the tubing I set up, and into plastic storage tanks. I'm going to try to talk Eb into letting me collect his sap and do the boiling for him at the Woodruff sugarhouse. He can't do it alone this year, and you've got your hands full wrapping up Cora's affairs."

"What happens if the sap doesn't get collected?" The sun was warm on her face, and despite being exhausted, she felt her mood lift.

"Eb loses a lot of money," Mitch said. "Just like us, he depends on the few thousand dollars the maple syrup brings in to keep the farm running."

Josie felt a stab of conscience, even as she added one more item to her long to-do list. "What should I be helping with?"

"No need, as long as I can get Eb to let *me* help him. I think if I tell him I'll boil his sap separately from Gramps's, he'll agree. He doesn't have much choice. With that bum leg, he can't carry the wood needed to keep the evaporator going."

"Mitch, thank you so much. I don't know what Eb, or Mom, or I would do without you." She felt a little flush of embarrassment creep up her cheeks. "Um, if you have time, could you check on Eb again this afternoon? I hate to ask, but I'm worried about him."

Mitch's brow furrowed. "Is that leg not healing? He's trying to do too much."

"He has an appointment with the orthopedic doctor next week. We'll find out then. It's probably just me." There was no point in saying anything to Mitch about what had happened last night until she'd spoken to Sharla. It was all speculation.

"Well, don't worry. I'll make up some excuse to come back." His eyes held hers just a moment longer than necessary. "I like it here."

Her stomach fluttered. Definitely time to go. "Thanks," was all she managed. He didn't have to be so nice. Mitch opened her car door and she got in, tossing her gloves on the passenger seat. He waved from the front porch as she drove away.

Evelyn was waiting for Josie on the steps of Miss Marple Knits when she arrived in town. "Hello, stranger," Evelyn said. "Long time no see."

"Hi, Evelyn." It was all Josie could do to keep from looking up at the windows across the street. "Thanks again for helping me."

Evelyn waved her hand dismissively. "Don't be silly. It's nice to be busy, and sorting yarn is almost as much fun as knitting it."

They entered the shop, which was full of February sunshine. "We should be able to finish the main part of the store today, then tomorrow we can start on the storeroom," Evelyn continued. "Maybe we'll even make the deadline." Josie wasn't so sure about that, but there was no sense saying it to her friend. Her maybe-friend.

An hour or so later, a knock sounded. Sharla, wearing mirrored sunglasses and dressed in her dark blue uniform pants and a matching coat, stepped across the threshold. Evelyn started. "I haven't forgotten Andrew today, have I?"

Sharla took off the glasses. She didn't look nearly so intimidating without them. Unzipping her coat, she smiled. "No, Mom, Andrew's at preschool today, and I'm off this afternoon." She inclined her head in Josie's direction. "Josie asked me to come in."

Evelyn's face paled. It was a good thing Sharla wasn't looking at her mother-in-law, or Evelyn would have had to do some explaining.

Hmm. Evelyn must think I'm about to rat her out. Josie had considered it, but decided to keep quiet for now. There was no proof of anything except that Evelyn had a secret. Which everybody did, of some kind. Not that curiosity wasn't killing her.

Josie turned toward Sharla. "Something happened last night,

on my way home. It's probably nothing, but I thought I should tell you." She related the events, and gave the officer a vague description of the other vehicle. "I couldn't see the license plate."

Sharla looked thoughtful. "That's not much to go on, you know. It was probably nothing, just some dope driving too fast for conditions. Still, to cover all the bases, why don't you come down to the station and put in a report?"

"You—" Josie's throat was tight, and she cleared it. "You don't think it could have anything to do with Lillian's murder?"

Sharla's voice was matter-of-fact. "I'm not going to lie to you. Until we catch the killer, I guess anything's possible."

"Do you have any suspects?" Evelyn piped in, asking the question on the tip of Josie's tongue. Evelyn's cheeks were pink again, and she seemed to have recovered.

Sharla dropped her chin and cut her eyes to the older woman. "If we did, I couldn't talk about it."

"Well," Evelyn harrumphed. "If there's a murderer loose in Dorset Falls, I'd say the townspeople have a right to know."

"You're right," Sharla said. "And just as soon as there's an arrest, there'll be a press conference at the town hall."

"Are there any suspects?" Josie said. "I'm not asking for names," she added quickly. There was no point in asking. Sharla was doing her job and keeping her mouth shut.

"We have some leads we're following up on. And I really can't say any more about it. Josie, come down to the station and fill out a report. Mom, you're coming for dinner tonight, right?"

Evelyn pursed her lips. "I don't know why you wouldn't let me cook for you. You deserve a day off, and I don't mind in the least."

"Not to worry, Mom. I put a pot roast in the slow cooker this morning. It'll be ready at six o'clock, and I'll let you do the dishes if it will make you feel better."

"It will," Evelyn declared. "Bye, honey."

Sharla grinned and suited back up to go outdoors. "Bye."

The rest of the morning passed quickly. At twelve forty-five, Josie blew her bangs out of her face and sat down heavily on the couch. Evelyn excused herself to the restroom.

They were finished. Finished with this room, at least. The cubbies and baskets were empty. The yarn was sorted, counted, and bagged. The patterns, tools, and supplies were inventoried and placed in several cardboard boxes salvaged from the storeroom. Josie's eyes roamed the walls and landed on the framed picture of Miss Marple. The actress—whose name Josie didn't know—seemed to be looking directly at Josie over her knitting. "All right," Josie said aloud. "You can stay for now. You'll be the last thing I take out." Miss Marple seemed to approve.

Evelyn returned, rubbing her hands together. "Shall we go get some lunch at the general store? I'm starving."

"Good idea. And we can see if they have any extra boxes. We're going to need them when we tackle the storeroom."

The g.s. was busier than normal. Josie understood why when she saw the lunch special: macaroni and cheese with a tomato salad. She ordered two, then sat down to wait. Evelyn was rearranging the Charity Knitters display, then disappeared down one of the aisles. She must have needed toothpaste or something.

"Josie, right? Mind if I join you? Most of the tables are full." The voice was familiar, but it took Josie a moment to remember whom it belonged to.

"Of course not, Gwen, sit down. I'm eating with Evelyn today." The mechanic's wife parked herself opposite Josie and took off her coat.

"Thanks. The only other empty seat is the one between Diantha Humphries and Courtney. And she hates me," Gwen said cheerfully.

Josie let out a snort of laughter. "Well, we have something in common then. I'm definitely not their favorite person, even though I've known them for all of a week or so."

"It's funny," Gwen said, pulling a couple of napkins from

the dispenser and setting them in front of her. "I should be the one to hate Courtney. She's always hitting on Rusty."

Josie had seen that herself, and she could well believe it hadn't been the first time. "Well, Rusty seems like a great guy." She hoped it was true.

"He is. And a great dad." Gwen smiled. "Courtney's just . . . proprietary. Her father owned the garage for years, and Rusty worked for him, learning the business. When her father decided to retire, he sold the business to Rusty and left for Florida. She was livid at the time. Thought her father should have left the business, including Rusty, to her."

"Even though she's married to Trey?"

Gwen chuckled. "*Because* she's married to Trey. Seriously. Put those two men side by side and tell me whom you'd pick. The only thing Trey has going for him is a good job."

Evelyn came over and sat down. "Gwen! Lovely to see you, dear. How are Rusty and the kids?"

Josie left them to chat while she retrieved the lunches. Lorna was busy, and, based on the number of dollars in her tip jar, she was having a pretty good day, so Josie just thanked her. She set the tray down on the table in front of her lunch companions.

They dug in. The pasta was bathed in a hot, gooey sea of cheese, topped by toasted bread crumbs. In a small white dish on the side was a fresh tomato and onion salad dressed with a light vinaigrette.

When she finished, Josie sat back in her chair, sated. It had probably been a mistake, though a delicious one. Her restless night combined with the heavy meal to make her sleepy. She stifled a yawn. "Need a coffee?" Gwen said sympathetically. "If you're like me, you probably don't have time for a nap. I'm going to order one for myself. I have to be on my toes when my kids come home."

"I'd love one," Josie said, grateful. She reached into her purse for her wallet.

"Don't worry about it," Gwen said. "I heard you were in the shop the other day with your car, so you're a client. Evelyn?" Evelyn nodded.

Gwen went to the counter to order the drinks, taking the empty dishes with her. Josie reached back into her purse to return the wallet. Her fingers touched something soft. What was that? She pulled out the skein of yarn she'd found in Cora's desk drawer back in the morning-borning room and offered it to Evelyn.

Evelyn took the yarn. "What's this?" Light dawned on her face as she examined it. "Of course! You found another skein of yarn to match your scarf. So you must have found Cora's notebook. Who had the yarn?"

Josie frowned. "I still haven't found the notebook. I don't have a clue where it might be. I found this back at the house and forgot to give it to you until now."

Evelyn's smile didn't quite reach her eyes. "Well," she said. "This might not be enough for the hat I have in mind for you. A slouchy tam, I think, would look right at home on the streets of New York or the streets of Dorset Falls. I'll need one more skein. So keep looking." She glanced around, then put the yarn into her purse.

Josie knew where at least one more skein of this yarn was—made into a cord and pulled tight around Lillian Woodruff's neck.

Josie didn't like the next thoughts that popped into her head. Why was Evelyn so insistent that Josie find Cora's sales notebook? Was she afraid of what Cora had recorded? Evelyn might have bought some of this same yarn herself. And she was hiding something across the street.

Acid churned in Josie's stomach. Could Evelyn have made the blue cord and killed Lillian? And if so, why?

Gwen returned with the coffees. Josie picked hers up and took a sip, grateful for the distraction. She was pretty sure it took a fair amount of upper body strength to strangle someone. Could a woman in her sixties manage it?

"You look like you just saw a ghost," Gwen remarked. "You okay?"

Josie snapped back from her musings. "Uh, yeah. I'm fine. Didn't sleep well last night." Her cell phone vibrated in her pocket. She pulled it out and read the display, which indicated a new text message. "Excuse me for a minute, will you? I don't mean to be rude."

It was from Monica, her friend back in New York. *Have found serious buyer for whole inventory. No need to ship. They'll arrange truck. $40K is the offer. Just take pix and send so they can verify.* Hallelujah.

Chapter 15

"So we're done?" Evelyn said, her eyebrows rising in surprise. "Just like that?"

"Just like that, and thanks for the help." Josie felt her body relax with relief on so many levels. Her trust in Evelyn was wavering, so Josie hadn't been all that enthused about working with her any longer. And though she had no idea how much the contents of the store were actually worth, forty thousand dollars sounded like a fair price, one she was sure Eb would accept. That money would more than make up for his lost maple syrup this year, if Mitch hadn't been able to convince Eb to take his help.

"I feel bad, leaving the job undone," Evelyn said, pulling out her knitting.

"Please don't. You've done so much already." Josie sipped at her coffee. "I'll just go back and take some photos this afternoon and send them off. The buyer will send movers to do the rest of the work."

Gwen looked at her watch. "I'm glad everything worked out for you. Time for me to scoot. I've got a couple of errands to run before the kiddies get home." She snapped a lid on her coffee cup. "Stop by next time you're in town visiting Eb. I'd love to show you the house."

Josie felt a pang of guilt. Once she got back to New York, would she ever think about coming back to see her great-uncle? Maybe. Maybe not. She wasn't exactly proud of that thought. "I'd like that," she said. Gwen moved quickly out the door.

"Well. I suppose if you really don't need me, I can find something to do this afternoon." Evelyn seemed just a bit testy. Why? Had she been working at the shop in hopes of finding and disposing of some kind of evidence, like Cora's notebook, because she was guilty of murder?

Evelyn put her knitting into her purse. "Let me know if you want to get together again before you leave. I'll miss you," she said, her voice breaking.

Josie's stomach clenched. Evelyn had been nothing but kind to her and Eb, and here Josie was mentally accusing the woman of dreadful things. The thought crossed Josie's mind that maybe Evelyn was just . . . bored. Making casseroles for Eb and Roy and helping out at the shop kept her occupied.

"I'll miss you, too," Josie said softly. "But I'm not going until Eb is back on his feet or my mother gets here." Whichever came first.

Evelyn nodded. *Please don't cry,* Josie thought. *I feel bad enough.*

"All right then," Evelyn said. "I'm off. And don't worry about tracking down that other skein of yarn. I'll find a pattern that will work with what we have." She patted Josie's hand, then left.

Josie took her time walking back to Miss Marple Knits. She had to stop thinking of it that way, as a business with a name. An identity. Soon the old building would be gone, and a new one would be built in its place. Miss Marple Knits would be just a memory. Like Cora. Josie's stomach knotted again as she opened the door.

Dropping her bag and coat on the couch, she headed directly for the storeroom to assess the contents. There didn't seem to be anything there that the movers couldn't take, other than the shelving, which Eb might want for his workshop. She made a mental note to ask him about that when she told him about the offer. Tonight she'd bag up Cora's yarn from the house and give that to Evelyn to divide up among the knitters of Dorset Falls as she saw fit.

The only place left to check was upstairs, where Cora might have stored an additional stash. If Josie could find it. Was there even an entrance from this shop, or was there an outside door fronting on Main Street, like the building across the street? The door wasn't in the front of the store, so she began to walk the perimeter of the back, scrutinizing the walls, most of which were covered with shelving and boxes. Finally, in the back left corner, a doorway presented itself.

Josie took a deep breath. The area was dimly lit, most of the fixtures being located toward the front wall. The dark-painted door swung open with a creak that made her fillings ache when Josie turned the knob. Reaching inside, praying she wasn't going to be grabbed by something unseen, she ran her fingers lightly along the interior wall until she located a switch and flipped it on.

She was looking at a stairway, all right. A very steep, very cobwebby stairway. Footprints were visible in the dust on the steps, probably from the crime-scene techs or the detective. There was a narrow pathway cleared through the cobwebs.

Josie returned to the shop area and retrieved a broom. Was this really necessary? Unfortunately, yes. She had to at least take a look at what Cora had stored up there before the building was demolished.

Applying the broom into the corners, Josie held her breath

and swept down the webs, which stuck to the broom like a serving of unappetizing cotton candy. Halfway up, she gave in and took a breath, immediately regretting it. The air was stale and musty. She coughed and soldiered on, finally reaching the top.

The stairs opened onto a landing about eight feet square. Natural light shone through a window on an outside wall. Moving counterclockwise, she poked her head into each of the rooms that rimmed the landing. There was a tiny kitchen with 1950s-era appliances and a black-and-white linoleum tile floor. An even tinier bathroom housed pink china fixtures and a claw-foot tub covered in peeling darker pink paint. Ick. She couldn't imagine taking a bath in that thing.

The last room was fairly large compared to the others, perhaps ten by twelve. It was probably meant to be a living room, since a bank of windows lined the front wall, leaving the room too exposed to be a bedroom. A ratty plaid couch sat in the middle of the space.

What a relief. Cora didn't have anything of value up here. Not that Josie had really expected to find anything. No self-respecting yarn junkie would subject her stash to this much dust and grime. Based on the condition of the second floor, checking the third seemed like a waste of time. But she needed to finish the job.

She returned to the landing and picked up her trusty broom. The stairs to the third floor twisted up and around, and her stick of cobweb candy grew even fatter as she ascended.

Instead of a series of small rooms, this set of stairs opened into a large, empty space. Nothing up here to bother with either. There was a bank of windows in front of her, identical to the ones on the second floor. She made her way toward them, then stepped back involuntarily. The windowsills were full of dessicated spiders and flies. Double ick.

From a safe distance, she looked out the windows. Three stories down, Main Street and the sidewalks that lined it wouldn't be visible unless she got closer. Which she was not about to do.

But she could see the individual bricks of the building across the street, outlined in whitish mortar.

A pigeon fluttered, then landed on the windowsill. Josie frowned. Was that the window where the light had been last night? It hadn't been her intent to come up here and look into the other building, but here she was.

And there it was.

She moved closer to the windows, avoiding looking at the bugs. The shades were pulled in all of the windows across the way. Nothing to see here, folks.

Or was there? She stared. She hadn't been mistaken. A third-floor shade moved, almost imperceptibly, as if a breeze had blown across it.

Josie moved quickly to a side wall, out of sight of anyone who might be watching. She felt horribly . . . visible. There were no shades or curtains at all here on this side of the street.

And yet, why should she be uncomfortable? She had every right to be up here, and she had nothing to hide. Still, if there were some Boo Radley watching, she didn't want to give him anything to . . . watch.

Except it wasn't Boo Radley. She was pretty sure it was Evelyn. Or Helen. Doing . . . something over there. Curiosity continued to gnaw at Josie. She forced her gaze from the window and took one last look around. There was nothing here that needed removing before the demolition, so she was done.

Back in the storeroom, she pulled out her cell phone and took a dozen or so photos of the contents, hoping the flash was bright enough to show acceptable detail. She did the same in the front, then bundled the pictures all into a folder, which she sent off to Monica to forward to the buyer.

Her eyes fell on the picture of Miss Marple on the wall. Suddenly, the movie sleuth didn't look friendly anymore. *Traitor*, she seemed to be saying from behind her knitting.

"What do you want me to do, Jane?" Josie said aloud. "I'm just the labor around here. It's not my decision to close." She took the picture off the wall and placed it face down on the counter. There. Just because she'd promised to let her stay until the end didn't mean she had to look at her.

Josie shut off the lights and locked the door on the way out.

"The offer is forty thousand dollars for the contents of the shop." Josie scooped out some of the not-so-Spanish rice casserole and added a dinner roll to Eb's plate, setting it down before him.

Her great-uncle tore the roll in half and slathered on a heart-attack-inducing amount of butter. "Take it. I'll maybe buy a new truck. Then you can go home."

Josie placed her own plate on the table and sat down. "Sick of me already? I'm not leaving till my mother gets here. Who else is going to do your laundry and listen to you complain?" She smiled.

"I don't complain. Why is there no salt on this table?"

She snorted, grateful she didn't have food in her mouth yet. "You're plenty salty. And you don't need more. It's bad for you."

"Hmmph." He stabbed his fork into his dinner.

"So, Eb. Did Cora have any family? Anyone else we might have to ask before we accept?"

His Adam's apple bobbed up then down as he swallowed. "Nope."

No one could ever accuse her uncle of giving too much information. "Mom's handling the estate paperwork, right? Who's the lawyer?"

"Your mother's in charge. Ask her."

"I can't ask her, Eb. She's on a cruise." Josie felt her jaw twitch with frustration. She was almost certain Eb could have answered all her questions, but just didn't want to be bothered. And there was a problem. Everything had to be moved out of the building ASAP because Trey was evicting them. If she couldn't broker this deal and get the buyer's movers here fast, she was going to have to figure out how—and where—to transport the inventory until they could come and pick it up.

"Yup."

Clearly Eb was going to be no help.

After dinner she settled herself into the morning-borning room and fired off another text to her mother. *Have offer on shop. Please call ASAP.* It was only to make herself feel better by taking some action. She'd already asked her mother to call, and her mother would call when she was able.

Eb didn't have any boxes lying around—he'd just grunted when she asked—so she'd grabbed some plastic trash bags from the kitchen. Chances were good that Evelyn would be so happy to get her hands on Cora's stash, she wouldn't mind the less-than-snazzy containers.

As Josie sorted and stuffed, she allowed the yarns to run through her fingers. Each skein had its own weight, its own texture. Her mind began to wander, imagining garments made from some of these skeins. A 1950s-style sweater with gently puffed short sleeves in raspberry, worn over a slim dark skirt and tights. A dove-gray knitted jacket, complete with lapels, belted over a pair of wide-legged pants in cream. A lacy emerald green stole wrapped over a perfectly fitted sheath dress in the same color—perfect for New Year's Eve. The images were clear in her mind.

She could picture them on a model. Or herself.

But she couldn't *make* them. At least, she couldn't make the knitted items. Her degree programs had required her to do some sewing along with her designing, so she would be able to produce only half of each outfit she'd imagined.

She could, however, *draw* the missing pieces. Josie opened up the bag of yarn she'd been working on and dumped it out onto the desk, then sat down, staring at the fuzzy lumps of color. Pulling some sheets of plain paper off a stack on the desk, she began to sketch.

And sketch.

And sketch some more. The pencil flew, and the sheets of paper stacked up with more designs than she'd produced in the last three years working for Otto. Of course, these were all just quick representations and would have to be refined before she gave them to Otto. And for now they were in black-and-white, but she made careful notes on each page about color and textures. Tomorrow when in town she'd see if she could get some colored pencils at the g.s.—even crayons would do, she supposed, in a pinch.

Not all of these designs would make it into her final fall collection. But she had a *concept*—a thing she'd never quite managed to get right before. Knitwear combined with modern garments, which would look just as good on the runway or the red carpet as they would on an average woman. For the runway show at least, the knitted components would need to be handmade. And she had a number of knitters at her disposal in Dorset Falls. Evelyn seemed like just the person for the job.

Josie's whole body was still tingling with excitement when she finally put down the pencil—which she'd sharpened enough times tonight that it had lost a third of its length. Gathering up the sketches, she tapped them against the surface of the desk and patted the top and sides until they were in a neat stack, set them down on the desk, then leaned back in the desk chair, exhausted. *This is a very comfortable chair,* she realized. *And a comfortable place to work, too.* Maybe this trip to the country was exactly what she'd needed to get her spark of creativity back.

Josie felt her face break into a smile of satisfaction. Everything was falling into place. Otto would love this collection. She'd get her job back—maybe even ask for a raise, if he didn't offer one. She'd packed up most of the shop and found a buyer for the contents. Her mother would be here in another week to handle the estate paperwork and take care of Eb until his cast came off.

Coco, who'd been sleeping on one corner of the desk on the stack of blank paper, stood, stretched, and pawed at a ball of yarn, which rolled off onto the carpet, leaving a long tail in its wake. Josie reached out a hand and stroked the dark fur. The cat began to purr as she paced back and forth across the designs, her tail undulating.

"We've got this, Coco," Josie said. "For the first time, I think we've got this. We're going back to the Big Apple a success."

She was definitely going to ask Otto for a raise. Visions of a shrinking student-loan balance danced across her mind. Less money out, more coming in, a positive cash flow meant more money for other things. Like designer handbags. There was a gorgeous red patent-leather Prada bag she'd been salivating over.

Is that what's really important? A voice had quietly infiltrated her lovely thoughts. Coco's green eyes were trained on her. Josie squirmed, just a little. "Well, yes," she said aloud, hoping Eb had gone to bed and wasn't listening to her talking to herself. "If you're in the fashion world, stuff like that *is* important."

Except, she knew it wasn't true.

A vision of Lillian Woodruff's lifeless body replaced the dollar signs in Josie's brain. She blinked to clear it, but it wouldn't go away.

She needed to find Cora's sales notebook. Then she would have done all she could to find Lillian's killer.

Perhaps her business in Dorset Falls wasn't finished, after all.

Chapter 16

Before she left for town the next morning with her daily egg quota washed and safely stashed into cardboard containers, Josie took a few minutes to bag up the rest of the yarn for Evelyn. She set the three bags by the front door. *Black sheep, black sheep, have you any wool? Yes sir, yes sir, three bags full.*

There was a black sheep in Dorset Falls. But who was it?

And why would anyone want to kill an old lady? It did no good to speculate, she thought as she loaded the eggs and bags into the trunk of her Saab in separate trips. She had only met Lillian once—*alive*. A shudder racked Josie's body, and she suspected it wasn't from the cold air of a February morning in Connecticut.

Josie was for all intents and purposes a stranger here, so she had no understanding of the intricacies of how this town and its residents functioned, how they connected with each other, how their special small-town symbiosis worked. And the police seemed to be doing their job. She supposed she should keep her nose out of things.

Still, one more look around the shop wouldn't hurt. If she could help the investigation by finding the notebook, she would.

She didn't. By midmorning, after searching the storeroom and the front of the shop again, she concluded that it simply wasn't there.

Could someone have taken it? The black sheep, maybe? The killer. Lillian had somehow gained access to Miss Marple Knits, and someone else had joined her in the shop, then murdered her. Or maybe the killer had been here first. Lillian saw activity, but instead of calling the police, decided to confront the burglar herself, getting killed in the process. Lillian had wanted this shop. It wasn't out of the realm of possibility that she might have felt a little proprietary toward it.

So how had anyone gotten in? Josie wasn't a trained investigator, but there didn't appear to have been a forced break-in, which meant that either the door had been left open—which she was quite certain she hadn't done—or someone had a key.

Reaching into her jacket pocket, she pulled out the key ring Eb had given her the first day she arrived in town. The two keys clanked together softly as she examined them. They were a dull brownish color, each with a slightly different shape. One fit the front door—she'd used it this morning. The other must go to the rear exit. Making her way to the back door, she stuck the key in, gave a turn, and heard the locking mechanism clunk.

So who else would have had keys to the shop? Eb, of course, might have had another set. But Josie had been with Eb almost the whole time between when she'd last seen Lillian alive, here at the shop, and the next day, when Lillian was found dead in the back. Leg still encased in a fiberglass cast, Eb couldn't drive his truck. And that ATV-thing of his made a fair amount of noise. Josie would have heard it leaving the barn. Not that she suspected Eb, really, but she needed to go through the possibilities.

Trey.

Her heart lurched.

Trey owned this building. It was entirely possible—likely, even—that he had a set of keys.

But what possible motive could he have for killing Lillian? She'd offered to buy Miss Marple Knits, but that wouldn't have put a kink into Trey's plans to raze the building and put up a fast-food restaurant. Even if Eb had wanted to sell the business to her, Lillian could have had her pick of any of the empty storefronts on Main Street to reopen. She didn't need this building.

Diantha? The old battle-ax was ornery enough she might not need an actual reason to kill someone. And she had access to Trey, who seemed to do whatever she wanted, and therefore had access to the keys, assuming Trey had some.

Diantha was also a knitter, and that cord wrapped around Lillian's neck had not come fresh and loose out of a skein of yarn. It had been neatly and expertly twisted into a rope, and the ends embellished with perfect tassels, like one might see holding back a formal drapery. Someone who knew what he—or she—was doing had made the murder weapon.

Of course, that didn't necessarily mean a knitter had perpetrated the crime. A knitter could have made the cord, put it into her knitting basket, and the killer could have taken it.

Josie's reasoning brought her right back to where she had been when she walked through the door. Josie was no Miss Marple. The idea that there was another set of keys was so obvious, there was no way the police weren't looking into it.

But even after her triumph last night—a flush of pride warmed her cheeks at the thought of her new designs—it was still going to be tough to go back to New York without knowing the truth. She hoped Sharla and Detective Potts, and probably the state police too, would hurry up and find the killer.

She pulled out her cell phone. "Evelyn? It's Josie. Can you meet me at the g.s. for lunch?" Truth was, she missed Evelyn's presence at the shop already. And maybe her friend had heard something new about the investigation.

* * *

Josie left her car parked in front of Miss Marple Knits—and she reminded herself to stop thinking of it like that. Soon it would be no more than a memory. She crossed the street and peeked into the alley behind the corner building. No cars back there. No cars except hers on Main Street. Five minutes later Josie was setting her coat and purse down on one of the metal mesh chairs in the café.

Evelyn still hadn't arrived, so Josie picked up a red plastic shopping basket with DOUGIE'S GENERAL STORE emblazoned along each side in white script letters. There was a tiny section of office supplies in the back corner. Notebook paper, ballpoint pens, paper clips, and number-ten envelopes constituted the selection. She headed for the short toy aisle and found what she was looking for: a pack of colored pencils. She picked up a few things for the house, set the basket by her feet, and sat down to wait.

Evelyn appeared a few minutes later, her cheeks pink from the cold. She removed her hat and smoothed her hair. "Colder than a witch's tatting shuttle out there," she said. "This isn't good for Eben and the rest of the syrup farmers. They need warm temperatures during the day." Her huge purse, almost certainly stuffed full of one knitting project or another, landed with a soft thud on an empty chair. "How is that dear man?"

Josie smiled, wondering what a tatting shuttle was. "He's fine. I checked with his doctor. He's due for x-rays in another week, then if his leg is healed, they'll remove the cast." Of course, she planned to be gone by then, but she'd be glad to know the old geezer was back on his feet.

Evelyn made a clucking noise. "I'll bring another casserole out to the house. You have enough going on without having to cook, too."

"I'm an expert warmer-upper," Josie said. "And I wouldn't say no."

"Good. That's settled."

They ordered. Pad Thai was the special of the day, which seemed an unlikely menu choice for Dorset Falls, but Lorna hadn't steered Josie wrong yet. Evelyn ordered the meatloaf and potatoes. While they waited, the two women chatted amiably.

"So," Evelyn said, "I talked to Sharla last night." Her eyes sparkled. Gossip. Just what Josie had been hoping for.

"And?" Josie sipped at her tea, which tasted of lemon with a hint of mint.

Evelyn leaned forward and dropped her voice. "Sharla tells me they're close to making an arrest." She dropped back, a frown creasing her bright pink lips. "And she won't—all right, *can't*—tell me who."

Josie felt a wash of relief. Thank goodness. Everything really was, now, falling into place, and she'd be able to leave with a clear conscience.

"I wonder if it's someone local," Josie mused.

"My daughter-in-law wouldn't even tell me that." Evelyn's frown deepened.

Josie smiled sympathetically. "Well, hopefully the arrest will be made soon, and we can all rest easier."

"Hey, ladies," Lorna called from behind the counter. "Lunch is up."

Josie retrieved the two plates from her friend. She couldn't decide which of the aromas wafting up toward her smelled more delicious, that of the peanutty Asian noodles or that of the stick-to-your-ribs meatloaf, with its shiny ketchup glaze and adjacent cratered scoop of mashed potatoes complete with gravy pooled in the middle and running down the sides, like lava from a volcano. Lorna could hold her own with any diner in New York, that was clear. Feeling guilty at having left Eb with a cold sandwich—even though that was what he'd requested—while she dined on delicious hot food, Josie ordered another plate of meatloaf to go. He could have a nice dinner.

"Do *you* have any ideas who it might be?" Josie asked, crunching on a tender-crisp carrot covered in tangy sauce.

Evelyn put down her fork. "I know who I'd *like* it to be," she said decisively.

Josie was glad she'd already swallowed, because she couldn't suppress a snort.

"Diantha," they said together, then glanced around to make sure no one had heard them.

"But to answer your question, no." Evelyn poked her fork into her mashed potatoes and brought the tines to her mouth, where they hung suspended while she spoke. "I've racked my brains trying to figure out why anyone would want to kill Lillian. I mean, she wasn't always Miss Mary Sunshine, but she had no real enemies that I know of."

Josie nodded, thoughtful. "She wasn't involved in anything . . . out of the ordinary?"

Evelyn started, just a little. Josie had struck some kind of nerve. Had Lillian been involved in whatever was going on across the street from Miss Marple Knits? That would mean Evelyn might be involved—might be in danger herself.

The older woman recovered. "I don't think so. We saw each other at least once a week at our Charity Knitters meetings. If she had been doing something she shouldn't have been, I have to think we would have rooted it out of her. We may be old, but we're savvy."

Josie laughed, twirling noodles around her fork. "Experience goes a long way."

After lunch, Josie returned to her car with her to-go box of dinner, while Evelyn stayed behind to rearrange the items on the Charity Knitters table, which had been looking a little messy, and, she said, to do some shopping.

Speaking of messy, Josie's car was looking that way too.

Since she'd arrived in Dorset Falls, she'd been on the go. And she'd let her car go, too. In New York, she never left, well, anything visible inside the vehicle. Since she parked on the street, it didn't do to give less-than-savory types the temptation.

She glanced at the bright blue door of Miss Marple Knits. Nope, there was no need to go back in. Until the deal with the buyer was finalized, and arrangements for the movers were made, she guessed she was done there. A twinge of sadness pinched her heart. But it was just as well. She had designs to complete. Lorna had confirmed that, for a small fee, she could convert the drawings into digital files at the g.s., then Josie would be able to e-mail them to Otto.

Her eyes scanned both directions, checking for traffic—fat chance of that in Dorset Falls—before she opened the driver's side door and left it ajar while she picked up an embarrassing number of empty candy wrappers and straw papers from the carpet. Wadding everything into a ball, she put the mess into a fast-food bag, closed the door, and moved around to the passenger side. She removed an empty soda cup from the center console and stuffed that in the bag as well, squashing it to make it fit. A stack of clean napkins she kept—those always came in handy.

Her fingers closed around the napkins. She touched cold metal. "Huh?" Pulling the napkins away, she saw a key ring. She laid the napkins on the dash and picked up the ring. Where had this come from? It must be Key Day, because she'd been thinking about keys only a few hours ago.

Right. This was Cora's key ring that Rusty at the car shop had given her. Josie had forgotten about it. She sat down in the passenger's seat and held the keys up to the light.

The fob was made of black plastic, had electronic buttons, and was clearly marked with the name of a car manufacturer. Cora must have had a newer model car. Josie's old Saab boasted no such luxury. Reaching into her coat pocket, she pulled out the ring she'd been using to let herself in and out of the shop. She compared the two sets and found matching keys. Here, at least, was one duplicate set. How many more were out there?

Several other keys were also on the ring. It was likely one, maybe two, went to Eb's house. One looked a lot like the key to the front door of Miss Marple, but the pattern didn't match. But it appeared to be the same vintage, and it had the same dull patina. Perhaps it went to one of the doors above the shop.

Her eyes fell on the building across the street, honing in on the door Evelyn and her friend Helen Crawford kept disappearing into. She looked at the key again. Evelyn, Helen, and Cora had been friends, as well as members of the Dorset Falls Charity Knitters Association together. Had Cora also been involved in whatever was going on up there?

The more Josie thought about it, the more she wondered.

It was none of Josie's business. Neither Evelyn nor Helen owed her any explanations. Friends could have secrets from each other—and she did consider Evelyn a friend.

And yet, Josie could just slip over there and try the key in the lock. No one was around. Her hand reached for the door handle.

Buzzzz. The ringing of her cell phone snapped her back to the present. She glanced at the display before connecting.

"Hi, Mitch," she said.

"Josie, come on home. I think Eb's had a heart attack."

Chapter 17

Josie threw the phone onto the passenger seat without even disconnecting the call, climbed over the gearshift into the driver's seat, and sped off toward the farm. *Please,* she thought. *Let my uncle be all right.* Somehow in the past few days she'd grown attached to Eben Lloyd. If anything happened to him, she'd never forgive herself for not being there. What was a shop full of balls of yarn or a car full of trash compared to a person's life?

She pulled past the driveway and parked on the edge of the road. Mitch's truck and Eb's truck took up a lot of room, and the EMTs needed to be able to get to Eb quickly, without her car being in the way. She slammed the car door shut and raced to the house, throwing open the front door.

"Uncle Eb? Mitch!" Her heart pounded inside her rib cage, so intense that she could practically hear each accelerated beat.

"Out here," Mitch called, his voice muffled. "In Eb's workshop."

She ran through the kitchen and out the back door, into a shed brightly lit with fluorescent fixtures. She hadn't been out here before, but she could see Mitch across the room, standing guard over Eb, who was seated in a chair. His bloodless face scowled when he saw her.

"Go on now, missy," he wheezed. "Nothin' to see here."

Josie ran over to him, gave him a hug. "Oh, Eb, there's plenty to see here. I'm just glad I'm seeing you alive." She looked into Mitch's eyes. "What happened?"

"I came over to, uh, borrow something." He nodded at Josie, over Eb's head. Right. He'd come to check on her uncle, bless him. "I found him sitting in this chair, complaining of chest pains, so I gave him an aspirin and called the EMTs, then you." Mitch looked out the window, which was free of shade or curtains and covered in a light grime. "Here's the ambulance now." She could hear the sirens approaching, thank goodness. Mitch looked at her again. "If you're all right, I'll go meet the ambulance in the driveway and lead the attendants back here."

Josie nodded, grateful. "Hope you're wearing clean underwear, old man." She dropped a kiss on top of his gray head. He was still conscious, so she had to believe the EMTs could stabilize him and get him to the hospital.

Within minutes two EMTs were rolling a gurney through the exterior door. They took a quick history. The female, clearly understanding that Eb would not respond well to sympathy, said, "How about an ambulance ride, Mr. Clooney? My partner here will hold off the paparazzi."

To Josie's surprise, Eb didn't protest. *He's actually afraid,* Josie thought. The female EMT helped him onto the gurney, then covered him with a blanket and wheeled him out toward the waiting ambulance. Josie and Mitch followed.

She shivered as they loaded him in, and Mitch put a warm arm around her shoulders. The male attendant spoke for the first time. "We'll be here for a few minutes making sure he's stable, then we're taking him to the hospital in West Torrington. You're welcome to ride along, of course." His expression was dubious. He clearly had Eb's number as well.

"Uh, I think he'd be more comfortable without me in such close quarters. He's very . . . private. I'll pack a bag for him, follow along, and meet you at the hospital. Is he going to be okay?" The EMT gave a grim smile. What had she expected? An older man with chest pains and shortness of breath—the EMT couldn't give her any guarantees that her great-uncle wasn't going to die any minute.

Tears welled as memories of her former life in Dorset Falls flooded her mind. Her mother would drag her out to see Eb most Sundays, or occasionally bring him into town to have dinner at their house if he'd allow it. Of course Josie had complained about going to the farm—she'd been a typical bratty teenager—but the truth was, she'd secretly liked it here where there was no pressure on her as the new kid in town to try to fit in with the established cliques. And where she could put aside the memories of her dead father, if only for an afternoon.

And she'd secretly liked Eb, too. He had kept a horse, and would often ask her to take Queenie for a ride as if Josie were doing Eb a favor. While they ate the dinner her mother had brought, Eb would needle Josie and she'd needle him back, less sharply under her mother's slightly disapproving eye. It was impossible to say for sure if Eb had enjoyed their company, but in retrospect, he must have. Otherwise, he'd have forbidden her and her mother from coming to visit. Or would have taken off somewhere when he knew they were coming.

Her mother had stayed in touch with him over the years. But after Josie had moved away, she barely thought of her great-uncle. She'd been bent on having fun and making a name for herself in the fashion world. The thought of how self-absorbed she'd been made her feel sick. Family mattered.

And now that she'd gotten to know Eben Lloyd again, her heart would break if she lost him.

Mitch squeezed a little tighter. "If you want," he said, "I'll drive you. My grandfather is playing cards tonight at the VFW. I'll probably need to pick him up later anyway."

Josie wiped at her eyes and felt a surge of gratitude. "Thanks, Mitch. I'd appreciate it."

They watched the ambulance speed away, then returned to the house through the workshop door. For the first time, she looked around. Every inch of wall space was covered in tools and other items hung from hooks on white pegboard. Fluorescent fixtures illuminated the room to a blinding degree. All around her were old cabinets and dressers being used as cabinets, all of varying sizes and color schemes. Sitting on top of the cabinets and cluttering up most of the floor were piles of wood and pieces of rusty metal, just like the ones now covered in snow in the front yard.

"What is all this?" Josie asked. "What does he do out here all day?"

Mitch laughed. "Most of what you're seeing here is old metal parts from machinery that hasn't been used on the farm for fifty years or more. He welds the stuff together into sculptures." He pointed toward a six-foot-tall . . . something that appeared to be made of wheels and what might have been a rusty metal tractor seat. There was something appealing about it, she had to admit. Whimsical, yet rustic. It would look good out on the front lawn, maybe with red geraniums and dark purple petunias planted around the base in the summertime.

"Are you telling me that my grouchy Yankee farmer uncle is a folk artist?"

Mitch laughed again. "That's exactly what I'm telling you. But don't let him hear you call him that. In his mind, he's just welding together bits and pieces of junk to keep himself busy during the winter. Come on, let's feed the pets, pack Eb a bag, and get to the hospital."

Mitch drove his car, which Josie had to admit was a lot more comfortable than the disintegrating fifteen-year-old leather seats of her Saab. She leaned back and closed her eyes. Mitch had said the trip would take thirty to forty minutes. Dorset Falls was a long way from a hospital.

"Try not to worry," Mitch said. "Eb's a fighter."

"By 'fighter,' do you mean he's too ornery to die?" Josie had to smile. It helped to think of her great-uncle as some kind of cranky superhero.

Mitch laughed gently. "I'm glad I got there when I did."

"Me too. And thanks. You probably saved his life."

"No thanks necessary. And my grandfather would never forgive me if I didn't do everything I could for Eb. Tormenting him is Roy's reason for living."

They pulled into the hospital visitors' parking lot just at the thirty-minute mark. Mitch was a good driver, and he seemed to know some shortcuts. He also seemed to know some of the hospital personnel, because when he and Josie approached the reception desk, the nurse greeted him by name.

"Mitch Woodruff, you handsome thing, you." She was sixty if she was a day, with short, gray, pixie-cut hair. Her scrubs were printed with bright yellow smiley faces. She set down the crocheting she'd been doing and beamed up at him.

"Muriel Capocci," he said, grinning. "You get more beautiful every day."

"Thanks for noticing. What brings you here?"

Mitch gestured to Josie. "This is Josie Blair. Her great-uncle, Eben Lloyd, was just brought in by ambulance. At least I hope they're here by now. I don't see how we could have beaten them."

Muriel punched at her keyboard. "It looks like they arrived a few minutes ago. They're putting him in a room now and lining up some tests. It'll be a while before you can see him, so you may as well get a cup of coffee and sit down to wait. We'll call you in when the doctor is ready to talk to you." She picked up her crocheting project and went back to work.

Josie had never felt so helpless in her life.

Mitch put his arm around her again and guided her to a seat in the waiting room. "How about if I get us something to drink? Coffee? Soda? Water?"

"Maybe a Mountain Dew, if they have it? We could be here for a while, and I'll probably need the caffeine."

Mitch strode off, his long, denim-clad legs carrying him down the hallway and quickly out of sight. She took a deep breath. Should she text her mother? There didn't seem to be any point. Katherine Blair was still out of cell range or she would have called by now. And it wasn't like she could do anything, even if she did get the message.

Josie flipped through the magazines on the side table. They all seemed to be about sports or parenting, neither of which interested her. Not a fashion magazine in sight. But that was just as well. She'd had the foresight to bring her preliminary sketches with her, so she pulled them out of the tote bag she'd found in the morning-borning room and began to shuffle through them.

By the time Mitch returned—with both drinks and homemade-looking chocolate chip cookies on a paper plate, which he set down beside her—she'd sorted the drawings into two piles. One was for the definite keepers, and the second was for the maybes.

Mitch picked up one of the maybes, examined it, and gave a low whistle. "Did you do this? It's amazing. I can see you wearing this."

Josie eyed him. Was that a line? No, he seemed genuinely interested, and she was fairly sure, based on their short acquaintance, that he was not the kind of guy who would try to take advantage of a situation like this.

"Um, yeah. This is what I went to school for. But my employer has been less than impressed with the other things I've offered him over the last few years." Probably because she hadn't been offering Otto the thing he really wanted, which had more to do with taking clothes off than wearing them. When she went back—if she went back—she wouldn't ignore his increasingly less subtle advances anymore. If she lost her job permanently, so be it. She'd figure something out.

"Well, I'm no expert, but this looks like talent to me." Mitch set the drawing back down on the stack.

Josie felt absurdly pleased. It had been a long time since anyone had complimented her work. Maybe, just maybe, she could make a go of this. She glanced toward the glass window behind Muriel's station. Two nurses were visible, and they appeared to be talking to each other. Josie felt her heart rate tick up again. "What do you suppose is happening?" she asked Mitch.

He gently patted her arm. "Try not to worry, okay? It has to be a good sign that he was conscious when we found him and the EMTs brought him in. I'll bet a nurse will be here any minute to have us fill out paperwork."

As if on cue, a door opened, and one of the nurses she'd just seen brought over a clipboard. "Are you the niece Eben told us about?"

Josie nodded.

"We need you to fill this out as best you can. Eb was here just a few weeks ago after the car accident, so his information should be up-to-date in our system. But it's procedure."

Josie took the clipboard the woman held out. "Can you tell me anything yet about his condition?"

The nurse—KELLY TAYLOR, her name badge read—shook her head so that her shiny hair bounced. "I'm afraid not. But you're in luck. The cardiologist hasn't gone home yet, so your uncle is being seen immediately by a specialist. I'm sure once the preliminary tests are finished, Dr. Andersen will be out to talk to you."

When the nurse returned to her station, Josie looked at the clipboard and groaned inwardly. The document was two full pages, plus some kind of consent form, which she was pretty sure she did not have the authority to sign for Eb. She filled out his name and address. Date of birth? Not a clue, a fact that she immediately felt guilty about. It would have been nice if she'd sent him a card now and then over the years, but she hadn't even considered it. Family medical history? Personal medical history? She had to answer both questions with *Unknown,* as well as virtually everything else. Finally, she scribbled her signature on the consent form. It was the best she could do.

"Want me to take that to Kelly for you?" Mitch asked, setting aside the magazine—sports—he'd been perusing.

Josie stood. "No, I will. At least it will feel like I'm doing *something.*"

She walked across the low-pile carpet and waited at the window until the nurse noticed her and slid back the glass. "Sorry. There's so much I don't know."

Kelly smiled sympathetically. "That's fine. We have everything we need."

"Would you mind if I borrowed the clipboard for a bit? I'll return it before I leave."

"That's fine. We've got plenty." She closed the glass window.

Josie sat down, pulled a fresh sheet of paper out of the tote bag, and clipped it onto the board. Then she fished out the box of colored pencils she'd bought at the general store and set it on the seat next to her.

"Are you going to draw?" Mitch asked. "Why don't we go wait in the cafeteria, where you'll have a table? Kelly will come and find us when the doctor's ready."

Josie shook her head. "Thanks, but no. I'm fine here. My apartment in Brooklyn is so small, I'm used to working like this." She picked up one of her keeper sketches, preparing to redraw it, this time with more detail, then looked into Mitch's blue eyes. "And thanks. For being there for Eb. And for me," she added. She never would have figured herself for the shy type, but this kind, good-looking alpaca farmer seemed to bring that out in her. Weird.

Mitch grinned. "You're welcome. Now get to work. It'll keep your mind off things."

Josie wasn't so sure about that, but it turned out to be true. She was just putting the finishing touches on her second drawing—the one of the emerald green New Year's Eve dress with the matching knitted stole—when a white-coated figure came to stand in front of her.

Josie looked up to see a petite woman with short, dark hair and big brown eyes behind tortoise-shell glasses. The woman stuck out her hand. "Dr. Andersen," she said. "I'm the cardiologist. Let's go into a private room so I can fill you in."

Josie got up to follow, turning to look at Mitch. "Will you come, too? I'd feel better with some moral support."

"You bet." He stood with alacrity and took her arm. They followed Dr. Andersen down a long hallway covered with brightly colored abstract art and into a small conference room.

When they were all seated, Dr. Andersen began. "Your uncle is quite lucky. The preliminary tests show that he most likely did not suffer a heart attack."

Josie blew out a breath of relief, then frowned. "But the chest pains and shortness of breath. What else could that be? Are you sure?" She wanted to clap her hand over her mouth. She'd probably just insulted this woman who was, in fact, clearly smart enough to have graduated from medical school.

Dr. Andersen chuckled. "Well, no. I'm not entirely sure yet, which is why I want to keep him overnight, maybe for a couple of days, for observation."

Mitch returned the chuckle. "Eb's not going to like that."

Josie straightened up in her chair. "Eb doesn't have any choice. He's staying until we figure out what's wrong." Her sudden bravado gave way to doubt. If Eb didn't want to stay, there wasn't a whole lot she could do about it. Except not provide him with a ride home.

"I like your spunk," Dr. Andersen said. "But seriously, I

want to run some more tests. We have him hooked up to a cardiac monitor, and it would be best to get some more data before we rule anything, like a heart attack, out. And I may have him looked at by a colleague tomorrow."

"Can we go see him?"

Dr. Andersen smiled. "You can. But afterward I suggest you go on home. We have your number in case anything changes—and my gut feeling is that it won't. He's stable, and he's in good hands here."

Josie felt her whole body relax. This doctor must have been at the top of her class in bedside manner. "I know. We'll just go in for a few minutes. He has a television in his room, right? It's almost time for that extreme fishing show he likes."

The doctor nodded. "This way."

Eb's room had pale yellow walls and two beds that could be separated by a floor-to-ceiling white curtain, which was currently open to reveal that Eb did not have a roommate. Which was good. For the missing roommate, at least. Her uncle was used to his solitude.

He wore a light green johnny and a matching bathrobe, and was sitting up in bed, his pale, hairy legs, one half encased in a cast, stretched out in front of him. "Woodruff," Eb said, "take her home."

Mitch, as always, was a good sport in the face of Eb's curt speech. "I will. But you know Josie. She had to come see for herself that you weren't dead."

Eb stared out at her from under his eyebrows, which seemed even grayer and longer than they had just a few days ago. "I ain't. Now get on out of here. My show's coming on, and I don't want you yammering so I can't hear it."

Josie leaned forward to give her great-uncle a hug, but he drew back. So Josie reached out and gave him a gentle punch in the upper arm. "Fine. I'm leaving. But I'll be back tomorrow."

"Suit yourself. Woodruff, make sure she takes care of the animals." Josie resisted the urge to roll her eyes. She'd been doing just fine taking care of the chickens, and Jethro, and Coco.

"Josie knows what she's doing. But I'll see that she gets home safely." Mitch grinned.

Eb's eyes narrowed. "See that you do." He leaned back against several big white pillows, then turned to Josie. "And you. Stop at the general store and bring me some more of those oatmeal cookies Lorna makes," he ordered.

"Aye, aye, captain," Josie said. "Bye, Eb. Behave and don't terrorize the nurses tonight, will you? I'll see you tomorrow." She stowed the overnight bag she'd brought for him on a visitor's chair and handed him the remote control.

"Later, Eb." Mitch picked up Josie's tote bag and slung it over his arm.

Eb frowned again. "Don't tell your damn grandfather about this. I'll never hear the end of it."

Chapter 18

Mitch and Josie had barely made it to the car when Josie's cell phone chirped. *Evelyn,* the display read. Mitch opened the car door for her and helped her in, then closed it and came around to the driver's side. She connected the call.

"Josie Blair," Evelyn said after they'd exchanged greetings. "What in heaven's name is going on? I heard the ambulance was sent out to Eben's this afternoon!"

Josie related what they knew, which turned out not to be that much. "So they're keeping him overnight for observation and some more tests tomorrow," she concluded.

Evelyn clucked. "That's terrible! I mean, it's good dear Eben probably didn't have a heart attack, of course. Come and stay with me tonight. I don't like to think of you rattling around that drafty old house by yourself."

Now that Evelyn mentioned it, Josie wasn't all that enthused about staying at the house alone, even with Jethro on guard. She'd seen a dog treat turn the beast into a harmless bunny rabbit, so she wasn't totally convinced he was up to the task. But no, she needed to go home. She had to take care of the animals, and get up early in the morning with the chickens.

"Thanks, Evelyn. That's awfully sweet of you. But I'll be fine." Probably. A vision of the night she was almost run off the road by an unknown vehicle flashed across her brain. Her heart rate ticked up.

"I won't take no for an answer. Are you with Mitchell?"

"Yes."

"Is he driving? Put him on." Josie dutifully handed the phone to Mitch, who was just turning on the ignition.

Mitch took the phone, brushing her hand lightly as he did so. Probably accidentally. But she liked it anyway.

"Hi, Evelyn," he said. "Uh-huh . . . uh-huh. I'll try." He rang off and handed the phone to Josie, who stowed it in her purse.

"Well," he said, grinning. "She won't take no for an answer. Which is good, because I was going to invite you to stay at the Hotel Woodruff, but that would have been . . . awkward."

Josie laughed. "Not known for your hospitality?"

Mitch turned on the radio, then turned down the volume so they could still converse. "Let's just say we're a couple of bachelor farmers, and leave it at that." His voice turned serious. "But I would feel better if you stayed at Evelyn's tonight. If you don't mind leaving me a key to the house, I'll fill up the woodstove, take care of the animals, and bring the eggs to you in town tomorrow morning."

A surge of emotion rose up into Josie's throat. People in this town really did care. She was for all intents and purposes an outsider, yet, aside from the Humphries family, people had been going out of their way to help her ever since she arrived. "Okay," she said, when she could finally speak. "Drop me at the farm so I can pack an overnight bag and say good-bye to Coco. I'll drive myself back to Evelyn's so I can go directly to the hospital tomorrow."

Mitch seemed satisfied. "Sounds like a plan."

A half hour later, they pulled into the Lloyd farm driveway. Dusk had fallen, and the house was dark. Jethro let out a high-pitched wail, then a series of barks. He must have some kind of hound in him.

Mitch walked her into the house and waited while she packed and found Coco. The cat twined around her feet, and she reached down to scratch between the cat's ears. "I'll be back tomorrow, Coco. Go find somewhere to sleep." Jethro came barreling through the dining room, sliding to a stop in front of Mitch. Coco took off like a shot. The dog panted and rubbed his head on Mitch's thigh until Mitch relented and gave him a pet. "Settle down, buster. Dinner's coming."

Between the two of them, Mitch and Josie made short work of the evening chores, and it wasn't long before Josie was stuffing her overnight bag into the full trunk of the car, alongside the three bags of yarn she needed to give to Evelyn. She'd forgotten all about them.

Mitch opened the car door, and Josie got in. "Would you mind giving me a quick text when you get there? It would make me feel better knowing you arrived safely."

"I will. And I won't make a comment about your being a mother hen, either." She smiled and punched his number into the contacts list of her phone.

He grinned back at her. "See you in town tomorrow." He stepped back as she put the car into reverse, her foot still on the brake pedal, holding her in place.

"Thanks, Mitch. For everything."

He nodded and put his hand up in a wave as she rolled out of the driveway.

"Antonio, listen up," she said, addressing her GPS unit. She probably could have found Evelyn's house without him, but she didn't feel like driving all over town. She spoke the address, and Antonio did his calculations.

Evelyn lived on Trelawney Court, a cul-de-sac containing a lot of neat Cape Cod–style houses with smallish lawns. While not new homes, most appeared to be well kept, and Evelyn's was no exception. The white siding could have used a power washing, but that was par for the course in New England in February, Josie supposed. Forest green shutters flanked each window, and the sharply pitched roof typical of the architectural style was covered in dark brown shingles. With flowers out front in the spring and summer, the home would have a cottagey appeal, she mused.

Evelyn opened the door between the main house and the attached garage before Josie even got to the steps. "Come in!" she warbled. "I've made us some dinner, since I'm sure you didn't have any." Evelyn peered over Josie's shoulder. "You didn't bring Mitchell with you? That's a shame. He's good-looking."

Josie entered the enclosed breezeway, dropped her bag on a bench, and hung up her jacket and scarf on the coat tree. She sloughed off her fur-lined clogs—which were rather worse for the wear after her time in Dorset Falls—and left them on the boot tray underneath the bench. Shouldering her bag, she followed Evelyn into a tiny kitchen.

Evelyn's kitchen was clean and tidy, but hadn't been updated in a while. The walls were papered in a busy teakettle design, and the window over the sink was curtained in a matching print. The cabinets were knotty pine, with black metal handles. Nineteen-sixties colonial.

"Sit down," Evelyn said, gesturing to the small dinette table along one wall. "Unless you need to freshen up before dinner?"

"I think I will just use your powder room first, if you don't mind?"

"Around the corner and down the hall, second door on your right. You can't miss it." She stirred something on the stove. "I hope you don't mind that I invited Sharla. Harrison took Andrew to a movie tonight."

Evelyn's powder room had probably been constructed from a closet, it was so small. It contained a commode and a tiny sink with a mirror over it. A bud vase with a single silk rose sat on the tiny counter. A spare roll of toilet paper sat on the toilet tank lid, topped with a crocheted cover.

Josie looked at herself in the mirror. Purple shadows rimmed her eyes. After the adrenaline rush of getting Eb to the hospital, she was now feeling the aftereffects and was bone tired. Her face flushed. Mitch had seen her looking like this. It was a wonder he hadn't run away screaming. Josie ran her fingers through her hair, smoothing it as best she could, and splashed some cold water on her face, then gave her hands a good washing with soap. Moderately refreshed, she realized she was starving. It had been a long time since lunch, and the cookie she had eaten at the hospital had long since worn off.

Returning to the kitchen, she sank gratefully into a chair next to Sharla, who had appeared in the meantime. Off-duty, she was dressed in civilian clothes, and her hair was down. "Hi, Josie. Good to see you again," she said.

Evelyn *tsked.* "You look exhausted. We'll get you to bed early tonight," she said. "Here. I have homemade chicken soup and hot biscuits." She ladled soup into bowls and set them in front of Josie and Sharla, then passed a plate of steaming biscuits.

"This looks delicious," Josie said, meaning it. "I hope you didn't go to any trouble. I know this was short notice." She spooned up some soup, catching a cube of white chicken and a bright orange carrot.

"Don't be silly," Evelyn said. "I had the soup in the freezer, and the biscuits are from a box mix. Easy peasy. But no peas in the soup! I don't like them. And," she added, "it's nice to have company. I'm glad you came. Both of you."

"Well, thank you. I'm glad too." Josie broke a biscuit in half and spread it with butter.

"How's Eben?" Sharla asked between mouthfuls. "I heard it come across the scanner that he'd been taken to the hospital."

That was probably how Evelyn had heard about it so fast. Josie relayed what had happened.

"So," Evelyn said. "Dear Eben can come home tomorrow?"

Josie and Sharla looked at each other and smiled. *Dear Eben.* "I don't know yet," Josie said. "We'll know once the tests are finished."

Evelyn's lips were now quite pale, her usual hot-pink lipstick now residing on the biscuit resting on her plate. She seemed older without the bright color lighting up her face. "Well, we'll hope it's nothing too serious. Especially now that he's Dorset Falls's most eligible bachelor."

Josie put her napkin to her mouth, stifling the snort that threatened to erupt. Sharla tapped her foot against Josie's under the table, like they were old girlfriends.

"Most eligible bachelor? I'd say that's Mitch Woodruff," Sharla deadpanned.

Evelyn tapped her napkin to her mouth. "If you're my age, it's Eben Lloyd."

"Really? Does Eb know that? I'm not sure he'd like it much," Josie pointed out.

Evelyn leveled her with a stare. "You're young, so you wouldn't understand. But let me tell you, when you're a widowed or divorced woman my age—and there are a lot of us in Dorset Falls—you strike while the iron is hot. You never know how many chances you'll get."

"Eb's kind of . . . difficult sometimes," Josie said. "What makes him such a catch?" She was honestly curious, though she did have one sneaking suspicion.

"He's alive," Sharla said with a giggle. Then her face went serious. "Sorry. I know he's in the hospital. But I'm sure he's going to be fine."

Evelyn shot her a look. "He *is* alive. In good health, up until today. Still has his teeth, though dentures and hair, or lack thereof, aren't deal breakers for most of us." She took a sip of water.

And he's got Cora's money, Josie thought.

"And of course, he's financially secure, unless he blows Cora's money, which seems unlikely, since he didn't do it while they were married." Evelyn looked into Josie's eyes. "Don't think the single seniors of this town are mercenary—well, some might be—but not all of our husbands left us with insurance policies or nest eggs, and remember most of us never worked outside the home in our own careers. Taxes and medical-insurance premiums go up every year. Money's a consideration."

Josie couldn't really find fault with that logic. Not everyone married for love. Although, she personally might like to one day.

"Cora's accident was such a shame," Evelyn continued. "And preventable."

Josie swallowed her surprise, along with a piece of buttered biscuit. "Preventable? How?"

"Well, I have to think if Eben had been driving instead of Cora, they might not have gone off the road. And if her air bag had deployed the way it was supposed to, well, things might have been very different."

Sharla shook her head. "We can't know that. And it's useless to speculate."

"You know, I was wondering about that," Josie said. "Did Cora often drive with Eb as a passenger? Somehow, I can't see him allowing that too often."

"No, which is what made that day such a perfect storm. Eb always drove if they were together, anytime I saw them, anyway. But that day Eb's truck was in the shop, you know, Rusty's? I think just for an oil change or maybe repairing something Roy Woodruff had done, so Cora picked him up to go to lunch at the winery over in Goshen while Rusty worked on the truck. She told Evelyn earlier that day that she was going to surprise Eben." Evelyn nodded her head in confirmation.

Josie turned to Sharla, the soup forgotten. "Did you ever

figure out what caused them to go off the road? Eb doesn't remember. And he never mentions the accident." She sat up straighter on the hard wooden chair. "If you can tell me, of course."

"Once an investigation into a traffic fatality is complete, it's public record, so yes, I can talk about it. Not that I did the investigation myself, but I read the report. As my mother-in-law has told you, I'd like to be a detective someday."

Josie leaned back. "You'll make a great detective," she predicted.

Sharla's grin was infectious. "Let's hope so. But to answer your question, there was gravel in the road at the spot where they started to skid, as well as some black ice. She hit that, lost control, and ended up in the ditch."

"And her air bag didn't deploy. Eb's did, and that saved him," Josie said. Her stomach clenched, thinking how awful that must have been. She hoped Cora had died instantly, and hadn't suffered.

Evelyn dipped a piece of non-lipsticky biscuit into her soup. "They were having bad luck with cars that week."

Josie inclined her head. "Bad luck?"

"Yes. Just a few days before the accident, I gave Cora a ride home from Rusty's. She was having some kind of engine problem, but Rusty fixed it. Gave the car a clean bill of health. He was fond of Cora."

"Do you think that could have been Roy Woodruff messing with Cora's car?" Josie was beginning to like that man less and less, even though she'd barely met him.

Evelyn shook her head emphatically. "Oh, no. The feud is strictly between Roy and Eben. There are lines they don't cross."

Josie wasn't so sure about that. "What about the air bags? Did Rusty check those too?"

Sharla answered. "The day before the accident, he tested all the systems and hooked the car up to the computer. Everything checked out, even the air bags. I've seen the printout."

"So what happened, then?" Josie frowned. "How could the car be fine one day and malfunction the next?"

"It's been known to happen. Sometimes things just go wrong. The car was inspected after the accident, of course. But the front-end damage was so heavy, some components were just destroyed."

"Poor Cora," Josie said through the lump in her throat.

There were several seconds of silence before Evelyn finally said, "Cora wouldn't have wanted us feeling sad about her, especially not when there's dessert sitting in the refrigerator. Let's have some."

Chapter 19

Sharla left after dessert, which turned out to be her favorite, lemon meringue pie. One thing Josie could say about Dorset Falls? People knew how to cook here. Despite Evelyn's best efforts, she'd been unable to get Sharla to divulge anything about the investigation into Lillian Woodruff's murder. By the time Josie and Evelyn had hand washed the dishes—Evelyn had no dishwasher, nor even a place in the cabinetry to put one—Josie was yawning.

Evelyn wiped her hands and hung the red-and-white-checked dish towel over the handle of the oven door to dry. "Let's get you to bed. Grab your bag, and we'll head upstairs."

"Really, Evelyn, I'd be fine with a pillow and blanket on the couch."

"Nonsense. I have a guest room. It's nice to have a guest to use it."

Josie followed Evelyn up the stairway and into the first room on the right. Her hostess must have been in a blue mood when she decorated, because the walls, curtains, and bedding were done in shades of that color. A very comfortable-looking double bed sat between two windows, covered in a puffy navy-colored quilt. "The bathroom is right next door. You'll find everything you need—towels, soap, shampoo. I'll be watching a movie if you need me." Evelyn went back downstairs, running her hand along the rail as she progressed.

Josie brushed her teeth in the bathroom—approximately the same vintage as the powder room downstairs, but slightly larger and containing a tub with a shower—changed into a T-shirt and fleece pajama pants, and lay down. The bed turned out to be as comfortable as it looked. Wafting up from downstairs was the unmistakable theme song from a James Bond movie. Josie pulled the comforter up around her neck and relaxed into the soft flannel sheets.

At least her body relaxed. Her mind took longer to quiet down.

It was ironic. She'd never given her great-uncle and Cora, the woman he'd married late in life, more than a passing thought as she finished school and tried to find her place in the fashion world. And now Eb and Cora were all she could think about. The accident that injured Eb and killed Cora. The air bag—why had it not deployed, potentially saving Cora's life? Josie should just accept Sharla's explanation that sometimes things go wrong. But it just seemed so random.

Random.

She sat up in bed. What if it hadn't been random?

Rusty had given the car a clean bill of health the day before the accident. Rusty had Eb's truck in the shop the day of the accident. What were the odds? What if someone had tampered with Cora's air bag after Rusty had inspected the car, but before she picked it up? Then had run her off the road—just as someone had tried to cause Josie to have an accident.

Something Evelyn had said that night came back to Josie. Eb was Dorset Falls's most eligible bachelor. And it might not have been because he still had his teeth and his hair.

It might have been because his wife had recently sold her house and was sitting on a pile of cash. Which he would inherit if Cora died, along with a whole shop full of yarn. Maybe even a life-insurance policy.

Helen Crawford. Evelyn Graves. Even Diantha Humphries. They'd all been fawning over Eb for the last week, and probably before Josie had even arrived. An ugly picture was forming. The single senior ladies of Dorset Falls had reason to want Cora out of the way.

And what else did these ladies have in common? They were all members of the Dorset Falls Charity Knitters Association.

Lillian Woodruff had died by being strangled with a twisted rope of yarn, one that would take a bit of special skill to make. And that pointed to a knitter.

But which one?

Josie's heart pounded in her chest. There was a connection between Cora's death and Lillian's murder. There had to be. And if someone in the Charity Knitters was bumping off other members of the group in an attempt to get to Eben, who would be next?

Josie swallowed a lump of panic. She was in Evelyn Graves's house, had eaten the dinner she cooked. Was Evelyn a potential victim? Or could she be the killer? Evelyn was hiding something in the abandoned building across the street from Miss Marple Knits, and Helen Crawford was in on it. What if Evelyn and Helen were working together to see who could marry Eb first, then kill him and split the money?

What if . . .

She lay back against the pillows. Clearly, she was insane. Her imagination was running wild after a long, stressful day and too many episodes of cop dramas on television back at her apartment in New York. Still, Josie wasn't stupid. She got up and moved an armchair up against the closed bedroom door. Just in case.

She climbed back into bed and fell into a fitful sleep.

* * *

Josie woke up early, groggy and unrested. This morning she would stop in at the police station and talk to Detective Potts about the horrible ideas that had come to her last night. She would rather have given the information to Sharla. But if there was even the slightest possibility that Evelyn was involved, Josie didn't want to put Sharla into the awkward position of having to choose her loyalties between her family and her job. Even though it might come to that anyway.

Josie moved the chair back into its spot by the window. Apparently it hadn't been necessary, which was a relief. Still, her plans did not include staying here any longer than she had to. She showered and dressed quickly, stripped the bed, stuffed the sheets into the hamper in the bathroom, then headed downstairs, overnight bag in hand.

Evelyn was already up, sitting at the kitchen table with a newspaper and a cup of coffee. "Good morning, sunshine," she said. "Sit down, and I'll make you some breakfast."

"Thanks, Evelyn. But I promised Mitch I'd meet him in town."

She smiled. "Very good. I'd rather look at his handsome face than a wrinkly old lady's any day, too."

"You're not that wrinkly. You must have good genes."

Evelyn got up and went to the cupboard. She pulled out a metal travel mug and filled it with coffee, then handed it to Josie with a spoon. "Cream and sugar's on the table. You can return the mug anytime. Or not at all. I have more than I need."

Josie fixed the coffee and gave it a stir, then popped the lid into place. She wasn't entirely sure she wanted to drink it. But then again, poison had not been the killer's MO up till this point. And she could use a jolt of caffeine.

"Thanks for dinner and for putting me up last night," Josie said, heading for the breezeway. "I really appreciate it." She shrugged into her jacket and put on her clogs.

Evelyn looked down at Josie's feet and frowned. It was clear some kind of maternal instinct had kicked in. "You'll want to get yourself some boots, if you didn't bring any with you. The weather's warming up during the day, and things are going to get muddy around here."

Things are already muddy around here, Josie thought. "Well, I don't expect to be here much longer. But I'll check Cora's closet. She probably had a pair that will be close enough in size."

Evelyn seemed satisfied. "All right then, out you go. You don't want to be late for your date."

"Thanks again." Josie opened the exterior door onto a bright, cold morning.

"Anytime. And tell dear Eben I said I hope he's on the mend soon." Evelyn's face was all innocence.

Evelyn's words, which Josie would have thought cute yesterday, now took on a more sinister meaning. Josie mentally shook her head. She had no proof of anything, only some wild ideas that didn't seem quite so plausible in the light of day. "Bye, Evelyn."

Josie made her way to the car and tossed her overnight bag into the backseat.

The coffee, hot, thick, and sweet, ran down her throat as she waited for the car to warm up. With the magic of caffeine, it only took a moment for her head to begin to clear. She checked her watch. It was just after eight o'clock. Mitch had said he'd meet her at the g.s. at nine with the eggs. She backed out of the driveway, raising her hand to Evelyn, who was waving to her from the living room bay window.

Go Directly to Jail. Do Not Pass Go. Do Not Collect Two-Hundred Dollars. Josie wasn't exactly going to jail, although she suspected the police station had at least a holding cell or two. She pulled into the shared parking lot between the police and the fire stations, which were located in the same block as the town hall, but facing Grove Street rather than Main.

She took a deep breath, got out of the car, locked it, and headed inside.

The officer on duty sat behind a sliding-glass partition, similar to the one at the hospital, though this one was probably bulletproof. His hair was short and dark, and a close-trimmed goatee outlined his mouth. His beefy dark arms strained at the hems of the short sleeves of his uniform as he pulled back the glass. "I'm Officer Denton. Can I help you?"

Josie swallowed. This was the second time she'd been in this police station, the first being when she'd reported the car's almost running her off the road. It was not less intimidating now, which she guessed was kind of the point. She cleared her throat. "I'd like to talk to Detective Potts."

Officer Denton's eyes were assessing, but his words were clipped. "Your name?"

"Josie. Josephine Blair." Her nerve was rapidly deserting her.

"The nature of your business with Detective Potts?"

What could she say? That she suspected some unidentified old woman was bumping off potential rivals for a Yankee farmer's affections? It sounded ridiculous, even to her.

"I'd like to talk to him"—she cleared her throat again—"about Lillian Woodruff's death." There.

"Do you have some information?" Officer Denton asked, his face expressionless.

"Look, is he here? It won't take long." She put her hand up to Cora's blue scarf and adjusted it. Stroking the soft fiber was almost as good at calming her as stroking Coco's fur.

He eyed her, then relented. "As it happens, he's not in yet. Leave me your name and phone number, and I'll have him call you."

A reprieve. But she'd been looking forward to getting the crazy theory out of her own head and into the hands of someone who could actually do something about it. "Josie Blair. B-L-A-I-R. He has my number, but I'll give it to you again."

She rattled it off, and Officer Denton dutifully wrote it down on a pink message pad. "When do you think he'll be in?"

"He doesn't report to me," Officer Denton said. "He'll call you."

"Thanks." *For nothing,* she thought, and headed back to her car.

The coffee was still hot as she sat in her car, once again waiting for the old engine to warm up. Potts's laughter was going to be audible from here to Hartford. Supposedly the police were close to making an arrest. Was she just throwing a monkey wrench into their investigation?

No, she owed it to Cora, and to Lillian, to say something. And Josie would, just as soon as Potts called her back.

She pulled out, drove around the block, and parked in front of Miss Marple Knits. The interior was dark, not that she'd expected anything different. It wasn't quite time to meet Mitch, so she might as well use the time productively. She fired off a text to her friend Monica, asking her again to put her in touch with the buyer. Josie put the key in the lock and entered the shop.

Setting the travel mug on the sales counter, she glanced around. The shop hadn't gotten any less forlorn, that was for sure. Miss Marple stared up at her from the confines of her frame.

Huh?

She looked at the picture again. It was faceup.

Last time she was in, she had left the picture facedown, because she didn't want to see Miss Marple's accusing stare.

Someone had been here.

She glanced around. The bags of yarn were lined up around the perimeter of the room. Impossible to tell if they'd been moved. Or was it? She pulled out her cell phone and called up the photos she'd taken for the buyer. She scrolled through them, comparing the photos to the scene in front of her. There were slight discrepancies. A bag farther away from the wall.

Another bag tipped over. A grouping of three where the pictures showed two should have been.

Adrenaline surged. She should check the back room, but common sense won out. What if the intruder was still here?

She grabbed the coffee mug and her purse and hightailed it out of there.

Chapter 20

The general store was full of people, or as full as Josie had ever seen it. Lorna was dispensing coffee and muffins to the on-their-way-to-work crowd. She waved to Josie, then went back to her customers.

Josie sat down in the rear of the café, facing the front entrance, with her back to the wall so no one could sneak up on her. She took several deep breaths, willing her heart to slow its racing beat.

Whoever had been in Miss Marple Knits was looking for something. And the only something she could think of was Cora's notebook, which still hadn't turned up. She fished around in her purse and pulled out a crumpled sheet of paper. After Detective Potts had released the crime scene to her, he'd handed her an inventory of what they had taken. She laid the paper on the table and smoothed it out with her hand. There was no mention of any notebook.

Which meant the authorities didn't have it, unless they'd secured it from somewhere else.

If the handwritten sales list in that notebook contained

what she thought it did—namely, a list of people who had bought that particular blue yarn that had been used to make the murder weapon—the killer would need the notebook to cover his or her tracks. And might stop at nothing to get it and destroy it.

As soon as she spoke to Detective Potts and called the hospital to check on Eb, she was going back to the farmhouse and would turn it upside down. The notebook had to be there somewhere.

Josie started, simultaneously sucking in a breath as a shadow fell across the table. She looked up to see Mitch standing over her. His smile quickly turned to a frown. "What's wrong?" He sat down, setting the container of eggs on the table. "Eb hasn't taken a turn for the worse, has he?"

Breathe, Josie. She forced her shoulders into a more relaxed posture and gave her neck a roll, attempting to dissipate the tension. "No, I haven't called the hospital yet, but they would have let me know if something had happened. I didn't sleep well last night and . . ."

"And?" Mitch prompted.

Could she trust him? Should she? Maybe it would be better to just head right back to the police station—*Go Directly To Jail. Do Not Pass Go*—and report the break-in. If it had been a break-in. The front door and windows were intact. But she hadn't checked the back door for damage. Not that it mattered. The killer had gotten in without breaking a window or forcing the lock when he'd killed Lillian, and he'd gotten in again.

"Josie," Mitch said, placing a reassuring hand on her arm. "Talk to me."

She lowered her voice. "Someone was in the shop again."

Mitch jumped into action. "You have to report this. I'll take you down to the police station right now."

"Thanks. But I already have a call in to Detective Potts. The desk sergeant said he'd have him call me when he came in. And I'm not going back to the shop today. In fact, I'm not going back there at all until the movers come to take away the inventory."

Mitch frowned. "I want you to stay in town today. I have an appointment I can't cancel, but you could stay here at the store until I come back, then I'll take you to the hospital."

She was touched. "Thanks. I'll probably take you up on that. Is everything okay at the house? How did the girls do this morning?" She opened the egg container, then the four individual boxes. Each contained the usual dozen brown shells nestled safely inside.

"They're fine. Clucking and squawking as usual. Oh, you must have had a visitor last night—" Mitch cut off, as something dawned on him. His face darkened. "When I went to feed Coco and Jethro this morning, there were fresh tracks in the snow leading up to the front porch." He frowned, thinking. "I didn't notice anything unusual other than the footprints, but I didn't investigate the whole house, either."

Josie's heart seemed to be taking up permanent residence in her throat.

"My guess is that nobody got in," Mitch continued. "If that's what the footprints meant. I didn't see any signs that the door locks had been forced, and if a window had been broken, it would have been awfully cold in the house. And of course, nobody gets past Jethro."

"You do." She felt awful. He'd been nothing but nice to her, and here she was practically accusing him of . . . something.

Mitch smiled. He didn't appear to have taken offense. "That's because I've been working on him for a long time. The dog associates me with food. He might even like me a little."

"That makes one of you," Josie said. "Two if you count Eb."

"Do you think there's a connection between the break-in at

Miss Marple Knits and this unknown person who came up your—Eb's—front steps?" Mitch sounded dubious.

"I honestly don't know. Maybe. It could be nothing, just a traveling vacuum-cleaner sales rep who knocked on the front door and found we weren't home." She hoped that was true. Maybe the person would come back. Eb's vacuum cleaner was on its last legs.

"Well, when you talk to Detective Potts, mention it, okay?"

"I will."

"I meant what I said. Stay here, or at least where there are other people around. I wouldn't want anything to happen to you." He looked into her eyes. Josie returned the gaze. Her stomach fluttered. "Because," he continued, "if you're not around, I'll have to see more of Eb than I already do."

Josie laughed, a genuine laugh that dissipated some of the tension she'd been feeling, at least for the moment.

"Okay," she said. "And thanks."

"I'll text you when I'm ready to take you to the hospital. Be careful." He strode off.

Good advice. Until the murderer was behind bars, the entire town of Dorset Falls should be careful.

Lorna came out from behind the counter, the breakfast rush taken care of. She brought the coffee pot and waved it toward Evelyn's travel mug. "Want me to fill that up for you?"

"Sure do." Josie took off the lid, and Lorna poured in the fragrant liquid.

"What was all that about? I haven't seen Mitch that serious in a long time. Is everything all right?" She glanced back toward the counter. There were no customers in line, so she sat down.

Josie sipped at the coffee. Much better hot than lukewarm. She considered how much to say to Lorna. It seemed prudent—a quality Josie had not heretofore ever been known for—to keep things quiet until she'd unburdened herself to Detective Potts. She'd rather look like a fool with her ridiculous theory to one person than to the whole town.

"Just worried about Eb," she finally said. "You've heard by now he's in the hospital? The doctors don't think he had a heart attack, but they still don't know what the problem is. Mitch is going to take me over later."

Lorna nodded. "Good idea. Are you going to wait for him here? You're welcome to stay. I've got a paperback in my purse, if you need something to read."

"Tempting, but I've actually got work to keep me busy. And I'm waiting for a phone call." She reached into her tote bag and pulled out the sketch she'd been working on at the hospital yesterday, still attached to the borrowed clipboard. She made a mental note to return it.

Lorna twisted her neck so she could get a better look. "I want that dress," she declared. "I may not have a date, but I could get one in that."

"Let's just hope my boss likes it," Josie said. Despite her earlier confidence, it was going to take some work to get herself unfired from the Haus of Heinrich. Something nagged at her. Did she really want to be unfired?

"He'd be crazy not to. I'll let you get back to it, and I should get back to work too." Lorna returned to her station.

Josie worked steadily for close to an hour, finishing the fifties look and starting in on the wide-legged pants with the fitted knit blazer. These drawings didn't need to be Metropolitan Museum of Art quality, so long as they captured the important details. But they did need to impress Otto, something she'd rather spectacularly failed to do up till now.

She held the sketch out at arm's length, added a few quick touches, and set it down, satisfied. She might just pull this off yet.

Her cell phone vibrated, indicating she had a text. Mitch? No, it was Monica.

Buyer wants to meet you in New York. Today, 4:00.

Today? Impossible. And why would this buyer need to meet Josie in person?

She texted back. *Can't. Tied up here. Have buyer call me. Need inventory picked up ASAP.*

Will see what I can do.

What was going on? This deal could *not* fall through or she'd have a bigger mess on her hands. She needed to have Miss Marple Knits emptied out in a few days, and there was no time to find another buyer. She did not relish the thought of packing up the entire store and moving it out to Eb's, but that's just what she'd have to do if she couldn't get the buyer to stop stalling.

She texted Monica again. *Get me buyer's name and phone number. I'll call myself.*

Josie had barely pressed *send* when the phone actually rang. She didn't recognize the number, but it was from the local area code. "Hello?"

"Ms. Blair? It's Detective Potts. You wanted to talk to me?"

Deep breath. "I'm at the general store. It's too public here. Can you meet me at Miss Marple Knits?"

There was a short pause. "Usually people come down to the station if they want to tell me something. But as it happens I need to pick up lunch. So yes, I'll meet you at the yarn shop in ten minutes." He rang off.

Josie packed up. She'd get this over with and hopefully out of her head. Because no matter how she mentally fiddled with them, the pieces fit. She waved to Lorna on her way out the door.

The temperature had risen into the forties, which felt positively tropical as Josie made her way along the sidewalk. She glanced at her phone. Detective Potts should be here in less than five minutes. But just to be on the safe side, she decided to wait in her car, which was parked on the street, instead of inside the shop.

She didn't bother to turn on the ignition, just sat there soaking in the sun radiating in through the glass. Main Street was virtually empty, as usual, not even a car traveling from somewhere else to somewhere else. Movement caught her eye across the street. The shade covering the third floor window shifted from side to side before settling back into place. Either there was a ghost, or a draft, or a person up there. She continued to watch from the corner of her eye, but the movement wasn't repeated.

At that moment, Detective Potts appeared. No more snooping for Josie. She got out of the car, grabbed her bag, and met him on the steps of Miss Marple Knits.

"Thanks for coming," Josie said, unlocking the door.

He followed her in, leaving his coat on, clearly not intending to stay long. Fine. She wanted this over quickly too.

"Now. What did you want to talk about? You know the investigation is ongoing and I can't talk about it, right?"

She nodded. "Of course. I wouldn't ask you for information you're not allowed to give. Let's sit down."

He twisted his lips to one side, clearly not wanting to stay any longer than he had to, but he complied.

"First," Josie continued, "someone has broken into this store again."

The detective leaned forward almost imperceptibly. "And what makes you say that?"

"Because the last time I was in here, I took a picture off the wall and laid it facedown on the counter. When I came in this morning, the picture was faceup. And these bags of yarn have been moved. I can show you the before and after photos."

He looked skeptical. "Were there any signs of forced entry? Broken locks or windows?"

She shook her head. "Well, not out front, at least. I didn't go into the storeroom or check the back entrance."

"Come on then," he said, heaving himself up from the couch. "Let's go check it out." He led her past the tiny bathroom and into the back. The electric EXIT sign was lit up, making the back door impossible to miss. He pulled out a flashlight and shone it on the floor and around the perimeter of the door, then honed in on the bar that served as a handle. He put his hand on the metal, testing it. The door didn't budge. Locked.

The detective eyed her. "Any other entrances to this building?"

Josie was pretty sure he already knew the answer to that question. He and his crime-scene techs had presumably done a thorough investigation after Lillian's body was found. "Not that I know of," she finally said.

"Well, you're wrong about that. There are fire-escape exits on the second and third floors, from when there used to be tenants up there. Let's go check those out."

Fortunately, the spiders had not had time to rebuild their evil webs in the stairwell. Detective Potts led the way. He'd shut off his big Mag flashlight, but held it out in front of him. If there was an intruder up there, which seemed unlikely, he had a weapon at the ready.

But it proved unnecessary. The two upstairs floors were as empty as they'd been the other day when Josie had looked around for items to remove before the demolition. The doors to the fire escapes, which Josie had not noticed before—probably because she hadn't been looking for them—were both locked.

Whoever was breaking into 13 Main Street, Dorset Falls, Connecticut, was teleporting in. Or using a key.

Detective Potts was careful not to touch the doorknobs, and told Josie not to do it either. He would send a tech over later to dust for fingerprints on the interior and exterior door handles.

"But I don't expect to find any," he warned. "If this is the same person who murdered Lillian Woodruff, he's smart enough to wear gloves. At least he did at the murder scene."

Josie noticed the cop had said "he." "Do you have a suspect?"

Detective Potts eyed her. "Where'd you hear that?"

She thought fast. She didn't want to get Sharla into trouble. Maybe Sharla wasn't supposed to reveal even that much. "At the general store. Isn't that where all the gossip in this town collects? Nobody's throwing around any names, though."

His face was impassive. "I'm not about to throw out any names, either."

"Of course not." Drat.

"Let's go back downstairs. Was this all you wanted to tell me? You said you had information about the Woodruff murder. And," he looked pointedly down at his watch, "we need to get a move on. I only get a short lunch today."

A couple of minutes later they were back in the seating area of the shop. Josie took a deep breath, then told him her theory.

He stared at her for a moment, then the corners of his mouth began to twitch. He was trying not to laugh at her. She was trying not to be insulted.

"So let me get this straight," he said. "You think one of the old ladies in this town is bumping off other old ladies who might be standing in the way of a romance with"—he worked to suppress a snort, but didn't quite succeed—"Eben Lloyd." Potts stowed his flashlight somewhere in the interior of his thigh-length topcoat. "Eben Lloyd, the crotchetiest SOB that ever lived, other than maybe Roy Woodruff. No offense to your uncle, of course."

"None taken." She'd known the detective would be skeptical, but she hadn't expected him to dismiss her outright, either. "I admit he has his moments. But he's also come into a lot of money since Cora died."

Potts looked thoughtful, then let out a sigh. "I'll review the evidence again, see if anything fits your theory, but that's the best I can do. I'll tell you right now we *do* have a suspect, and evidence, and an arrest is going to be made any day now. So I'd advise you to put this idea out of your head. It's interesting. It would make a good television movie. But it's wrong."

She should have felt relieved. So why did she feel so unsatisfied?

Chapter 21

Josie locked up the shop behind her, careful to close the door with her sleeve rather than her fingers, the way Detective Potts had showed her. Although if there were fingerprints on the front door, it was likely she'd smeared them already.

Mitch pulled up out front just as she stepped onto the sidewalk. He rolled down the window. "Perfect timing?" he said.

"Perfect timing." She took the big step up into the SUV, closed the door, and buckled up.

"You weren't alone in there, were you?" His tone somehow managed to admonish and show concern at the same time.

She shook her head. "No, I had Detective Potts with me. He's going to have the place dusted for fingerprints again."

"Good. I'd hate to have to yell at you for doing something dangerous." He flashed her a smile that showed a lot of white, even teeth. He either had excellent genes, or had had excellent orthodontic work as a kid.

"Danger's my middle name," she said, putting on a cheesy British accent. Ugh. Why had she done that? It was so lame. But Mitch just laughed.

"Ready? Let's go see Eb."

It was a beautiful day for a drive. The sky was blue and nearly cloudless, and enough snow had melted off the lawns and fields that patches of brown grass were visible. Maybe spring really would come to Dorset Falls, someday. Josie closed her eyes and leaned back in the seat. She dozed off.

When she woke, they were pulling into the parking lot of the hospital. Her head jerked up. "Oh, I'm so sorry. I guess I'm not very good company."

Mitch moved the gearshift into park. "Don't worry about it. You said you didn't sleep well last night. And I'm not surprised, with everything you've been going through."

"Well, I hope, at least, I didn't snore." That would be embarrassing.

"Nope. You sleep pretty as a picture. Not that I noticed. I was keeping my eyes on the road, I swear."

Warmth crept up her neck and over her cheeks. She opened the door and stepped out, grateful for the cooler air. "All right, you charmer, come on," she said across the hood. "Let's go see the other charmer in my life."

A different receptionist was on duty today. She raised her eyebrows when Josie told her whom they were visiting, but she was too much of a professional to say anything more than, "He's been moved to Room 216. Elevators are down this hall and to the right."

They found Eb sitting up in bed. Someone, a nurse probably, had found him the newspaper, and he was dutifully filling in boxes on the daily crossword. Josie felt a stab of guilt. She should have remembered to bring him the paper. He didn't look up as they came in, even though he couldn't have failed to see them.

"Eb?" Josie said. "How's it going?"

He made one more notation, then finally deigned to acknowledge their presence over the tops of his cheaters. "Did you bring my cookies?"

She felt worse about the cookies than about the paper. She'd completely forgotten. "Uh, no. Sorry."

He pursed up his lips. "Did you remember to feed the dog?"

"All taken care of," Mitch said. "So. What does the doctor say?"

"Not a heart attack. I've got the ticker of a teenager."

Josie felt a surge of relief. "What else did she say?"

Eb was prevented from answering by the arrival of the cardiologist, Dr. Andersen. "I'm glad you're here. Let's pull up a chair, shall we?" Her tone was friendly and efficient, same as it had been yesterday.

"Uncle Eb says it definitely wasn't a heart attack," Josie said.

Dr. Andersen smiled. "No. His heart is quite healthy. We did a number of tests to rule out things like angina. I'm glad to say that Eb is in extremely good shape for a man of his age."

"Which I told you when I first came in, Doc." Eb folded his arms across his stomach.

"Yes, you certainly did." The doctor cut her eyes to Josie. "He's quite articulate about his needs and wants."

"No argument there," Josie said. "So if it wasn't a heart attack or angina, what was it?"

"Heartburn," Eb piped up, triumphant. "Could have just taken a spoonful of baking soda mixed in warm water instead of being poked and prodded for the last twenty-four hours."

Josie turned to the doctor. "Really? That's it?"

Mitch was smiling broadly in the chair next to her.

"That's it," Dr. Andersen said. "What's he been eating lately?"

Evelyn's never-ending casserole, that was what. "So you're telling me that green peppers and tomato sauce cause heart-attack-like symptoms?"

The doctor nodded. "Severe indigestion certainly can. I don't recommend the bicarbonate of soda remedy, though. There are better choices." She wrote down the name of an over-the-counter medication on a slip of paper and handed it to Josie. "You can get this at any drugstore. Just keep it on hand."

"So can we bring him home?" Josie asked.

"Well," the doctor responded, "since we have him here, I thought we could have his leg x-rayed. It's been six weeks since the accident, and we may be able to get him out of that cast sooner than his next appointment."

Eb sat up straighter. "Where's the machine? Take your picture and bring in the saw and let's get it done, Doc."

Dr. Andersen chuckled. "I'm a cardiologist, Eben. The orthopedist won't be in until tomorrow. So if you'd like to be our guest for one more night, you won't have to come back next week as long as Dr. Robbins gives you the okay."

Eb leaned back against the pillows, considering. "Fine. Bed's comfortable. There's Jell-O and mashed potatoes at every meal. Even at breakfast if you want it. I'll stay." He leveled a stare at the doctor. "But this block of cement"—he indicated his cast—"better be off tomorrow." His tone was ominous.

The doctor seemed slightly amused. "Well, I can't promise anything. That'll be up to Dr. Robbins to decide."

"Hmmph." Eb was obviously done talking. But he made no move to get out of bed, so Josie thought it was safe to assume he planned to stay.

Unfortunately, that also meant that she'd be staying alone at the farm tonight, a thought that did not exactly thrill her. Maybe she could get Jethro to sleep in her room. She certainly wasn't going back to Evelyn's. No matter what Detective Potts thought about the other ladies of the Charity Knitters, Evelyn was hiding something. And until Josie found out for sure that it wasn't murder, she was going to stay on her guard.

The doctor rose. "That's settled, then. Dr. Robbins will see you on his rounds tomorrow." She turned to Mitch and Josie.

"I'll look in on Eb again in the morning, but as long as he doesn't have any further problems, I won't need to see him anymore. Just watch what he eats. Avoid greasy and high-acid foods if possible."

When the doctor had gone, Josie turned to Eb, who had picked up his crossword puzzle and was studiously filling it in. "We're here to visit, Eb. You wanna play cards or something?" Of course, the only card game she could remember how to play was Go Fish, but she might be able to manage rummy or Crazy Eights, if someone gave her a refresher.

He didn't look up. "Nope. Don't want to play cards. Do want you to go home. You got the stuff in the shop sold yet?"

Nuts. She'd forgotten. Monica hadn't texted her back with the buyer's contact information. "Uh, I told you there was an offer."

"An offer ain't money in the bank."

"I'm working on it, okay?" She felt her hackles rise. She hadn't asked for this job.

"Eb," Mitch cut in. "I'm going to take her home now. We'll call in the morning." He took Josie's arm. "Let's go and leave Eb to the nurses."

She took a deep breath.

"I'll see you tomorrow, Eb. And I'll make sure we have cookies at home." But her uncle had already gone back to his puzzle. He didn't look up as she and Mitch left.

Josie looked at the set of keys in her hand. Mitch had dropped her off at home to pick up her car, then she'd driven to the general store, where she tried to work on her drawings. But it was impossible to concentrate. Detective Potts had dismissed her theory about a lady of Dorset Falls bumping off other ladies in an effort to get at Josie's great-uncle's new fortune. Potts had all but confirmed that the suspect about to be arrested was a man. And yet, she was not going to be able to dismiss her theory herself until she found out what was going on in that building across the street from Miss Marple Knits.

There was no time like the present. She'd just stick each key into the lock in turn, and see if one worked. If it did, she'd go upstairs, quickly find out what was going on up there, and the mystery would be solved. Her implied promise to Mitch that she wouldn't go anywhere alone would only be bent, not broken, if Evelyn or Helen were upstairs. Josie's ever-present canister of Mace was in her purse in case she got into trouble.

If none of the keys worked, she'd give it up, do her best to forget about it. Either way, maybe she could get some closure.

A rare car drove down Main Street, causing her to step back out of its path. She checked both ways, gave a glance to the shaded third floor window, and crossed the street.

Some of the keys didn't need trying. The key to Cora's wrecked car. The keys that she knew fit the front and back doors of Miss Marple Knits. The ones that went to Eb's farmhouse. She pressed the next remaining key to the lock. No luck with that or the second one. On the third try, the metal slid in, causing her to gasp softly. Honestly, she hadn't really thought this would work.

The key turned, and the tumblers clicked. Dropping Evelyn's travel mug, Josie's excuse for barging in, into her bag, she tried the door's old-fashioned knob. The door swung open.

Breathe, Josie. Here you go. She stepped inside.

She found herself on a tiny landing, only a few feet square. A metal light fixture hung from a chain overhead, illuminating the space with a dim light. She put a clog on the first riser, then put one foot in front of the other, ascending the stairs. At the halfway point, she grabbed the railing and looked over her shoulder. It wasn't too late. She could turn back. But she didn't.

Josie stepped off onto a landing on the third floor, not as large as its counterpart across the street. This one was ringed with doors, each bearing a metal number from one to five. Door number four was ajar. She approached it.

Through the crack, she could see what appeared to be a living room. Perhaps these were efficiency apartments. None could be terribly large if there were five units in this smallish space. She gave the door a push with her foot, and it swung open. Feeling like Goldilocks, and wondering what she was walking into, Josie went in.

A floral-upholstered living-room set, each fabric surface fitted with a clear plastic covering, took up the center of the room. Two 1960s-style end tables in a blond wood, with a matching coffee table decorated with a bowl of plastic sequined fruit, completed the grouping. Was someone living here? If so, it was someone with a taste for kitschy furniture, or someone with a tag-sale budget.

To the right, through a pass-through cut into the wall, she could see a tiny kitchen. Even for a noncook such as herself, the space would have been tough to use. Only a couple of cabinets were visible. She trained her ear toward the kitchen, where she could hear a faint burbling noise, followed by a hiss, as of steam. The coffeepot was on.

If the coffeepot was on, someone was home.

A fact that was confirmed by a gray herringbone wool coat hung neatly on a peg on one wall, a cherry-red scarf draped under the lapels.

Evelyn's coat.

Josie wasn't sure why that surprised her. Evelyn's car was parked outside in the alley.

A laptop computer sat on a small, Formica-topped table with chrome trim. The screen was on. She glanced at it, then back again, frowning. It seemed to be some kind of video feed. Examining the image more closely, she realized it was being transmitted from a security camera trained on the waiting room of a business of some kind.

A business that looked familiar, because she'd been inside it only a few days ago.

Rusty's car repair shop.

Josie wasn't sure what she'd expected to find, but it wasn't this. She watched as Rusty came into the picture behind the counter, his tall, bulky frame clearly recognizable. A woman approached the counter. All Josie could see was the woman's back. There was no audio, but she didn't need sound to know whom she was looking at.

It was Josie herself.

The loop repeated, and Josie walked back onto the screen.

The realization slammed into her with the force of a meteorite hitting the earth and shattering into a thousand pieces. Evelyn had been spying on her. The older woman had been pretending to be her friend, but had somehow been keeping tabs on her. Was she afraid Josie was getting too close to the truth about Cora's and Lillian's deaths?

Josie backed away, stunned. This couldn't be right. How had Evelyn gotten hold of Rusty's security footage? Evelyn couldn't have known that Josie would visit Rusty's that day.

Or could she have? Josie's fingers closed around the can of Mace.

Was it possible Evelyn had fiddled with Josie's car, causing the wonky ignition, knowing that Josie would take it in for repair? The vision of Evelyn in a mechanic's jumpsuit, applying a greasy wrench to Josie's Saab, flashed across Josie's brain. Ridiculous.

What reason could Evelyn have for keeping tabs on Josie? Not a single thing came to mind.

Josie started as the front door opened. Helen Crawford did a double take, her hand flying up to her throat. "Josie?"

"Helen?" Josie's heart rate skyrocketed.

Helen set down her shopping bag and stared. "What are you doing here?" she finally said, looking more surprised than confused. "Did Evelyn bring you? I thought we'd decided no one was allowed up here. Ever."

Josie decided to play dumb. Which was not far from the truth. She had no idea what was going on here. Couldn't even begin to guess.

"I had a set of Cora's keys. I wanted to see what they went to." It was the truth. Mostly.

"Does Evelyn know you're here?" Helen pulled a tray of cookies out of the bag and set them on the table, next to the laptop. Molasses, maybe, with a sparkly sugar coating.

Josie shook her head. "I just arrived."

"Well then," Helen said, her voice crisp, "you may as well see everything." She beckoned Josie to follow across the green shag carpet to a closed interior door. Helen knocked softly, then opened the door and stepped aside.

The room, which had probably been a bedroom when this was a proper apartment, was taken up by three six-foot folding tables set in a horseshoe shape around the perimeter. The tables were covered with various pieces of electronic equipment, as well as several large screens, all of which seemed to be playing video feeds like the one on the laptop out front. In a wheeled stenographer's chair in front of the screens sat Evelyn, an enormous pair of headphones covering her ears. She seemed oblivious to their presence.

Josie felt her mouth drop open. What in the name of Gucci was this? It looked like the set of a movie.

Helen stepped forward and reached out a hand to tap Evelyn's shoulder. "Evvy?" she said. Evelyn spun around, the cord from the headphones crossing her body like a bandolier. Her face went pale as she focused on Josie.

"Code red," Helen said.

"How—? What are you doing here?" Evelyn spluttered. "This place is secret!" Her face went as scarlet as the scarf around her coat in the outer room.

Helen's voice was matter-of-fact. "She had Cora's key. She must have seen your car in the alley and figured it out. I told you to stop parking there."

Josie just stood there, agape, until she finally found her voice. "I don't understand. Do you run some kind of surveillance business here? I thought you were both retired."

Helen and Evelyn looked at each other. "Sort of," Evelyn said. "Can we trust you?"

"Do you have a choice?" Josie responded. "I've already seen it."

Evelyn gave her an assessing look. "Fine. Let's go talk."

The three women trooped out to the front room. Josie sat down on one of the plastic-covered chairs, which gave off a little puff of air as she did so. Evelyn followed suit, choosing the couch.

"Cream and sugar in your coffee?" Helen called out from the kitchenette. "Never mind. I'll just bring a tray, and you can fix it yourself." She reappeared a moment later and set the tray on the coffee table. There were real china cups and saucers, as well as the cookies on a platter. Helen sat down on the chair opposite Josie and reached for a cup.

Josie didn't know what to say. She wondered briefly if she were a guest at the Mad Hatter's tea party.

Evelyn poured herself a cup of coffee, then began. "I suppose you're wondering what all this is." She swept her free hand around the room. "Helen owns this building."

"Hasn't been rented in years," Helen said, through a mouthful of cookie. "I've been using it as a tax write-off."

Josie butted in. "Where did you get all this equipment? It must have cost a fortune." Her suspicions resurfaced. Did these two need money to keep this little operation going, whatever this little operation was? And were they looking at Eb as the banker?

"Spygrannies.com," Helen said, looking pleased with herself. "You can buy anything on the Internet, including used surveillance equipment."

Josie was at a loss for words. Whatever she had imagined was going on in this third-floor apartment, senior ladies playing with spy gadgets had not even been on the radar. "So what—or whom—are you spying on?" she finally managed.

Evelyn and Helen exchanged a look. "If we tell you, you are sworn to absolute secrecy."

"I can't make that promise. If you're doing something dangerous, or illegal, I'll have to report it."

Evelyn sighed.

"You might as well tell her," Helen said. "She's already discovered us. If she wants to rat us out, we can't stop her."

"I suppose you're right." But Evelyn didn't look happy. "We're spying on Diantha."

"Not just Diantha," Helen piped in. "Courtney too."

Whatever Josie had expected, this wasn't it. "But why?"

Evelyn said, "Do you mean other than the fact that Diantha's uppity and thinks she can run the Charity Knitters—and the whole town of Dorset Falls—the way she likes? We thought if we could catch her doing something illegal, or at least unsavory, we could blackmail her with it and get her to step down from the Charity Knitters presidency."

"And from the town council," Helen added.

These ladies were probably breaking all kinds of laws. But Josie wouldn't exactly be against seeing Diantha taken down a peg or two. "Have you found anything?"

Evelyn frowned. "Unfortunately, no. So we moved on to Courtney. Diantha's so concerned with appearances, if we could dig up some kind of dirt on Courtney, and hold it over Diantha's head, it would be just as good."

"We think Courtney's having an affair with Rusty," Helen said. "But we can't prove it yet. That's why we put surveillance in the car repair shop."

"Cora set it up while I distracted Rusty." Evelyn nibbled at a cookie.

"Cora?" Of course Cora had been involved. Otherwise she wouldn't have had a key to this . . . inner sanctum.

"Well, Cora was president of the Charity Knitters. So for her it was just about getting Diantha to resign from the town council." Evelyn sipped at her coffee, then set the cup down in its saucer. "She died before we had enough data to confront Diantha."

"So now you're carrying on without Cora?" Josie said. Cora would be pleased, Josie assumed.

"Honestly, we're having some problems." Evelyn's face lit up. "I know! Since you've found us out, maybe you can help."

Whoa. As much as Josie would like to see Diantha deposed, and her little daughter-in-law too, this operation was out of her comfort zone. "I'd like to help, but—"

"Wonderful!" Evelyn actually clapped her hands. "Cora was our tech goddess. If she had been in the movies, she'd have been the character who hacks into the government's computers. I'll bet you've got the same skills."

"Evelyn, Helen, I know enough about computers to get by. But I'm no expert."

"Well, you know more than we do. We put tracking devices on Diantha's and Courtney's cars, but we don't know how to get the data off them."

Tracking devices? Good grief. Josie was definitely down the rabbit hole.

Helen jumped up with alacrity and came back with a thick booklet, which she handed to Josie. "The instruction manual," she said. "Just read this."

Um, yeah. Josie would get right on that. Because she didn't know what else to do, she took the manual and tucked it into her tote bag. Her fingers touched metal, and Josie pulled out the travel mug, which she set on the coffee table. "I wanted to return this to you," she said.

Evelyn cut her eyes to Josie. "Very good. An excellent excuse for following me up to the Lair." She turned to Helen. "You know something? I'm glad Josie found us. She'll make a great member of the team."

Helen nodded. "I believe you're right. Go ahead and keep the keys. You can come up here whenever you like. And," she added, "the sooner you figure out how to get the information off the tracking devices, the better."

Josie smiled ruefully. "You know I won't be here much longer, right?"

"You're here for at least a few more days, right? So you can help us while you're still in town."

Sure. Even if she did agree to apply her less than stellar computer skills to this little enterprise, would she be doing anything illegal? She wasn't actually doing the surveilling herself. But that was probably splitting hairs. The end result was the same.

"I'll try," Josie finally said, after taking a sip of the coffee, which was very strong. These ladies could hold their caffeine. Or maybe they needed to keep themselves awake while they surveilled Diantha and Courtney. "Oh, I have something for you. I bagged up the yarn from Cora's office at the farmhouse. It's in the trunk of my car. You two can divide it up."

Helen leaned forward, the yarn lust glittering in her eyes. Evelyn smiled, then looked at Helen. "That'll be some prime stuff. I know what Cora had at home."

A lightbulb seemed to materialize over Helen's pale blond head. "I know! Why don't we bring it up here and sort it out? Then we can leave some here to use while we're . . . working."

"Excellent idea," Evelyn said. "Shall we go get it?"

The members of the Charity Knitters did not waste time when yarn was at stake.

"Aren't you afraid someone will see you?" If Josie had noticed these two coming and going from this building, other people would too.

"Well," Helen said, "we have a cover story. If anybody sees us and mentions it—not that anyone has yet—we'll say that we're taking care of the cat I have living up here to keep the mice out of the building. Every once in a while one of us brings up a bag of cat litter or food, just in case someone's watching."

Josie chuckled. "Is there a cat?"

Evelyn shook her head. "But we really are thinking of getting one. We spend a lot of time here, and it would be nice to have a pet."

"Now," Helen said. "Why don't you bring your car around to the back, and we'll relieve you of the burden of Cora's yarn."

Josie descended the stairs, opened the front door gingerly, and looked both ways down Main Street. The coast seemed clear, so she closed the door behind her and went across the street to her car. She drove it around to the alley behind Helen's building and parked it. She hoped Evelyn wouldn't need to make a quick getaway, because Josie's car was blocking her in.

Josie popped open the trunk. The three bags of yarn would require two trips up two flights of stairs. Helen and Evelyn had not offered to help. Well, Josie thought, she was thirty-five years younger than these ladies, and the exercise would do her good.

She pulled two bags out and set them on the ground as she closed the trunk lid. She picked them up again and started her trek up the garishly lit stairwell. Josie squinted at the bright light. There was no consistency in this town. Either the stairs were dim and cobwebby, or blindingly brilliant.

By the time she reached the second-floor landing, her breath was ragged and a painful stitch lanced her side. Seriously? How out of shape was she? Once she got back to New York, it was back to healthier eating and the gym. No more Yankee food.

She set the bags down, stretched her cramped fingers, and picked the bags up in a better grip to continue her trek to the Lair.

Were Evelyn and Helen telling the truth about what they were actually doing in this not-so-abandoned building? And had Cora really been involved? The story had the ring of truth to it. Josie drew a deep breath as she dragged the bags up the last few steps, hoping the plastic wouldn't rupture, but her arms were too tired to lift the bags any higher. She liked Evelyn. Helen, too. She hoped their story was true. And that they weren't going to get themselves into a whole heap of trouble.

A shuffling noise came from behind the door to number four, and Helen opened it. Her eyes fell on one plastic bag, stuffed full, then moved on to the other. "I'll take those," she said, and reached out. The older woman had the moderately heavy bags inside the door in an instant. "Is there more?"

"One more bag. I'll go get it, then I should be on my way. I need to get back to the farm." Helen closed the door unceremoniously.

Josie returned to her car and brought up the last bag, less winded this time. There was no welcoming committee, so she tried the knob with her free hand. It turned easily, and the door swung open.

Evelyn and Helen had dumped the contents of both bags of yarn all over the couch and the small dining table. Their hands flew through the skeins of yarn, touching and sorting. "Ahem." Josie cleared her throat. The ladies didn't look up until she said, louder, "Evelyn? Helen?"

Evelyn looked up, her eyes glassy with yarn lust. Her gaze fell on the third sack. "Just bring that over here, will you, and dump it on the couch with the rest? We'll go through it. And thanks," she added, gratitude clearly an afterthought.

Josie couldn't fault her. She got the same feeling about handbags and designer clothes.

She left the two ladies singlemindedly pawing through the piles. They didn't seem to notice when she opened the door and shut it behind her.

Fifteen minutes later, her car rolled to a stop. She inhaled with a whoosh when she saw a strange truck in Eb's driveway, then let it out when Mitch appeared on the front steps. He raised his hand in a wave as she parked and met him on the porch.

"Sorry," he said. "I hope I didn't scare you. I've got my grandfather's truck this afternoon. Needed to go to the feed store, and we can fit more in the truck than in my SUV."

"Nope, not scared," she fibbed.

"I didn't know what time you were getting back, so I came over to take care of the animals. Hope you don't mind, but I found some of Lorna's meatloaf in the fridge, and I helped myself. There's some left," he said, sheepish.

"That's fine. I'm not very hungry. I'll probably just have a bowl of cereal later."

They stepped inside the house, which for once was not blazing hot. Mitch, it seemed, had a way with woodstoves as well as a way with pets, livestock, and old men. Probably women too, though he'd never mentioned a girlfriend. But if the nurses at the hospital were any indication, he charmed everyone and everything.

"Josie," he began, then faltered. He picked up his dirty plate and silverware from the dining room table and stood there.

"What is it?" She flipped through Eb's mail, which sat on a corner of the table.

"Don't take this the wrong way. But even if the police are about to make an arrest, it's still not made. And I still don't want you staying out here alone. I was thinking I should stay here tonight. On the couch," he added quickly.

Awkward. She barely knew Mitch Woodruff. Her New York sensibilities flashed *Bad Idea* like an illuminated billboard across her mind. But Mitch had proven himself nothing but trustworthy over the last few days. And it *was* a bad idea to stay alone. She supposed Evelyn would offer her a place to stay again tonight. But for some reason, she wanted to stay in the room upstairs. Sleep under the quilt and flannel sheets with Coco curled up on her feet so she couldn't move without disturbing her. After just a few days, the little bedroom she'd commandeered felt like *hers*.

And would she feel more comfortable with or without Mitch downstairs?

More comfortable with, definitely.

"I'd like that," she finally said. "And thanks."

His face relaxed into a smile. This self-assured farmer had been nervous about suggesting the innocent arrangement. It was kind of cute.

"Oh, I meant to tell you. I took a phone message earlier. I put it on the fridge under the Dorset Falls Volunteer Fire Department magnet."

A landline phone message? She couldn't remember the last time she'd gotten one of those. "I suppose I'd better go see who it is."

"It was from Denise Burke's office. She's a lawyer a couple of towns over."

Josie frowned. "A lawyer? Oh! Maybe it's Cora's estate lawyer. My mother's really handling everything for Eb, but I suppose I should return the call. Not that there's probably anything I can do." She glanced down at her watch. "It's just before five. I'll give her a call now."

Mitch went to the kitchen and retrieved the message. He read off the numbers as Josie punched them into her phone, then set the message on the table and excused himself. "I'll go let Jethro out," he said, and left her in privacy.

When Josie identified herself, the receptionist stated that Attorney Burke had left for the day. "Would you like to speak to her assistant? She's still here for a few more minutes."

"Sure." If Denise Burke's assistant was like most assistants in Josie's acquaintance, she would know as much as her boss.

"I'll patch you through."

Two clicks sounded on the line before the assistant picked up. "Sue Davis," she said in a no-nonsense, professional tone of voice.

"Hi, Ms. Davis. This is Josie Blair. Attorney Burke left a message at Eben Lloyd's home."

"Ms. Blair . . . oh yes. Your mother and your great-uncle have authorized us to communicate with you. The attorney wanted to let you know that she's completed her research on the lawsuit we were preparing for Cora before her death. Unfortunately, her heirs do not have standing to continue the suit on her behalf. So we are not going to be able to file the complaint."

Lawsuit? What type of lawsuit could Cora have been involved in?

"I'm afraid I don't know anything about the lawsuit. My mother and my uncle didn't mention it to me, and neither of them is available at the moment. Could you tell me what it was about?"

Josie heard the faint clicking of a keyboard on the other end of the line. "Mrs. Lloyd brought a lawsuit against Tristan Humphries III."

"Trey?" Why would Cora be suing Trey? "What kind of suit?"

"She brought the suit in her capacity as a member of the Dorset Falls Historic Preservation Commission. Her intent was to stop the demolition of 13 Main Street."

Chapter 22

Josie sat down hard on a dining room chair. A puzzle piece had shifted into a new place, and she didn't like the way it fit. Trey owned the building where Miss Marple Knits was housed. He wanted to tear down the building and put up a fast-food restaurant, presumably making a huge profit in the process. But Cora had been ready to file a lawsuit to prevent him from doing it.

As a tenant, Cora probably couldn't do a darn thing if Trey, the owner, wanted to kick her out. But if she'd been a member of the Historic Preservation Commission—and Josie remembered seeing a folder in the morning-borning room marked that, though it had been empty—Cora could try to stop him in her official capacity.

But had Trey tried to stop Cora from thwarting his plans? Permanently? Josie's heart raced.

"Ms. Blair? Are you still there? If you give me your cell number, I'll have the attorney call you. It might not be for a few days. She's in court most of this week."

Josie's mind raced. "Uh, yes. That will be fine." She rang off.

She stared off into space, running what she knew through her mind.

Mitch came back in and sat down at the table across from her. "Josie. What's wrong? Talk to me."

Josie looked past him, then her gaze landed on his face. "Do you know anything about the Historic Preservation Commission?"

Mitch's brow furrowed. "Well, I know they don't have a lot to do. They get involved when someone wants to remodel the kitchen of their colonial home, or put on an addition. Of course, they're on hold right now. Can't do anything with only one out of three members left."

Josie's suspicions were on high alert. "Cora was one. Who are the other members?" She had a sinking feeling she knew who one of the other members had been.

Mitch ran a hand over his chin. "Albert Blandford is the only one left now that Cora and Lillian are dead."

A knot formed in Josie's stomach and pulled tight. There had to be a connection between Cora's and Lillian's deaths. And it wasn't because they were members of the Dorset Falls Charity Knitters Association.

Or because they had designs on her newly rich great-uncle.

It was because they were both members of the Dorset Falls Historic Preservation Commission. Or had been.

And they had stood in the way of Trey Humphries's getting what he wanted.

Trey probably had keys to Miss Marple Knits. He could have lured Lillian there on some pretext. Where had he gotten the murder weapon, the cord made of that distinctive blue yarn? He could have gotten it anywhere, Josie supposed. Cora might even have had it lying around the shop.

Could he have somehow tampered with Cora's car? Disconnected the air bag after Rusty had given the car a clean bill of health, then run her off the road? Josie didn't know how he'd done it, but she did know a couple of things.

Two women were dead.

Trey Humphries had means, motive, and opportunity to have killed both of them.

Mitch reached across the table and put his hand over hers. She refocused, and realized she'd broken out into a light sweat.

"I think I know who killed Lillian Woodruff. And I don't think Cora's car accident was an accident at all." There. She'd said it.

"What? Wait. Let me get you a cold drink. You look like you could use one."

"I don't suppose Eb keeps the ingredients for a cosmo here?" she said hopefully.

Mitch gave a snort. "How about a beer? I saw some in the fridge."

"That'll be fine." She sat back and drew in a deep breath while Mitch was in the kitchen. Thank goodness he was here. Not that she felt like she was in immediate danger. But it seemed likely that if someone had been looking for incriminating evidence at Miss Marple, something he assumed the police had overlooked, like Cora's notebook, the next obvious place—perhaps the only place left—to search would be this farmhouse.

Mitch returned and set a beer and a glass in front of her. Condensation had already formed on the bottle. It was no craft microbrew like she could get in the city, but it was cold and the bitter taste seemed to focus her thoughts. She was right. She knew it.

"Now," Mitch said, "start from the beginning and tell me everything."

She laid out her suspicions. Mitch leaned forward, listening intently. His face was dead serious when she finished.

"You have to take this to the police," he finally said.

"You're right, but I'm not sure they'll listen to me. Detective Potts was less than impressed with the last theory I gave him about Lillian's murder." Her brow furrowed. "Which I guess was pretty far-fetched, now that I think about it. It was so silly, I don't even want to tell you what it was."

Mitch sipped his beer. "You don't have to. But how about Sharla? You could talk to her."

"I'll call her tonight. But it's not like I have any new evidence."

"But you put together what you knew. Just in case, you owe it to Lillian and Cora to say something."

Josie sat up straight. "This Albert. The last member of the Historic Preservation Commission. He's in danger. He's the only person left who could still bring a lawsuit to stop Trey."

She picked up her cell phone and dialed. "Evelyn? Oh, hi. Yes, I'm fine. Say, could you give me Sharla's number?" She paused. "No, of course it's not about that. I just wanted to ask her a question, that's all. Um-hmm. Um-hmm. Great, thanks."

Sharla answered on the second ring. "Hi, Josie. Let me just step out into the hall. I'm watching Andrew take his swim lessons." A moment later, the background noise greatly reduced, she said, "What can I do for you?"

Josie told her what she'd been thinking. "So you have to investigate Trey," she concluded.

There was a longish pause. "Josie, you understand that I can't tell you anything, right?"

"I know."

"So I will just say that we're looking into all angles regarding Lillian's murder. *All* angles. Do you understand what I'm saying?"

Josie breathed a sigh of relief. "So I don't have to worry about this? You've got it?"

There was another pause. "Don't worry," was all Sharla said.

"Okay." Josie met Mitch's eyes and nodded. He'd been

watching her intently. "I won't worry. But what about Albert? You're keeping an eye on him, right?"

Pause. "Don't worry. This will all be over soon. In the meantime, please keep any . . . ideas you have to yourself, okay?"

"I understand. I won't say anything. Thanks, Sharla. I feel much better now."

Mitch gave Josie a quizzical look when she hung up. "Well? What did she say?"

"It was more what she didn't say. We've heard the police were close to making an arrest. Pretty sure we can guess who that's going to be. But she asked me not to tell anyone else. So I have to swear you to secrecy—even though we don't know anything for sure."

"That makes sense. We don't want to jeopardize the investigation or the arrest. My lips are sealed. And Albert? He's safe?"

"It sounds like the police have this well in hand."

Mitch leaned back in his chair. "That's a relief. Dorset Falls isn't Mayberry, but major crime is unusual here just the same."

"How will Eb react, I wonder, when he finds out Cora might have been murdered?"

Mitch shrugged. "Same way Eb reacts to anything, probably. Still, he could have been killed right along with Cora. He'll *have* to feel something—anger, frustration, fear—even if he doesn't express it."

"Well, I guess I'm off the hook until an arrest is made. I told Sharla I'd keep it quiet, and that means from Eb too. What should we do tonight? Watch some television? *Project Runway* is on later."

Mitch raised his eyebrows. "Uh, sure. I'm game."

Josie let out a laugh. It felt good after the tension of the day. "I'm kidding. *Project Runway* is in reruns until the new season starts. But I should work on my sketches. If Eb gets his cast off tomorrow, I could be going back to New York sooner than I thought." Her stomach clenched. Wasn't that what she wanted? To get back to New York?

Mitch's face was impassive. "I've got the new edition of *Alpaca Today* in the truck. I'll keep myself occupied while you work."

"Wow. They have whole magazines devoted to alpacas?"

"They do." He turned toward the kitchen and gave a sharp whistle. "Jethro! Come on." The dog bounded into the room and skidded to a stop at the front door. Mitch followed. "Be right back," he said to Josie.

Josie considered calling the hospital, but decided against it. It wasn't like Eb would want to talk to her—she'd never seen him use a telephone of any kind—and if there was anything she needed to know, the staff would have called her.

By the time Mitch returned, she'd settled herself at the table and gotten to work. He held his magazine in one hand and hesitated by Eb's chair. "Oh, go ahead," she said. "Eb won't mind if you sit there. Or at least, he won't know about it."

Mitch grinned and lowered himself onto the dark orange velour. "Not a bad chair. Squishy." He opened his magazine and began to read.

Josie glanced over at him. Instead of feeling awkward, or uncomfortable, as she would have thought she might, she found that Mitch's presence was comfortable. Comforting, even. As though she'd known him a long time. She gave her head a slight shake and reminded herself, once again, that it was no good getting attached to people or places. Still, she'd made up her mind somewhere in the last few days, though she couldn't have said where or how, to make time to come and visit Eb once she returned to the city. She was fairly sure that under the cantankerous demeanor, he liked her, just a little.

Josie returned to her sketch. She made a few efficient strokes, outlining the puff-sleeved sweater and long slim skirt she'd drafted a few days ago. She added some color, then began to shade in the details. A couple more looks, which she could finish tonight, and she'd have enough to take back to Otto. And maybe, just maybe, she'd finally feel like she was doing what she was supposed to be doing. Josephine Blair—fashion designer. It had a nice ring.

"Well, isn't this cozy?" Josie looked up from her table at the general store into the disdainful face of Diantha Humphries. Just the person she wanted to see while she was eating breakfast. "You don't waste any time, do you?" Diantha turned to Mitch. "Watch out for this one."

"I'll consider myself warned," Mitch said, grinning. He smeared some cream cheese on his toasted bagel and took a bite. "What brings you out on this fine morning?"

Diantha's face creased into a self-satisfied smile. "Oh, just out and about. Preparing for the town council meeting tonight. Big things are going to start happening in Dorset Falls."

Big things or the Big House? Josie wondered how Diantha would take the news when her precious son was arrested for murder. How much did Diantha know, anyway? Was she so secure in her position in Dorset Falls society that she'd condone—or at least look the other way on—two murders? Somehow, Josie didn't think so. But she hoped the police leaned on the old battle-ax pretty hard, just the same. It would be lovely to see Diantha sweat.

Diantha turned to Josie, tapping a finger on the face of her watch. "The clock is ticking. When are you going to be out of that building?"

If Josie's hackles weren't already up, they were at attention now. *Keep it calm, Josie. Don't let her bait you.* She smiled sweetly. "Oh, any day now. Don't you worry. I'll be out on time."

"See that you are." Diantha turned on her heel and walked out, her large red leather purse swinging in a slow arc in her wake.

Mitch and Josie exchanged a glance. Neither one could say

aloud in this public place what he or she was thinking, but words seemed unnecessary. *She'll get what's coming to her.* Josie wished there were something she could do to make that happen.

"I should be going," Mitch said after swallowing the last bite of his bagel and draining his coffee. "I promised my cousins I'd meet them at the funeral home to help finalize the arrangements for Aunt Lillian. You—" His gaze held hers. "Be careful and don't go anywhere alone."

Josie nodded. "I know, I know. And I happen to agree with you. I hate to ask, but would you go with me to the hospital to pick up Eb this afternoon? He likes you more than he likes me."

Mitch gave a soft chuckle. "Not true. But of course I'll help. How about if I pick you up here around one?"

"Sounds great. See you then."

Josie watched his tall form as Mitch retreated out the door.

Maybe there *was* something she could do to make sure Trey, and Diantha, if necessary, got what was coming to them.

But first she needed to take care of some business. She fired off a text to Monica. *Need buyer's phone number ASAP.* Why had Monica not sent the number the first time Josie asked? Monica must have it, or at least an e-mail address, if she was communicating with him or her.

Josie pulled a manila folder from her tote bag sitting on the chair next to her. "Lorna?"

Lorna looked up from wiping the counter. "What's up? You had an interesting breakfast companion this morning." She raised an eyebrow.

"Oh, stop. Totally innocent." But Josie felt a warm tingle just the same. Mitch was good-looking, and good company. If he lived in the city, she would have enjoyed getting to know him a little better. *If you lived here, you could get to know him.* She put the thought aside.

Josie set her stack of drawings on the clean surface of the

counter. "Do you have time now to scan these so I can send them to my boss in New York?"

"Sure, but only if I can look at them first." Lorna dried her hands on her apron and spun the drawings so they were right side up. She sucked in a breath. "Are you kidding me? These are gorgeous!"

Josie's heart swelled, just a little. Validation was something she'd not experienced much of while working for Otto Heinrich. Of course, it remained to be seen what Otto would think. A strange feeling came over her, one she struggled to identify. And then it came to her. Confidence. Confidence in her own ability. Did it really matter what Otto thought? *She* liked the drawings. Unfortunately, that did not pay the bills.

"Thanks. I have a flash drive. Can you put the document on it?"

"Coming right up." After checking to see that she didn't have any customers lurking at the counter, Lorna took the drawings and the flash drive to the back of the store, where the combination scanner-copier-fax machine sat along the back wall. She came back a few minutes later and handed the items back to Josie. "Here you go. Knock him dead!"

Josie grinned, replacing the drawings into the folder and sliding it into her bag next to her laptop. "There's no Wi-Fi here, is there?"

"Hardly. I've been trying to get Dougie to put it in, but even the argument that it will bring in customers hasn't worked. There's public Wi-Fi at the library."

"Thanks. I'll be back in later." But Josie wasn't going to the library. She was headed for the Lair.

Chapter 23

Josie walked briskly down Main Street, pausing only slightly at the door to the ladies' secret hideout. Better to go around back and use the alley door. One of Cora's keys must fit it. Josie was aware that she was breaking her promise to Mitch again, but it was only temporary. Once she got upstairs she would call Evelyn and ask her to come in.

Josie tried several keys on Cora's ring before she found the one that worked. She slipped inside, closing the door behind her, and began her march up the two flights of moderately steep stairs. At least this time she wasn't carrying awkward bags of yarn.

She knocked softly on the door to Apartment 4. When no one answered, she tried several keys until the door swung open.

The couch, chair, and coffee table were still covered in piles of yarn, but now the piles were neatly sorted by color and style. There was no need to call Evelyn. She was in the control room with her back to the door, her headphones firmly in place. A video feed played on one of the monitors in front of her. Evelyn stiffened, then turned around slowly. "Josie! You gave me a fright. What are you doing here?"

"I could ask you the same thing," she replied, "but I'm not sure I want to know. I didn't see your car in the alley."

"It's parked at Helen's house, a block away. She convinced me it would be better to leave it there and come on foot. She's probably right, even though Main Street is dead as a post."

Josie replied, "I was hoping to use your Wi-Fi to send an e-mail?" She showed her friend the laptop she'd brought with her.

Evelyn seemed to relax. "Of course. Set up anywhere you like. The password is Bondgirl61." She went back to her surveillance.

Josie sat down at the small table that held the first computer she'd seen yesterday, the one that had been playing the loop of Josie herself in Rusty's car repair shop. She moved that laptop aside and opened her own. As she waited for her machine to boot up, she watched the other screen. The camera remained trained on Rusty's counter. He stood behind it, copper-red head down, typing. There was no sound. Perhaps this splinter group of the Dorset Falls Charity Knitters Association had not yet bought sound recording equipment from Spygrannies.com. Rusty looked up, and his face fell into a frown when a woman approached the counter. Although the woman's back was to the camera, Josie would have bet money it was Courtney, Trey's wife. She put her keys on the counter, leaving her hand out . . . why? Just in case he wanted to pick it up and kiss it? Josie couldn't tell if this was old footage or new. She shook her head and returned to her own computer.

She pulled up her e-mail, deleting all the junk as the flash drive engaged with a soft whir. *Otto,* she typed. *Am so excited about these new designs. Let me know what you think. I should be back next week, and I'll finish the collection.* She attached the file with the drawings, paused a moment, and hit *send*. There. It was out of her hands.

A red light blinked from the coffeemaker in the kitchen. She got up, poured herself a cup, and sat back down. Reaching into her tote bag, she pulled out the instruction manual Helen had given to her yesterday. The one that explained the tracking devices Cora, Evelyn, and Helen had somehow managed to place on the cars driven by members of the Humphries family.

She clicked on the desktop icon on the Lair laptop. Scanning the shortcuts lined up in a neat row along the left side, she double clicked on the one marked *GrannyTrack*. A screen opened up, and her heart sank. Evelyn had been right. This program might not be terribly user-friendly. Still, she'd give it a whirl.

Thumbing through the pages of the manual, she skipped over the section on "Installing the GrannyTrack Device." Presumably, they'd figured that part out. Ah, here it was. "Downloading Data." She followed the instructions, which turned out to be not that difficult for someone who had grown up around computers, like Josie. Punching in a few more keystrokes, she was rewarded when three columns of data filled the screen.

Each column contained dates and times written in military format, along with what appeared to be GPS coordinates. When the columns finished populating, a pop-up appeared on the screen. *Interpret Coordinates?* Sure. Why not? She didn't bother to look up what that meant in the manual, just clicked *Yes*. The columns shifted, and a line appeared in orange under each entry. Street addresses.

Josie sat back, satisfied and horrified at the same time. She'd figured this out fairly easily. But it was unsettling to think that this kind of technology was available to just anybody. There could be a tracking device on her car right now, and she wouldn't even know it.

She scanned the data more closely, then shook her head. Evelyn would be a pretty incompetent surveiller if she handed Josie the instruction manual and asked her to download data on herself. But that didn't mean somebody else couldn't have done it. She tried to put the thought out of her head. There was no discernible reason anyone would want to be following her.

Josie took a sip of her coffee, then got up and went into the control room. She touched Evelyn lightly on the shoulder. The older woman started, then punched a button on her keyboard, which paused the screen in front of her. Evelyn removed her headphones and spun around to Josie.

Her eyes lit up. "Did you figure it out?"

"I did. I'm not sure I know what it means, but you'll want to take a look at it."

Evelyn rose and hustled over to the screen. Josie pointed to one of the columns. "I assume there's one column for each car, but I'm not sure how we'll tell which one is which."

Evelyn leaned in, adjusting her reading glasses. The brightly beaded chain around each earpiece swung as she did so. "Easy," she declared. "Column 1 is Trey. See where he's mostly been the last few days? To his office at the insurance agency and home. Column 2 must be Diantha. She's made a number of trips to 121 Main Street. That's the town hall."

"So the third column must be Courtney. She's been all over. Isn't that the address of Rusty's car repair shop? And look how many times she's been to this address in Uncasville, wherever that is."

Evelyn rolled her eyes. "That's Mohegan Sun. The casino. Personally, I prefer Foxwoods, but to each her own. She's probably having lunch there, then heading over to the outlet malls. That seems to be her favorite pastime."

"So have you caught anything on video?" Josie said. She'd hoped to find something she could use to tip off the police, give them something to go on, without actually revealing the existence of any of these tapes and digital files. She didn't want to blow the ladies' cover or, worse yet, get them into legal trouble.

"No." Evelyn frowned. "Rusty seems to be resisting Courtney's advances. I'm glad for his wife, of course, but it's a little disappointing. We wanted dirt on Courtney and Trey to try to disgrace Diantha, but so far, we've got nothing."

Which meant Josie had nothing. Well, it had been worth a try. She looked at her watch. It was time to go to the hospital to see about Eb.

Josie walked back to the general store to wait for Mitch. She was sitting at a table tapping her fingers, thinking about what she'd just seen, when he walked in. "Ready to go?" he asked.

"As I'll ever be. I miss Eb."

Mitch grinned as he helped her into her jacket. "I do too. And it's been tough keeping Eb's whereabouts secret from my grandfather. Although from the smug look he's been wearing the last couple of days, I'm pretty sure he knows."

"I just need to stop at my car and pick up the bag of clean clothes I packed for him."

Mitch drove around the block and parked in front of Josie's car. She got out and popped open her trunk, giving a long look to the façade of Miss Marple Knits. Its dark, empty windows contrasted with the bright blue front door, and she felt a pang of sadness. The town meeting was tonight. The meeting that would decide the fate of this old building. She gritted her teeth in frustration. There wasn't a darn thing she could do to save it. The town council was apparently stacked in favor of Trey's petition, and even though Diantha would have to abstain from the vote due to her relationship with Trey, from everything Josie had heard around town, the vote was a shoo-in. She wouldn't even be allowed to get up and speak her mind since she wasn't a resident of Dorset Falls.

She pulled the overnight bag out of her trunk. Something farther back caught her eye. Oh, right. The box of yarn Rusty had given her, the one from the trunk of Cora's wrecked car. Josie pulled it forward. When she got back, she would run this box up to the Lair. Josie had a feeling that there would never be a saturation point for Evelyn and Helen. No amount of yarn could satisfy their lust. She closed the lid, wondering if this was how crack dealers felt.

"The town meeting is tonight," Josie said.

Mitch nodded, pulling out of the parking spot. "I plan to be there. You coming?"

"There doesn't seem to be much point. They wouldn't let me speak. And even if they did, nobody knows me here. What could I possibly say to sway a town council whose mind is already made up?" She blew out a frustrated breath.

Mitch was silent for a moment. "You might not be able to speak, but there are plenty of people who could. I've already made some phone calls asking people to attend the meeting. They don't have to listen to us, of course, but at least we'll have tried."

"But," she said, catching her lower lip between her teeth, "as ugly as it's going to be—and I'm just playing devil's advocate here—maybe the town would be better off with a restaurant on the corner. It would create jobs. It might even bring in people from the highway, if signs were put up." She didn't believe it, but felt like she had to put it out there.

"Nope." She turned toward Mitch as he shook his head. "A fast-food restaurant won't save this town."

Josie felt relief and sadness at the same time. "Can anything?"

"Bringing back small businesses to Main Street, that's what we need."

"Small specialty shops," she mused. "Like Miss Marple Knits. To attract tourists. Leaf peepers."

"Skiers. There's an old ski slope a couple of miles north. I've always hoped someone would come in with some money and get it going again. And we've got an old sleigh out in one of our barns. I'd love to fix that up and give sleigh rides in the winter."

Josie smiled. Such a lovely picture they were painting of a

charming Connecticut Main Street, restored to its former bustling glory. If there were a restaurant or two, and enough lodging, a boutique hotel, perhaps, and some bed-and-breakfasts, people would come up from the city for weekend getaways. It wasn't so far out of the realm of possibility.

And tonight's town council vote could take away that potential forever.

Josie was surprised when they pulled into the hospital parking lot, she'd been so lost in thought. Nurse Capocci waved at them as they passed her on the way to the elevators.

"Let's hope he's ready to go," Josie said.

"Eb was ready to go the minute he got here," Mitch replied. "But the prospect of getting that cast off must have made it tolerable."

Eb was sitting up in a chair when they got to the room. His pale, hairy legs were bare over gray slippers, one leg noticeably thinner than the other. The cast was gone.

He glared at them from under those eyebrows, which had not gotten any less bushy in the time he'd been here. "About time you showed up. I've been ready for an hour."

A doctor Josie had not met before came in and stuck out his hand. "Doctor Robbins," he said in a hearty voice. "The orthopedist."

Josie took the proffered hand, which the doctor pumped up and down. "So my uncle is good to go?" She glanced at Eb, who was fidgeting in the chair.

"I'm only good to go if you brought me some damn clothes," Eb growled.

Mitch held up the bag so Eb could see it. "Josie thinks of everything."

"Hmmph," Eb said. "Give 'em to me so I can get dressed."

The doctor chuckled. "Hold on a moment, Mr. Lloyd. I need to give you your discharge instructions. Which you will follow," he added, his voice suddenly taking on a commanding timbre, "to the letter, unless you want to end up back in a cast. And next time, I'll make you stay in it longer."

Eb sat there, frowning. "Out with it, then." Turning to Josie, he said, "You take notes."

The doctor rattled off some instructions. "But don't worry about remembering everything. It's all written down." He handed a sheet of paper to Josie. "Just have him get dressed, and then call the nurse. And stop at the window on your way out and have whoever's on duty give you an appointment for physical therapy and a follow-up in two weeks."

As soon as the doctor left, Eb was on his feet. The man was wiry and agile, even at diminished capacity. She bet he was a force to be reckoned with when he was at full throttle. Eb grabbed the handle of the overnight bag and raced for the bathroom.

"Guess he's ready to go," Mitch drawled.

Josie laughed. "Guess so." She read the instructions. "Nothing too onerous here. Ooh, he'll love this part: Use of a cane is recommended for the next two weeks until strength returns to the muscles of the leg."

The bathroom door opened, and Eb stepped out, fully dressed, in a pair of dark blue, sturdy-looking pants, a green T-shirt with a yellow John Deere tractor logo on the front, and a blue and white plaid flannel shirt unbuttoned over the top. He wouldn't win any fashion awards, but he looked comfortable. "Where's my cap?" he accused.

"Oh, I forgot. Wait, didn't you come in wearing one? It must be here somewhere." Josie located a plastic bag. "Here it is. And it could have been worse, Eb. At least I brought you a pair of shoes, since you came in here only wearing one."

"Hmmph. Get moving. I want to see my dog."

Mitch chuckled. "Jethro misses you, too. I'll go get the nurse."

He returned a few minutes later with a nurse, who was followed by an orderly pushing a wheelchair.

Eb's lips were set in a hard line. "Nope." He glared at the wheelchair as if it were an actual person, not an innocent, inanimate object.

The orderly smiled, showing a lot of very white teeth. "Yup!" he said. "You ride, or you're our guest forever. We're like the Hotel California. What'll it be?" He gave the wheelchair a little push toward Eb.

"Just do it," Josie said. "You want to leave, right? It's for five minutes, tops."

Eb's scowl deepened. He stalled, apparently considering, then finally gave in and lowered himself into the chair.

"Feet in the stirrups," the orderly said, checking the position of Eb's lower extremities. "Let's go." The orderly wheeled Eb around and rolled him out the door. "Race you to the elevators," he called over his shoulder.

Mitch picked up the bag of clothes Eb had come in with and stuffed it inside the bag Josie had packed earlier. "I was a track star in high school. I could beat them. But today they win," he said. "Ready?"

Josie gave one last look around. The room appeared to be empty of all Eb's personal effects. "Ready," she said. "Let's get the old boy home."

Mitch left to bring his SUV around under the canopy. Josie made Eb's appointment, while Eb sat fidgeting, tapping his knobby fingers on the arm of the wheelchair. The glass doors slid open with a barely audible *snick* and the orderly—his name was Bentley, according to his name tag—wheeled Eb out. Bentley settled him in the front seat, while Josie climbed into the back. Mitch pulled away as Josie waved to Bentley. Eb stared straight ahead.

"Do you have a cane at home?" Mitch asked. "Otherwise I'll stop at a pharmacy on the way home, and we'll pick one up."

Eb harrumphed. "I ain't using a cane."

"Oh yes you are," Josie piped up. "Two weeks. That's what

the doctor said. You want to fall and break a hip out of sheer stubbornness? Then you'll be laid up until summer. And I am *not* coming back here to bale your hay or take care of your pumpkins." Secretly, she thought she might come back for a few days in the fall, if Eb would allow it. Pumpkins made her happy.

Mitch must have taken Eb's refusal to say anything more as acquiescence, because he pulled in at a drugstore and parked. "I'll go in," Josie said. "I need a couple of items myself." She was low on shampoo, and she needed deodorant too.

When she came back out a few minutes later and stowed herself and her purchases—including a cane—in the SUV, Eb and Mitch were arguing good-naturedly about the chances of the Yankees winning a pennant this year. It was Greek to her. She didn't know anything about sports teams, but Mitch and Eb seemed to be enjoying themselves.

"Find everything you needed?" Mitch said, putting the car into reverse and backing out expertly.

"Yes." A grunt of disgust came from the front seat. "It's only for a little while, Eb. Cheer up. You're cleared to drive again."

"Woodruff better not have been anywhere near my truck while I've been on vacation," Eb said darkly.

"He's been busy splitting and stacking wood in the sugarhouse," Mitch said. "But I'll take a look at your truck before you drive it if you want." He pulled the SUV out onto the two-lane state route heading back to Dorset Falls.

Josie didn't need to see Eb's face to know that his hairy eyebrows were drawn together. The conversation in the front seat continued about maple syrup and trucks. "Whaddya think about the new Chevys? Might buy one," Eb said.

That reminded Josie. She pulled out her cell phone and punched in Monica's number. *Still waiting for buyer's phone number. Need ASAP!!!* She hoped Monica was all right. It wasn't like her to ignore a text.

Her cell phone gave a little chirp, indicating a new message. *Buyer arranging for movers. Will call you when it's in place, probably tomorrow.*

Okay, Josie texted back, although it was anything but. If the new owner of the contents of the yarn shop didn't contact her tomorrow, she'd have to start identifying city yarn shops and making calls to potential buyers herself. Monica had already gone above and beyond the duties of friendship for her, and there was no more time to waste waiting on a deal that showed no signs of happening. Eb might have to wait a little longer for his new truck.

When they pulled into Eb's driveway twenty minutes later and Mitch shut off the engine, Josie could hear Jethro's muffled howl coming from inside the house. She smiled. Man and dog would be together again. The cane hadn't been removed from its packaging, so Josie was grateful when Mitch innocently came around to Eb's side of the SUV and walked alongside him up onto the sagging front porch and escorted him inside.

Josie grabbed her bag from the drugstore, her tote bag, and her purse, then shouldered the strap of the duffel bag she'd brought Eb's boots and clean clothes in. Mitch met her at the door of the house and reached for one of the bags. "Sorry," he said. "I was coming back out to help."

She smiled at him, feeling a surge of gratitude. "I'm fine. Thanks for helping Eb. And for everything you've done for us," she added.

"My pleasure." Mitch tilted his head to one side. "Well, maybe not a pleasure," he said, lowering his voice so Eb wouldn't overhear. Not that Eb would have minded. Josie was pretty sure Eb enjoyed his reputation as a curmudgeon. "But I've known Eb since I was a kid. And I need him back in commission so he can keep my grandfather occupied. Roy's been at loose ends since Eb's been running on reduced power."

When she entered the house, she found Eb already in his armchair, Jethro stretched out on the floor by his side, panting and looking up adoringly with his big brown eyes at Eb, who stroked his head. "How about some coffee?" Eb said in her direction.

"Tea?" Lorna still hadn't gotten to the big-box store to get Josie the automatic drip machine.

Mitch laughed. "I could go for some coffee, too, Eb. I'll start the percolator." He grinned at Josie, and she grinned back.

"Guess I'll watch how you make it this time," she said, a bit sheepishly. "Eb, will you be all right here if I run into town this afternoon? I need to check on some things at the shop." No sense borrowing trouble by telling him the yarn deal wasn't yet solid. But she planned to scrounge as many boxes as she could from Lorna at the general store, just in case she had to empty the storeroom herself. And she'd get Eb his oatmeal raisin cookies while she was at it.

Mitch raised his eyebrows. "You should call Evelyn to meet you there," he said. "Or I can come with you."

Josie nodded. "I'll call Evelyn."

Chapter 24

"Thanks, Lorna," Josie said.

Lorna, bless her, had a number of boxes in the back of the store. "I've been stockpiling them, just in case you needed them," she said. "Are you going to the town meeting tonight?"

Josie frowned. "I'm not sure. It might be frustrating, not being allowed to speak my opinion. Not that my opinion really matters, I guess. I don't live here."

"Well, if you're not doing anything else, maybe you could come anyway. I'm trying to get as many Dorset Falls-ites to go as I can. The more people who see and understand what Trey is trying to do, the better. And extra bodies at the meeting won't hurt."

Josie took the bag of a dozen oversized cookies Lorna handed her, and put some cash on the counter. "I'll think about it."

Lorna glanced around. The store was mostly empty. "Come on. I'll help you load some of these boxes into your car. You can come back for the rest later."

When they got outside, balancing boxes, Josie popped open the trunk of her car. She shoved in one of her boxes, but met resistance. She shoved a little harder, but the box still wouldn't go in, so she set it on the ground and looked inside.

Ah. The last box of Cora's yarn—or at least the last of Cora's stash that Josie had located. The one that Rusty had pulled from the trunk of Cora's wrecked car. Josie reached in and dragged it forward on the carpet, then took it out. It was heavier than she had expected it would be, and something slid around on the bottom of the box. Something definitely unyarnlike. Probably a small tool kit or emergency supplies Cora kept in her trunk. Or just a weight of some kind—pattern books, maybe—to keep the box from tipping over. She handed the box to Lorna and asked her to put it on the front seat.

They loaded up as many boxes as would fit, then Lorna stood up straight, wiping her hands on her apron. "I should get back inside. Looks like a customer just arrived."

"Thanks for the help," Josie said. "And I'll think about coming to the meeting tonight." Lorna waved, then headed back to the store.

Josie drove around the block and parked in front of Miss Marple Knits. Would it hurt to go in alone, just to unload? She chewed her lower lip. It was probably a dumb move. Instead, she texted Evelyn. *Have more yarn. Can you meet me?*

An immediate text came back. *Already at the Lair. Come on up. Erase this text.*

Josie smiled. Evelyn took her spy stuff seriously. Josie hit *delete*.

Checking both directions to make sure there were no cars or pedestrians on the street who might see her, Josie carried the box around to the alley behind Helen's building and went upstairs. If someone did see her, she would keep it simple and say Helen had asked her to look in on the cat. It was as good an excuse as any. It might even fly.

Evelyn met her at the door, taking the box from her hands. "Come in," she said cheerfully. Was there yarn lust in her eyes?

It was not as intense as Josie had seen before, maybe due to the fact that there were only a dozen or so skeins. But there was a definite gleam.

Josie had barely taken off her jacket and laid it over the back of one of the plastic-covered armchairs—which was still full of the sorted yarn from the morning-borning room at Eb's farmhouse—when Evelyn turned the box over and dumped the contents on the couch.

"Yes!" Evelyn did a very uncharacteristic fist pump. "Here it is!"

Josie leaned in closer. Lying on top of the pile of yarn was a black three-ring binder. That had been the weight in the bottom of the box. Evelyn locked eyes with her.

"Cora's notebook," they said in unison. Evelyn hesitated a moment, then handed it to Josie. "You should be the one to look at it first," Evelyn said.

"We'll look at it together," Josie said firmly. "Come on over to the table, and we'll see what it says."

Prickles of anticipation raced up Josie's arms. Would this simple black binder contain evidence that would cement the police's case against Trey? She flipped it open, and she and Evelyn began to read.

But there was a problem. At least for Josie. Cora had dutifully noted the customer's name—and the members of the Dorset Falls Charity Knitters Association made up the majority—the quantity, the price, and a description of the yarn bought in each transaction. But Josie knew nothing about brands of yarn. If someone had bought a skein of the blue yarn that had been fashioned into the murder weapon, she'd never recognize it. Reluctantly, she handed the notebook to Evelyn.

"You'll have to do it," she said. "I'm no help."

Evelyn *tsked*. "Nonsense. You take half and look for the color name; that way, we can narrow it down. It'll be something like 'Azure Skies' or 'Ocean Variegated.' Something that sounds blue." She opened the binder rings with a snap and handed Josie half of the contents.

They scanned the pages for several minutes. Josie dogeared the corner of any pages that contained a promising color name. When Evelyn finished her stack, she could check Josie's pages to see if she recognized the correct brand. The entries abruptly cut off six weeks ago—Cora's last sale had been to Helen Crawford, who bought something called Cuddles sport weight, peach variegated, 2 skeins.

But there were still papers in the binder to peruse, after the sales data cut off. The next was titled *The History of Needlework,* by Cora Lloyd. Josie smiled as she thumbed through the sheets of lined paper, covered in a beautiful handwritten script. Cora had been writing a reference book.

Before Josie could show it to Evelyn, her companion let out a whoop. "This is it. It has to be. 'Paca-Sheep Softie, worsted weight, aurora borealis, 1 skein." Her eyes met Josie's, triumphant. "And guess whom it was sold to?" she trilled.

Josie's heart rate ticked up. "Don't keep me in suspense, Evelyn. Whom?" Josie leaned forward.

"Diantha Humphries!"

Josie smiled. Gotcha, Trey. That put the murder weapon squarely within Trey's grasp. Diantha had made the cord for whatever reason, to tie back a curtain or something, and Trey had taken it from her house. Or Diantha had made it and given it to Trey, perhaps to use in his office. There could be any number of scenarios, but Josie would leave it to the police to figure out the details. "Shall we call Sharla?"

Evelyn looked thoughtful. "Sharla's chaperoning Andrew's field trip to the butterfly conservatory today. I'd rather not bother her."

"Well, Detective Potts it is, then. But I'll say it was Sharla's idea to look for the notebook in the first place."

Evelyn nodded, satisfied. "But let's be thorough before you

call him. I'll go through the rest of the entries, just to be sure." She began to flip pages from the rest of her stack, then Josie's. When she finished, she said, "That's it." She rubbed her hands together, gleeful. "Oh, wait until I tell Helen! Diantha will be so mortified, she'll step down immediately. Her day has finally come." Evelyn reached into the pocket of her sweater, presumably for her phone.

"We should probably hold off telling anyone other than Detective Potts," Josie said.

Evelyn nodded. "I suppose you're right. I know! I'll invite Helen over for dinner tonight and make it a surprise. Do you want to come?"

"I'd love to, but I shouldn't. Eb came home from the hospital today."

The older woman clapped her hands again. "Wonderful! Did the cast come off? I'll bring over another casserole."

"Uh, that would be lovely. Could you make it for the freezer, though? I just bought a lot of groceries." A small fib was okay in the name of friendship, right? And, she realized, she could count Evelyn as a friend, now that Josie's suspicions had been erased with the discovery of the additional evidence against Trey. It felt good.

Josie pulled out her cell phone. She dialed Detective Potts's number. "Detective? It's Josie Blair. I've discovered something that might help the investigation into Lillian Woodruff's death. Can you call me?" She rang off.

"Shouldn't we just take it to the police station?" Evelyn said.

"I thought about that. But I'm not comfortable delivering this to anyone other than Detective Potts, or Sharla if she's available. They . . . think I'm a kook down at the station, and I don't want them sticking this on a shelf and forgetting about it."

"I'm sure that's not true, dear." Evelyn patted Josie's hand.

Josie was sure it was, and the proof of it stood in front of her. Evelyn had been one of the ladies she'd suspected of bumping off other ladies in an effort to get at Eb and his money. If Detective Potts thought Josie was a kook, well, there might have been a grain of truth in it.

"Well, just to be sure, I'll wait for him personally."

"Whatever you think is best. Now. I think Helen left brownies here yesterday. Let's have one to celebrate."

Josie adjusted the flame under the pan, then gave the turkey and rice stew she'd brought home from the general store a stir. Detective Potts still had not called, confirming her suspicion that he thought she was a flake. She dished up the stew and took two bowls to the dining room table, which had grown another crop of stuff in the few hours since Eb had been home. Finding a more or less clear spot, she set them down.

Eb got up with alacrity and came to the table. She'd given in about the cane, which he refused to use around the house. It had become clear that it was always best to pick her battles with Eb. As long as he used the cane outside on the rough or icy ground, he'd probably be okay.

Eb slurped up some stew. "Pretty good," he said, breaking off a piece of roll and dipping it in.

Josie put the spoon in her bowl and made figure-eight patterns. Her stomach was jumpy, and probably would be until she turned over that notebook, which was currently locked in the trunk of her Saab. She pushed the bowl away. It was no use. She couldn't eat until this was taken care of. "Eb, I'm going into town tonight. Will you be all right?"

He looked at her from under the ledge of his eyebrows. "I think I can take care of myself. But," he said, taking another bite of stew, "I'm going into town too. Council meeting."

Josie had planned to drive around town looking for Detective Potts's unmarked police car. As tempting as it was, she'd decided not to go to the meeting. She didn't think she could face Trey without giving something away. But she couldn't very well take Eb with her on her mission to find Detective Potts. Eb would pump her for information and might not take "no comment" for an answer.

He stared at her. "I'll drive myself."

"What? No." The man had just come home from the hospital today. He shouldn't be driving.

"I'll drive myself," he repeated. "Doc said I could do my normal activities. And driving is one of my normal activities."

She blew out a sigh. There was no way to stop him if he was determined to do it, which it appeared he was. "Fine. I had no idea you were so interested in local politics. What time are you going?"

"Meeting's at seven. No sense getting there early." He went back to his dinner.

Josie calculated. That meant he'd leave about six forty-five, which would give her plenty of time, if she left now, to look for Potts, then come back and secretly follow Eb into town. She could park down the road, toward the Woodruff farm, and watch for him to pull out. It would work.

"I'm going now," she announced. "Leave the dishes, and I'll tend to them later."

Josie drove into Dorset Falls, keeping her eyes open for the unmarked car. But she quickly realized her plan was flawed. It was after five o'clock, and it was February in Connecticut. Which meant night had already fallen, making the job of identifying any car much more difficult. She took a few turns around the block, and went down a few side streets, but she didn't even know where the detective lived. This had not been one of her brighter ideas.

Parking at the police station, she steeled herself and went inside.

Officer Denton sat in all his beefy glory behind the glass

window. His eyebrows rose when he saw her. "What is it now, Ms. Blair?"

She cleared her throat. "I'm looking for Detective Potts."

One eyebrow lowered. "Why?" he drawled.

"I have something I need to talk to him about, okay? Is he here?" She was pretty sure Officer Denton knew all about her previous theory.

"He's not."

Jerk. This train was headed for Frustrationville. There was no sense leaving a message. She'd already done that on Potts's cell phone. "Thanks," she said. "You've been a big help."

He grinned. "We aim to please, Ms. Blair."

She spun on her heel and went back to the Saab, cheeks burning despite the cold air.

Chapter 25

The parking lot of the town hall was full when she pulled in. She'd driven around the block so as not to arrive at the same time as Eb, and watched him from a distance as he ascended the stone steps, cane in hand. Not on the ground, but in his hand. She couldn't force him to use it, but at least he'd brought it with him.

Josie glanced around the parking lot. Jackpot. If she wasn't mistaken, Detective Potts's car sat under the yellow glare of a streetlight.

That settled it. Trey or no Trey, she was going to the town meeting.

The meeting room was packed. Eb had found—or someone had given him—an aisle seat. Josie found an empty seat a couple of rows back. She looked around.

Diantha sat facing the townsfolk, her back straight as a board and her face wearing a smug expression. She was clearly in her element, lording it over the little people. Dougie Brewster sat next to her, a placard reading MAYOR BREWSTER next to a glass of water in front of him. The other members of the council, none of whom Josie recognized, fanned out along the crescent-shaped dais.

Lorna waved when she saw Josie, then shrugged as if to apologize for not being able to sit with her. Evelyn and Helen sat toward the front, and even though their backs were to Josie, it was clear from the rise and fall of their shoulders that they were knitting away. Josie looked to her left, and her eyes fell on Courtney. She was also knitting, her head bent in concentration. Trey sat next to her, fidgeting. Since his item was last on the agenda, he had a long evening ahead of him. As did everyone else in the room, Josie supposed.

Detective Potts sat in the last row, in an end seat right in front of the door. She put her purse on her chair to hold the place and made her way toward him.

He looked up as she approached, his face unreadable. Sharla Coogan, in full uniform, entered the room at the same time, and stood along the wall on one side. Her eyes locked with Josie's. Josie gave a tiny nod of acknowledgment. Then she returned her gaze to Officer Potts.

"Could I talk to you? It'll only take a minute."

Potts's lips were set in a hard line. He shook his head, almost imperceptibly. "I got your voice mail. I'll call you tomorrow."

"It's . . . important."

"Not now," he growled through gritted teeth. "Go sit down."

What the heck was going on? She looked from Sharla to Detective Potts. There was no need to have police presence at a town meeting, was there? Not unless they were expecting trouble.

Or unless they were planning to make an arrest. In which case they already had enough evidence for a warrant. Cora's notebook would help, but it apparently wasn't absolutely necessary to the case.

"Okay," she said. "Call me when you can." She returned to her seat, just as Mitch and Roy came in. They located seats and sat down. Mitch smiled when he saw her, and she returned the smile.

Dougie Brewster looked at the big round wall clock behind

him. At the stroke of seven, he rapped a gavel on the table in front of him. "Dorset Falls town council meeting is called to order. First order of business . . ."

He droned on, his speech occasionally punctuated by other members of the council giving their opinions. The heat was turned up in the room, and Josie wiped a bead of sweat from her forehead. Moments later, her chin dropped toward her chest, and she jerked it back up. Wow. No wonder people avoided these meetings. They were dead boring. Her mind wandered.

"Next item. Vacancies on the Historic Preservation Commission."

Diantha piped up. "I move that we table till the next meeting. We're still interviewing candidates."

Dougie pulled at his chin, making a show of thinking about his response. He looked into the front row. "Albert, are there any pending applications that would be unreasonably delayed by tabling this item for another month?"

A man in the front row stood up. "I suppose not." He sat down. It appeared Albert and Eb were cut from the same cloth.

"Second," one of the council members Josie didn't know said.

Josie was livid. It was crystal clear what was happening here. By not appointing new members to the Historic Preservation Commission, the town council had hamstrung it. The only person with standing to bring a suit to stop Trey's demolition was one old man, Albert Blandford, who, if he wasn't already, should be afraid for his life.

Josie wanted desperately to jump up and protest. But she looked over at Detective Potts and Sharla, and clamped down on her impulses. They had things under control, it appeared, and she wasn't about to mess things up for them.

"Motion carried," Dougie Brewster said. "Next item."

As the meeting dragged on, people began to trickle out. Diantha's and Dougie's tactic of putting Trey's application last on the agenda seemed to be working. Now that the room had emptied a bit, Josie had a clear view of Rusty who, even sitting, towered over everyone in the room. Courtney looked up occasionally from her knitting to stare at the back of Rusty's head. Trey shifted in his seat, then shifted again, but kept his eyes focused straight ahead. Sharla and Detective Potts remained in their positions, faces impassive.

Finally, Dougie Brewster sat back in his chair. "Final item. Demolition permit requested for 13 Main Street. Permit issued by the building department, requires council approval."

Trey sat up straighter. Courtney continued to knit, keeping her eyes on her work.

"Is there any discussion?" Dougie said.

Albert stood up and made his way to the chair, small table, and microphone facing the members of the council. He adjusted the microphone and, as he did so, a ring of keys fell to the carpet from his pocket with a soft metallic jingle. He bent down, picked them up, and put them on the table in front of him.

"State your name and address for the record," Dougie said.

"Albert Blandford. 235 Ashworth Drive."

"Proceed." Diantha glared at Albert from one direction, while Trey glared at him from behind.

"As the sole member of the Historic Preservation Commission, I object to this permit's being granted. If Mr. Humphries wants a chicken joint in town, he doesn't have to knock down a hundred-year-old building to do it. He'd be better off putting it out on the connector road."

A murmur went up around the room. If the remaining folks of Dorset Falls had been bored into comas by the meeting, they were awakening now. Heads began to nod in agreement with Albert's words.

Josie glanced at Sharla and Detective Potts. Their stances had changed, stiffened. Both appeared to be on high alert. Trey was clearly nervous. Courtney continued to look at her knitting, secure, perhaps, in the knowledge that the approval rested with the town council, not the members of the community.

Albert continued to talk, his voice growing more strident as he got warmed up. "Do you know what downtown Dorset Falls is going to look like with that monstrosity on the corner?" he demanded. "I want it stated on the record that I'm not afraid."

He turned, smiling triumphantly at the rest of the crowd, as a large man strode forward toward the town clerk, who was busily typing into her computer. The large man stopped in front of the woman and dropped a set of stapled papers in front of her. She looked at the front page of the packet, her face unreadable, and passed the packet down the town council table.

Albert leaned toward the microphone. "Consider yourselves served! We'll let the Superior Court of the State of Connecticut decide whether or not Trey Humphries can tear down that building!" He slammed his fist on the table with enough force that the keys rattled in front of him.

Somebody let out a whoop, and the people of Dorset Falls began to clap. Diantha's face had gone white with anger. Dougie rapped hard with the gavel, trying to restore order.

Albert picked up his keys and put them in his pocket, grinning as he walked back to his seat.

Keys. Something nagged at Josie. Car keys. Shop keys. Her eyes fell on Rusty, then went involuntarily to Trey and Courtney.

Trey stood up, shaking. "You—you can't do this!" he finally squeezed out.

The marshal who had served the papers positioned himself in the doorway, blocking the exit, as Sharla and Detective Potts moved toward Trey.

Trey rushed toward Albert, who had not made it back to his seat. Trey tripped over an empty chair, slowing him down long enough for Potts to tackle him to the floor, while Sharla pulled handcuffs from her belt.

"Don't you dare handcuff my son!" Diantha shrieked. "I'll sue you for everything you've got. Both of you!"

Sharla snapped on the cuffs. "Go for it," she said. They helped Trey to his feet and began marching him toward the back of the room.

Trey looked stricken. "I didn't do anything! You can't arrest me! I never touched Albert Blandford."

Potts's face was grim. "You're under arrest for the murder of Lillian Woodruff, and suspicion of murder of Cora Lloyd."

"What? I didn't kill anyone!" Trey struggled, but made no headway against the iron grips of the officers.

While every eye was turned toward Trey being led out of the room, Josie's went to Courtney. Her face was white as the snow capping the shrubbery outside. She made no move to follow her husband.

Following.

Keys.

Pieces of the puzzle shifted again, and Josie's mind raced to fit them together in a new way.

She stood up. "Wait!" Every head turned toward her. Potts and Sharla stopped short, keeping their grip on Trey.

"It might not have been Trey!" Josie blurted. "Courtney could have done it!"

Courtney's eyes narrowed to slits. "Shut up, you witch. Don't you think this is hard enough for me?" she hissed.

Diantha raced over to stand next to Courtney. Diantha hauled back, then propelled her arm toward Josie to strike her. Josie was quicker and grabbed Diantha's wrist. She faced them both.

"What are you thinking, Josie?" Sharla prompted.

Josie took just a moment to get it straight before she laid everything out.

"She's got nothing," Diantha spat out.

"But I do," Josie said. "Cora and Lillian were members of

the Historic Preservation Commission. Cora had consulted with a lawyer about stopping the demolition of 13 Main Street, but she died when the air bag failed to deploy in her car, even after the car had been given a clean bill of health just the day before. Lillian Woodruff was strangled at Miss Marple Knits, but there was no sign of a break-in."

"So what?" Courtney sneered. "There's no connection."

"Really? We know Lillian was strangled with a cord made from yarn that came from Cora's shop. I have proof of who bought that yarn."

Potts stared at her. "Is that what you wanted to tell me?"

Josie nodded. "I'll give you the documentation later." She continued. "If someone tampered with Cora's car, it was someone with access—keys—to Rusty's shop. Someone also had keys to Miss Marple Knits. Detective Potts, I think if you investigate further, you'll find that Courtney had access to both sets of keys."

Courtney's face went livid. "You can't prove anything."

"Courtney's father owned Rusty's garage before Rusty bought it." Josie turned to Rusty. "Did you change the locks after you took over?"

Rusty's face went as red as his hair. He shook his head. "I never thought of it."

Josie went on. "So if Courtney still had a set of keys to Rusty's, she could have tampered with Cora's car. And she could have taken Cora's keys, using them to lure Lillian into Miss Marple Knits and kill her."

Potts was silent for a moment, working through the details. "Okay," he said. "I see the opportunity, and you say you know who bought the yarn, so once you tell me we'll have the means. But what's the motive?"

Josie chewed her lower lip. She had to be careful, or she'd give away Evelyn and Helen's secret. "If I were you, I'd look into Courtney's financial records. She's been spending a lot of time at the casinos. If I had to guess, I'd say she's racked up some gambling debts, or she's been doing a whole lot of shopping. The sale of 13 Main Street to a national fast-food chain would have netted her and Trey some significant money."

Courtney, who'd been standing there frozen as Josie laid out her theories, suddenly bolted. Josie reached for her, but Diantha grabbed Josie and held her back.

The marshal left his post at the door and rushed over.

Suddenly, Eb's cane went flying. Courtney flailed as she tripped over the obstacle, and the marshal grabbed her before she hit the floor. Eb stood up, walked into the aisle, and retrieved the cane. "This might not be useless after all," he said.

Chapter 26

Josie sat at her favorite table in the general store the next morning. Lorna made Josie go through the entire scenario again, just to make sure she had it correct. "I wonder if Trey knew about Courtney?" Lorna said, taking a bite of muffin.

"He was so hot to see the deal go through with the developer, he must have known he and Courtney were in financial trouble. Whether he knew about the murders, I guess we'll have to leave to the professionals to find out."

Her cell phone chirped. A text from Monica. Finally. There was a phone number for the buyer, but no name. *Don't hate me. I swear I didn't know.* What did that mean? "Excuse me, will you? I have to make a call."

Lorna waved her away. "Go use the office if you want to. Dougie's not in today."

Josie punched in the number as she walked to the back of the store. The urgency was off. It didn't seem likely that Trey would be able to enforce the eviction from jail, where he was currently sitting while Diantha scrambled to post bail for both Courtney and Trey. But it was time for Josie to go back to New York, and the sooner she got this over with, the better.

She just wished the hollow feeling she had when she thought about it would go away.

After several rings, a voice answered. "Haus of Heinrich."

Huh? She looked at the display on her screen and reviewed the number. How had she missed that when she dialed? The hollow feeling was replaced by rage. What was this? Some kind of joke?

"Haus of Heinrich," the voice repeated. Anastasia, the aspiring model Otto had recently dumped, was still as snippy as ever.

"Put me through to Otto," Josie demanded. "Now."

There was a whooshing sound as Anastasia sucked in a breath. "Josie? Is that you? What's wrong?"

"I'll tell you later. Just put Otto on." Josie took a few deep breaths.

The line clicked. "Josie," Otto said. "It's about time you called me. Those drawings you sent me were . . . adequate."

"What do you want with the inventory of a yarn shop?" She struggled to keep her anger in check.

He chuckled. "What *would* I want with all that raw material? Nothing. But I want *you* to come back."

For the love of Prada. He thought he could manipulate her into returning to work by buying the inventory of Miss Marple Knits. "Otto, you're my employer. Or at least, you used to be. I'm not interested in any kind of relationship with you but business. I've never encouraged you. Do you understand?"

"Not really," he said, his voice almost cheerful under his guttural Germanic phrasing. "That's what makes you interesting. You're a challenge."

"Were my designs *ever* any good?"

"Eh, you're not too bad. But I can't have anyone doing better work than me."

She shook her head. Why had she ever thought she wanted to go back to that job? She'd be eating noodles from a cup and might have to move in with her mother, but there was no way she was going back to the Haus of Heinrich.

"Otto, the deal's off. I don't want your damn money." She was aware, as she said it, that Eb would not be getting his new truck. "And I quit. Permanently."

His voice went serious. She could picture him on the other end of the phone, going into international businessman mode. "You'll never work at another design house. Anywhere. Ever."

"Fine by me." She hung up.

"I'm headed over to the shop, Lorna," she said, placing a five-dollar bill on the table. "Talk to you later."

Josie walked past the empty storefronts of Main Street, barely registering her surroundings, until she got to the bright blue door of Miss Marple Knits. Her thoughts raced. Finally, she put her key in the lock. The door swung open, and her eyes roamed the space. The yarn was still bagged up around the perimeter of the room, the cubbies still empty.

You can do this, a voice said inside her head. A feeling suffused her like a warm embrace. She ran her hand along the sales counter until her fingers closed on the frame of the picture of Miss Marple. The old woman no longer looked threatening or accusing. She looked almost . . . smug.

Josie hung the picture back on its nail and gave the actress a chuck under the chin with her index finger. "What do you say, Janie? Let's give it a go."

Epilogue

"The shop looks beautiful," Evelyn said. "I'm so glad you decided to stay. Cora would have been so proud."

Josie pulled two tissues out of a box on the counter, handed one to Evelyn, and dabbed at her own eyes with the other. It didn't matter that Josie had never met Cora in life. Cora was everywhere, and Josie knew she was smiling down on the grand reopening of Miss Marple Knits from that giant yarn shop in the sky.

Eb was sitting on the couch, looking decidedly uncomfortable. Helen Crawford sat next to him, chatting away. Eb was a very popular man among the ladies of Dorset Falls, whether he wanted to be or not.

And there were plenty of ladies, and even a few men, milling about Miss Marple Knits. Some had shopping baskets piled high with yarn and looped over their arms. Others were taking advantage of the refreshments Lorna had provided. Josie was pleased to see that there were plenty of people she didn't recognize—new customers from outside Dorset Falls, she figured. The marketing she'd done seemed to be paying off.

Evelyn stared at Eb. "I'd better go rescue dear Eben from Helen. She'll talk his ear off."

Josie smiled. "He'll appreciate that." Actually, he wouldn't appreciate it at all. But it would be fun to watch. "And thanks for all your help, Evelyn. I couldn't have gotten the shop ready without you."

"Nonsense," she said, waving her hand dismissively. "I was happy to do it. And I'm even happier to have a job. I'll see you tomorrow morning at nine o'clock sharp." She strode off toward the couple on the couch.

Josie shook her head, then made her way behind the counter. A brand new cash register had been installed, one that could both process credit cards and keep track of inventory. A million ideas had been swirling around in her head since she made the decision to make Dorset Falls her home.

Her mother laid a skein of raspberry-colored cashmere on the counter. "I'd like to be your first customer," she said. "I'm so happy for you, pumpkin." Her smile lit up her whole face.

"Thanks, Mom. And thanks for sending me here. I feel like I have a whole new life ahead of me." She rang up the sale, grateful for the training the technician had given her when he installed the machine. She'd get the hang of this, she was sure.

"Speaking of new life," a male voice said. Josie looked up to see Mitch Woodruff smiling down at her. She felt her face flush, just a little. *Must be the crowd. All that body heat*. "Guess what?" he said.

"Don't make me guess." Josie placed her mother's skein of yarn into a brown paper bag marked MISS MARPLE KNITS. "Things are a little crazy around here." She handed the yarn to her mother, who was still smiling, and was now looking at Mitch with interest. "Crazy in the best possible way."

Mitch shrugged out of his coat and draped it casually over his arm. He looked like he was staying for a while. Josie felt a little pool of warmth form in her chest. Having played a role in figuring out what had really happened to Cora and Lillian, she no longer felt like an outsider in this town. Dorset Falls was starting to feel like home.

"Then I won't keep you in suspense. I went out to feed the herd and found Lulubelle lying on her side."

"Oh no!" Josie said, her heart sinking. "The poor thing. Will she be all right?"

Mitch grinned. "She's fine. She's done this before. Her cria was born this morning."

Josie grinned back, relieved. "Did you bring me a picture?"

"I sure did." He pulled out his cell phone and handed it to her. She held the phone so her mom could see too.

"Well, that is about the cutest thing I ever saw," Katherine declared. "Look at that little face and all that beautiful fur."

"Fiber," Josie and Mitch said in unison, then laughed.

Katherine shook her head. "Whatever, you two. I'm going to go try one of Lorna's cookies." She turned and walked toward the refreshment table.

"So," Mitch said, "I thought since the cria was born on your opening day, you'd like to name her. Of course, she'll have her formal Alpaca Registry name, but you could give her her nickname."

Josie felt her face split into a wide grin. "Really? I'd love to." She tapped her fingers on her chin. "Let's see. Vera? Donatella? I've got it. Stella."

"Stella," Mitch said. "I like it. You'll have to come and see her."

"I'll be over as soon as I get off work."

"If you're nice to me, I might even let you muck out the paddock."

Josie wrinkled her nose. "Sorry, Mitch. I'm not *that* far removed from the city. But I'll enjoy watching you." She felt herself flush again. That hadn't come out quite right.

Eb appeared next to Mitch. Josie was grateful for the interruption. "Nice doings," he said, nodding in what Josie could only assume was approval.

"She's done a great job," Mitch agreed.

Eb fished around in the front inside pocket of his jacket. He pulled out a folded piece of paper and handed it to Josie.

"What's this?" She opened the document. *Quitclaim Deed* was printed at the top. She looked at him, puzzled. "I don't understand."

"I bought this building from Humphries. He needed the money to pay for the lawyers. But I've got no interest in being a landlord," Eb said.

Josie's mouth hung open. "You're giving me the building?"

"And the business. Got no interest in that either."

Tears welled up in Josie's eyes. "I don't know what to say, Unc."

Eb snorted. "Then shut up and don't say anything, for Pete's sake. Just keep those old biddies away from me." He turned and headed for the refreshment table.

Josie surveyed the shop through her tears. "I think I'm going to like owning my own business."

"And I'm going to like having you here," Mitch said. "Now I'll move aside. I think you've got customers to wait on."

She pulled a bag out from under the counter and grinned at the woman on the other side. "Can I help you?"

Knitting Patterns

SCRAP YARN TEA WALLET

Helen Crawford is fussy about her tea. There are only a few brands she likes, so she carries her own tea bags with her and just buys a cup of hot water in restaurants. When one too many tea bags broke loose and made a mess of her purse, she knitted up a pretty tea wallet to hold them neatly. Now she never goes anywhere without it.

Requirements

- Small amount of scrap worsted-weight yarn, approximately 20 yards
- Size 5 knitting needles
- A pretty button, approximately ¾ to 1 inch in diameter
- Crochet hook, size G

Gauge: Not important for this project.

Cast on 26 stitches using your preferred method. Knit in stockinette stitch for 36 rows. Bind off 25 stitches, leaving the last stitch on the needle. Do not break yarn.

To create envelope, place crochet hook in last stitch, setting knitting needle aside. With wrong side facing you, pull up a stitch in the opposite corner, yarn over, then pull through both loops on hook.

Make approximately 22 single crochets (enough to give you a nice edge that lies flat) along one long edge of the work (flap), working over yarn ends so they won't have to be woven in later. Make 1 single crochet in point. Chain 11 to make button loop, then make 1 single crochet in the same stitch on the point to close loop and turn corner. Make 22 single crochets along the other side, again working over any ends.

Continuing down one of the open edges, make 11 slip stitches. Turn. Bring opposite edge toward slip-stitched edge and join with 11 single crochets. Continue on and join the remaining open edges with 11 single crochets. Break off, and weave in the remaining loose end.

Sew a decorative button (a shank-style button works best) under the loop. Fill with your favorite tea bags.

LAVENDER SACHET

Cora knitted lavender-filled sachets and placed them in the drawers of the antique dresser in the guest room, where Josie found them. Josie wants to knit up lots of them in pretty colors and place them in a basket in the yarn shop, right by the cash register. She thinks they'll sell well.

Requirements

- Small amount of worsted-weight yarn, approximately 9 yards
- Size 5 knitting needles
- Dried lavender

Gauge: Not important for this project.

Cast on 15 stitches using your preferred method. Knit in stockinette stitch for 32 rows. Bind off, leaving a tail for sewing.

Fold piece in half, right sides together, and sew together two sides, plus half of the remaining side. Leaving yarn attached, turn piece right side out. Fill sachet through the hole with dried lavender (a kitchen funnel works well for this), then sew up hole. Weave in ends.

FELTED WOOL HANDBAG

Josie found a beautiful forest-green felted handbag in Cora's closet. She loved it so much she decided to keep it. Evelyn, after examining the bag closely, wrote up this pattern for the shop.

Requirements

- Two skeins worsted-weight 100% wool yarn (must be wool, no substitutes)
- Size 8 knitting needles
- One pair purchased circular handbag handles, plastic or acrylic (not bamboo)
- Vintage brooch, preferably something sparkly

Gauge: Not important for this project. However, felting works best with a looser stitch, so if you tend to knit tightly, go up to a size 9 needle.

Handle Casings: (Make 2) Cast on 25 stitches using your preferred method. Knit in stockinette stitch for 16 rows. Bind off, leaving a tail for sewing.

Body of Bag: (Make 1) Cast on 60 stitches using your preferred method. Knit in stockinette stitch until piece measures 26 inches. Bind off loosely. Fold piece in half, right sides together, matching bound off and cast on ends. Sew or crochet the sides together to form a bag. Mark center of each open (top) edge.

Mark center of one long edge of each handle casing, and pin or clip to marked top of bag, matching centers. Sew or crochet handle casing to bag on one long edge, fold handle casing over the handle, and sew or crochet the other long edge to the bag, encasing the handle. Repeat on other side. Weave in ends.

To felt, place entire bag, handles and all (this is why acrylic or plastic handles are called for, not bamboo), into a lingerie bag and run it through a regular washing machine cycle. You can wash other clothes with the bag—towels work well. When load is done, remove wet felted handbag from lingerie bag and lay out on a towel. The piece will have shrunk, and the knitted fabric will have thickened and tightened. This is exactly what you want. Stretch bag gently into a symmetrical shape and allow to air dry. This may take a day or two. Do not put in dryer.

When bag is dry, affix vintage brooch to one side. Evelyn suggests using sewing thread to attach the brooch securely so it doesn't accidentally come unfastened. If you don't have a sparkly pin, you could also attach a silk flower or a satin ribbon bow, or tie a colorful silky scarf around the handles to cascade down. Use your imagination and decorate your bag however you wish.

* * *

These patterns are copyrighted by Sadie Hartwell and are free for your personal use. You are welcome to make and sell items made from these patterns, but Sadie would appreciate a link back to her Web site. You can see photos of all the projects at www.sadiehartwell.com. Sadie would love to see your projects too!